WHY I WAS BACHMAN

By Stephen King

Between 1977 and 1984 I published five novels under the pseudonym of Richard Bachman. These were *Rage* (1977), *The Long Walk* (1979), *Roadwork* (1981), *The Running Man* (1982), and *Thinner* (1984). There were two reasons I was finally linked with Bachman: first, because the first four books, all paperback originals, were dedicated to people associated with my life, and second, because my name appeared on the copyright forms of one book. Now people are asking me why I did it, and I don't seem to have any very satisfactory answers. Good thing I didn't murder anyone, isn't it?

From the Introduction to *The Bachman Books* by Stephen King.

PRAISE FOR STEPHEN KING

'An incredibly gifted writer' – *Guardian*

'A writer of excellence . . . King is one of the most fertile storytellers of the modern novel . . . brilliantly done'
– *The Sunday Times*

'Splendid entertainment . . . Stephen King is one of those natural storytellers . . . getting hooked is easy'
– Frances Fyfield, *Express*

'A sophisticated literary craftsman' – *Observer*

'Genuinely masterful' – *Daily Telegraph*

PRAISE FOR STEPHEN KING

'Not since Dickens has a writer had so many readers by the throat . . . King's imagination is vast. He knows how to engage the deepest sympathies of his readers . . . one of the great storytellers of our time' – *Guardian*

'You can't help admiring King's narrative skills and his versatility as a storyteller' – *Sunday Telegraph*

'King cannot be faulted as a yarn-spinner' – *The Times*

'Stephen King is one of America's finest writers' – *Scotsman*

ABOUT THE AUTHOR

Stephen King was born in Portland, Maine, in 1947. He won a scholarship award to the University of Maine and later taught English, while his wife, Tabitha, got her degree.

It was the publication of his first novel *Carrie* and its subsequent film adaptation that set him on his way to his present position as perhaps the bestselling author in the world.

Carrie was followed by a string of bestsellers including *The Shining*, *It*, *Misery*, *Bag of Bones*, *On Writing* (A Memoir of the Craft) and *Dreamcatcher*.

He lives in Bangor, Maine, with his wife, novelist Tabitha King.

stephen
KING

writing as Richard Bachman

THE RUNNING MAN

NEW ENGLISH LIBRARY
Hodder & Stoughton

First published in Great Britain in 1983 by New English Library
First published in paperback in 1984 by New English Library
A division of Hodder Headline

A New English Library Paperback

30 29 28 27 26 25 24 23 22

A CIP catalogue record is available from the British Library

ISBN 0 450 05642 2

Typeset by Rowland Phototypesetting Ltd,
Bury St Edmunds, Suffolk
Printed and bound in Great Britain by
Clays Ltd, St Ives plc

Hodder and Stoughton
A division of Hodder Headline
338 Euston Road
London NW1 3BH

THE RUNNING MAN

... MINUS 100 and COUNTING ...

She was squinting at the thermometer in the white light coming through the window. Beyond her, in the drizzle, the other highrises in Co-Op City rose like the gray turrets of a penitentiary. Below, in the airshaft, clothesline flapped with ragged wash. Rats and plump alley cats circulated through the garbage.

She looked at her husband. He was seated at the table, staring up at the Free-Vee with steady, vacant concentration. He had been watching it for weeks now. It wasn't like him. He hated it, always had. Of course, every Development apartment had one — it was the law — but it was still legal to turn them off. The Compulsory Benefit Bill of 2021 had failed to get the required two-thirds majority by six votes. Ordinarily they never watched it. But ever since Cathy had gotten sick, he had been watching the big-money giveaways. It filled her with sick fear.

Behind the compulsive shrieking of the half-time announcer narrating the latest newsie flick, Cathy's flu-hoarsened wailing went on and on.

'How bad is it?' Richards asked.

'Not so bad.'

'Don't shit me.'

'It's a hundred and four.'

He brought both fists down on the table. A plastic dish jumped into the air and clattered down.

'We'll get a doctor. Try not to worry so much. Listen —' She began to babble frantically to distract him; he had turned around and was watching the Free-Vee again. Half-time was over, and the game was on again.

1

This wasn't one of the big ones, of course, just a cheap daytime come-on called *Treadmill to Bucks*. They accepted only chronic heart, liver, or lung patients, sometimes throwing in a crip for comic relief. Every minute the contestant could stay on the treadmill (keeping up a steady flow of chatter with the emcee), he won ten dollars. Every two minutes the emcee asked a Bonus Question in the contestant's category (the current pal, a heart-murmur from Hackensack, was an American history buff) which was worth fifty dollars. If the contestant, dizzy, out of breath, heart doing fantastic rubber acrobatics in his chest, missed the question, fifty dollars was deducted from his winnings and the treadmill was speeded up.

'We'll get along, Ben. We will. Really. I . . . I'll . . .'

'You'll what?' He looked at her brutally. 'Hustle? No more, Sheila. She's got to have a real doctor. No more block midwife with dirty hands and whiskey breath. All the modern equipment. I'm going to see to it.'

He crossed the room, eyes swiveling hypnotically to the Free-Vee bolted into one peeling wall above the sink. He took his cheap denim jacket off its hook and pulled it on with fretful gestures.

'No! No, I won't . . . won't allow it. You're not going to—'

'Why not? At worst you can get a few oldbucks as the head of a fatherless house. One way or the other you'll have enough to see her through this.'

She had never really been a handsome woman, and in the years since her husband had not worked she had grown scrawny, but in this moment she looked beautiful . . . imperious. 'I won't take it. I'd rather sell the govie a two-dollar piece of tail when he comes to the door and send him back with his dirty blood money in his pocket. Should I take a bounty on my man?'

He turned on her, grim and humorless, clutching something that set him apart, an invisible something for which the Network had ruthlessly calculated. He was a dinosaur in this time. Not a big one, but still a throwback, an embarrassment. Perhaps a danger. Big clouds condense around small particles.

He gestured at the bedroom. 'How about her in an unmarked pauper's grave? Does that appeal to you?'

It left her with only the argument of insensate sorrow. Her face cracked and dissolved into tears.

'Ben, this is just what they want, for people like us, like you—'

'Maybe they won't take me,' he said, opening the door. 'Maybe I don't have whatever it is they look for.'

'If you go now, they'll kill you. And I'll be here watching it. Do you want me watching that with her in the next room?' She was hardly coherent through her tears.

'I want her to go on living.' He tried to close the door, but she put her body in the way.

'Give me a kiss before you go, then.'

He kissed her. Down the hall, Mrs Jenner opened her door and peered out. The rich odor of corned beef and cabbage, tantalizing, maddening, drifted to them. Mrs Jenner did well – she helped out at the local discount drug and had an almost uncanny eye for illegal-card carriers.

'You'll take the money?' Richards asked. 'You won't do anything stupid?'

'I'll take it,' she whispered. 'You know I'll take it.'

He clutched her awkwardly, then turned away quickly, with no grace, and plunged down the crazily slanting, ill-lighted stairwell.

She stood in the doorway, shaken by soundless sobs, until she heard the door slam hollowly five flights down, and then she put her apron up to her face. She was still clutching the thermometer she had used to take the baby's temperature.

Mrs Jenner crept up softly and twitched the apron. 'Dearie,' she whispered, 'I can put you onto black market penicillin when the money gets here ... real cheap ... good quality—'

'Get out!' She screamed at her.

Mrs Jenner recoiled, her upper lip raising instinctively away from the blackened stumps of her teeth. 'Just trying to help,' she muttered, and scurried back to her room.

Barely muffled by the thin plastiwood, Cathy's wails continued. Mrs Jenner's Free-Vee blared and hooted. The contestant on *Treadmill to Bucks* had just missed a Bonus Question and had had a heart attack simultaneously. He was being carried off on a rubber stretcher while the audience applauded.

Upper lip rising and falling metronomically, Mrs Jenner wrote Sheila Richards's name down in her notebook. 'We'll see,' she said to no one. 'We'll just see, Mrs Smell-So-Sweet.'

She closed the notebook with a vicious snap and settled down to watch the next game.

... MINUS 099 and COUNTING ...

The drizzle had deepened into a steady rain by the time Richards hit the street. The big Smoke Dokes for Hallucinogenic Jokes thermometer across the street stood at fifty-one degrees. (*Just the Right Temp to Stoke Up a Doke – High to the Nth Degree!*) That might make it sixty in their apartment. And Cathy had the flu.

A rat trotted lazily, lousily, across the cracked and blistered cement of the street. Across the way, the ancient and rusted skeleton of a 2013 Humber stood on decayed axles. It had been completely stripped, even to the wheel bearings and motor mounts, but the cops didn't take it away. The cops rarely ventured south of the Canal anymore. Co-Op City stood in a radiating rat warren of parking lots, deserted shops, Urban Centers, and paved playgrounds. The cycle gangs were the law here, and all those newsie items about the intrepid Block Police of South City were nothing but a pile of warm crap. The streets were ghostly, silent. If you went out, you took the pneumo bus or you carried a gas cylinder.

He walked fast, not looking around, not thinking. The air was sulphurous and thick. Four cycles roared past and someone threw a ragged hunk of asphalt paving. Richards ducked easily. Two pneumo buses passed him, buffeting him with air, but he did not flag them. The week's twenty-dollar unemployment allotment (oldbucks) had been spent. There was no money to buy a token. He supposed the roving packs could sense his poverty. He was not molested.

Highrises, Developments, chain-link fences, parking lots empty except for stripped derelicts, obscenities scrawled on the pavement in soft chalk and now blurring with the rain. Crashed-out windows, rats, wet bags of garbage splashed over the sidewalks and into the gutters. Graffiti written jaggedly on crumbling gray walls: HONKY DON'T LET THE SUN SET ON YOU HEAR. HOME FOLKS BLOW DOKES. YOUR MOMMY ITCHES. SKIN YOUR BANANA. TOMMY'S PUSHING. HITLER WAS COOL. MARY. SID. KILL ALL KIKES. The old G.A. sodium lights put up in the 70s busted with rocks and hunks of paving. No technico was going to replace them down here; they were on the New Credit Dollar. Technicos stay uptown, baby. Uptown's cool. Everything silent

5

except for the rising-then-descending whoosh of the pneumo buses and the echoing clack of Richards's footfalls. This battlefield only lights up at night. In the day it is a deserted gray silence which contains no movement but the cats and rats and fat white maggots trundling across the garbage. No smell but the decaying reek of this brave year 2025. The Free-Vee cables are safely buried under the streets and no one but an idiot or a revolutionary would want to vandalize them. Free-Vee is the stuff of dreams, the bread of life. Scag is twelve oldbucks a bag, Frisco Push goes for twenty a tab, but the Free-Vee will freak you for nothing. Farther along, on the other side of the Canal, the dream machine runs twenty-four hours a day . . . but it runs on New Dollars, and only employed people have any. There are four million others, almost all of them unemployed, south of the Canal in Co-Op City.

Richards walked three miles and the occasional liquor stores and smoke shops, at first heavily grilled, became more numerous. Then the X-Houses (*!!24 Perversions – Count 'Em 24!!*), the Hockeries, the Blood Emporiums. Greasers sitting on cycles at every corner, the gutters buried in snow-drifts of roach ends. Rich Blokes Smoke Dokes.

He could see the skyscrapers rising into the clouds now, high and clean. The highest of all was the Network Games Building, one hundred stories, the top half buried in cloud and smog cover. He fixed his eyes on it and walked another mile. Now the more expensive movie houses, and smoke shops with no grills (but Rent-A-Pigs stood outside, electric move-alongs hanging from their Sam Browne belts). A city cop on every corner. The People's Fountain Park: Admission 75¢. Well-dressed mothers watching their children as they frolicked on the astroturf behind chain-link fencing. A cop on either side of the gate. A tiny, pathetic glimpse of the fountain.

He crossed the Canal.

As he got closer to the Games Building it grew taller, more and more improbable with its impersonal tiers of rising office windows, its polished stonework. Cops watching him, ready to hustle him along or bust him if he tried to commit loitering. Uptown there was only one function for a man in baggy gray pants and a cheap bowl haircut and sunken eyes. That purpose was the Games.

The qualifying examinations began promptly at noon, and when Ben Richards stepped behind the last man in line, he was almost in the umbra of the Games Building. But the building was still nine blocks and over a mile away. The line stretched before him like an eternal snake. Soon others joined it behind him. The police watched them, hands on either gun butts or move-alongs. They smiled anonymous, contemptuous smiles.

—That one look like a half-wit to you, Frank? Looks like one to me.

—Guy down there ast me if there was a place where he could go to the bathroom. Canya magine it?

—Sons of bitches ain't—

—Kill their own mothers for a—

—Smelled like he didn't have a bath for—

—Ain't nothin like a freak show I always—

Heads down against the rain, they shuffled aimlessly, and after a while the line began to move.

. . . MINUS 098 and COUNTING . . .

It was after four when Ben Richards got to the main desk and was routed to Desk 9 (Q-R). The woman sitting at the rumbling plastipunch looked tired and cruel and impersonal. She looked at him and saw no one.

'Name, last–first–middle.'

'Richards, Benjamin Stuart.'

Her fingers raced over the keys. *Clitter-clitter-clitter* went the machine.

'Age–height–weight.'

'Twenty–eight, six–two, one–sixty–five.'

Clitter-clitter-clitter

'Certified IQ by Weschler test if you know it, and age tested.'

'One twenty–six. Age of fourteen.'

Clitter-clitter-clitter

The huge lobby was an echoing, rebounding tomb of sound. Questions being asked and answered. People were being led out weeping. People were being thrown out. Hoarse voices were raised in protest. A scream or two. Questions. Always questions.

'Last school attended?'

'Manual Trades.'

'Did you graduate?'

'No.'

'How many years, and at what age did you leave?'

'Two years. Sixteen years old.'

'Reasons for leaving?'

'I got married.'

Clitter-clitter-clitter

'Name and age of spouse if any.'

'Sheila Catherine Richards, twenty–six.'

'Names and ages of children, if any.'

'Catherine Sarah Richards, eighteen months.'

Clitter-clitter-clitter

'Last question, mister. Don't bother lying; they'll pick it up during the physical and disqualify you there. Have you ever used heroin or the synthetic–amphetamine hallucinogen called San Francisco Push?'

'No.'

Clitter

A plastic card popped out and she handed it to him. 'Don't lose this, big fella. If you do, you have to start back at go next week.' She was looking at him now, seeing his face, the angry eyes, lanky body. Not bad looking. At least some intelligence. Good stats.

She took his card back abruptly and punched off the upper right-hand corner, giving it an odd milled appearance.

'What was that for?'

'Never mind. Somebody will tell you later. Maybe.' She pointed over his shoulder at a long hall which led toward a bank of elevators. Dozens of men fresh from the desks were being stopped, showing their plastic IDs and moving on. As Richards watched, a trembling, sallow-faced Push freak was stopped by a cop and shown the door. The freak began to cry. But he went.

'Tough old world, big fella,' the woman behind the desk said without sympathy. 'Move along.'

Richards moved along. Behind him, the litany was already beginning again.

... MINUS 097   and COUNTING ...

A hard, callused hand slapped his shoulder at the head of the hall beyond the desks. 'Card, buddy.'

Richards showed it. The cop relaxed, his face subtle and Chinese with disappointment.

'You like turning them back, don't you?' Richards asked. 'It really gives you a charge, doesn't it?'

'You want to go downtown, maggot?'

Richards walked past him, and the cop made no move.

He stopped halfway to the bank of elevators and looked back. 'Hey. Cop.'

The cop looked at him truculently.

'Got a family? It could be you next week.'

'Move on!' the cop shouted furiously.

With a smile, Richards moved on.

There was a line of perhaps twenty applicants waiting at the elevators. Richards showed one of the cops on duty his card and the cop looked at him closely. 'You a hardass, sonny?'

'Hard enough,' Richards said, and smiled.

The cop gave him back his card. 'They'll kick it soft again. How smart do you talk with holes in your head, sonny?'

'Just about as smart as you talk without that gun on your leg and your pants down around your ankles,' Richards said, still smiling. 'Want to try it?'

For a moment he thought the cop was going to swing at him. 'They'll fix you,' the cop said. 'You'll do some walking on your knees before you're done.'

The cop swaggered over to three new arrivals and demanded to see their cards.

The man ahead of Richards turned around. He had a nervous, unhappy face and curly hair that came down in a widow's peak. 'Say, you don't want to antagonize them, fella. They've got a grapevine.'

'Is that so?' Richards asked, looking at him mildly.

The man turned away.

Abruptly the elevator doors snapped open. A black cop with a huge gut stood protecting the bank of push buttons. Another cop sat on a small stool reading a 3-D pervert mag in a small bulletproof cubicle the size of a telephone booth at the rear of the large car. A sawed-off shotgun rested between his knees. Shells were lined up beside him within easy reach.

'Step to the rear!' the fat cop cried with bored importance. 'Step to the rear! Step to the rear!'

They crowded in to a depth where a deep breath was impossible. Sad flesh walled Richards on every side. They went up to the second floor. The doors snapped open. Richards, who stood a head taller than anyone else in the car, saw a huge waiting room with many chairs dominated by a huge Free-Vee. A cigarette dispenser stood in one corner.

'Step out! Step out! Show ID cards to your left!'

They stepped out, holding out their ID cards to the impersonal lens of a camera. Three cops stood close by. For some reason, a buzzer went off at the sight of some dozen cards, and the holders were jerked out of line and hustled away.

Richards showed his card and was waved on. He went to the cigarette machine, got a package of Blams and sat down as far from the Free-Vee as possible. He lit up a smoke and exhaled, coughing. He hadn't had a cigarette in almost six months.

... MINUS 096 and COUNTING ...

They called the A's for the physical almost immediately, and about two dozen men got up and filed through a door beyond the Free-Vee. A large sign tacked over the door read THIS WAY. There was an arrow below the legend, pointing at the door. The literacy of Games applicants was notoriously low.

They were taking a new letter every fifteen minutes or so. Ben Richards had sat down at about five, and so he estimated it would be quarter of nine before they got to him. He wished he had brought a book, but he supposed things were just as well as they were. Books were regarded with suspicion at best, especially when carried by someone from south of the Canal. Pervert Mags were safer.

He watched the six o'clock newsie restlessly (the fighting in Ecuador was worse, new cannibal riots had broken out in India, the Detroit Tigers had taken the Harding Catamounts by a score of 6–2 in an afternoon game), and when the first of the evening's big-money games came on at six-thirty, he went restlessly to the window and looked out. Now that his mind was made up, the Games bored him again. Most of the others, however, were watching *Fun Guns* with a dreadful fascination. Next week it might be them.

Outside, daylight was bleeding slowly toward dusk. The els were slamming at high speed through the power rings above the second-floor window, their powerful headlights searching the gray air. On the sidewalks below, crowds of men and women (most of them, of course, technicos or Network bureaucrats) were beginning their evening's prowl in search of entertainment. A Certified Pusher was hawking his wares on the corner across the street. A man with a sabled dolly on each arm passed below him; the trio was laughing about something.

He had a sudden awful wave of homesickness for Sheila and Cathy, and wished he could call them. He didn't think it was allowed. He could still walk out, of course; several men already had. They walked across the room, grinning obscurely at nothing, to use the door marked TO STREET. Back to the flat with his daughter glowing fever-bright in the other room? No. Couldn't. Couldn't.

He stood at the window a little while longer, then went back and sat down. The new game, *Dig Your Grave*, was beginning.

The fellow sitting next to Richards twitched his arm

anxiously. 'Is it true that they wash out over thirty percent just on the physicals?'

'I don't know,' Richards said.

'Jesus,' the fellow said. 'I got bronchitis. Maybe *Tread-mill to Bucks . . .*'

Richards could think of nothing to say. The pal's respiration sounded like a faraway truck trying to climb a steep hill.

'I got a fambly,' the man said with soft desperation.

Richards looked at the Free-Vee as if it interested him.

The fellow was quiet for a long time. When the program changed again at seven-thirty, Richards heard him asking the man on his other side about the physical.

It was full dark outside now. Richards wondered if it was still raining. It seemed like a very long evening.

. . . MINUS 095   and COUNTING . . .

When the *R*'s went through the door under the red arrow and into the examination room it was just a few minutes after nine-thirty. A lot of the initial excitement had worn off, and people were either watching the Free-Vee avidly, with none of their prior dread, or dozing. The man with the noisy chest had a name that began with *L* and had been called over an hour before. Richards wondered idly if he had been cut.

The examination room was long and tiled, lit with fluorescent tubes. It looked like an assembly line, with bored doctors standing at various stations along the way.

Would any of you like to check my little girl? Richards thought bitterly.

The applicants showed their cards to another camera eye embedded in the wall and were ordered to stop by a row of clotheshooks. A doctor in a long white lab coat walked over to them, clipboard tucked under one arm.

'Strip,' he said. 'Hang your clothes on the hooks. Remember the number over your hook and give the number to the orderly at the far end. Don't worry about your valuables. Nobody here wants them.'

Valuables. That was a hot one, Richards thought, unbuttoning his shirt. He had an empty wallet with a few pictures of Sheila and Cathy, a receipt for a shoe sole he had had replaced at the local cobbler's six months ago, a keyring with no keys on it except for the doorkey, a baby sock that he did not remember putting in there, and the package of Blams he had gotten from the machine.

He was wearing tattered skivvies because Sheila was too stubborn to let him go without, but many of the men were buck under their pants. Soon they all stood stripped and anonymous, penises dangling between their legs like forgotten war-clubs. Everyone held his card in one hand. Some shuffled their feet as if the floor were cold, although it was not. The faint, impersonally nostalgic odor of alcohol drifted through.

'Stay in line,' the doctor with the clipboard was instructing. 'Always show your card. Follow instructions.'

The line moved forward. Richards saw there was a cop with each doctor along the way. He dropped his eyes and waited passively.

'Card.'

He gave his card over. The first doctor noted the number, then said: 'Open your mouth.'

Richards opened it. His tongue was depressed.

The next doctor peered into his pupils with a tiny bright light, and then stared in his ears.

The next placed the cold circle of a stethoscope on his chest. 'Cough.'

Richards coughed. Down the line a man was being

hauled away. He needed the money, they couldn't do it, he'd get his lawyer on them.

The doctor moved his stethoscope. 'Cough.'

Richards coughed. The doctor turned him around and put the stethoscope on his back.

'Take a deep breath and hold it.' The stethoscope moved.

'Exhale.'

Richards exhaled.

'Move along.'

His blood pressure was taken by a grinning doctor with an eyepatch. He was given a short-arm inspection by a bald medico who had several large brown freckles, like liverspots, on his pate. The doctor placed a cool hand between the sac of his scrotum and his upper thigh.

'Cough.'

Richards coughed.

'Move along.'

His temperature was taken. He was asked to spit in a cup. Halfway, now. Halfway down the hall. Two or three men had already finished up, and an orderly with a pasty face and rabbit teeth was bringing them their clothes in wire baskets. Half a dozen more had been pulled out of the line and shown the stairs.

'Bend over and spread your cheeks.'

Richards bent and spread. A finger coated with plastic invaded his rectal channel, explored, retreated.

'Move along.'

He stepped into a booth with curtains on three sides, like the old voting booths – voting booths had been done away with by computer election eleven years ago – and urinated in a blue beaker. The doctor took it and put it in a wire rack.

At the next stop he looked at an eye-chart. 'Read,' the doctor said.

'E – A,L – D,M,F – S,P,M,Z – K,L,A,C,D – U,S,G,A—'

'That's enough. Move along.'

He entered another pseudo voting booth and put earphones over his head. He was told to push the white button when he heard something and the red button when he didn't hear it anymore. The sound was very high and faint – like a dog whistle that had been pitch-lowered into just audible human range. Richards pushed buttons until he was told to stop.

He was weighed. His arches were examined. He stood in front of a fluoroscope and put on a lead apron. A doctor, chewing gum and singing something tunelessly under his breath, took several pictures and noted his card number.

Richards had come in with a group of about thirty. Twelve had made it to the far end of the room. Some were dressed and waiting for the elevator. About a dozen more had been hauled out of line. One of them tried to attack the doctor that had cut him and was felled by a policeman wielding a move-along at full charge. The pal fell as if poleaxed.

Richards stood at a low table and was asked if he had had some fifty different diseases. Most of them were respiratory in nature. The doctor looked up sharply when Richards said there was a case of influenza in the family.

'Wife?'

'No. My daughter.'

'Age?'

'A year and a half.'

'Have you been immunized? Don't try to lie!' the doctor shouted suddenly, as if Richards had already tried to lie. 'We'll check your health stats.'

'Immunized July 2023. Booster September 2023. Block health clinic.'

'Move along.'

Richards had a sudden urge to reach over the table and pop the maggot's neck. Instead, he moved along.

At the last stop, a severe-looking woman doctor with close-cropped hair and an Electric Juicer plugged into one ear asked him if he was a homosexual.

'No.'

'Have you ever been arrested on a felony charge?'

'No.'

'Do you have any severe phobias? By that I mean—'

'No.'

'You better listen to the definition,' she said with a faint touch of condescension. 'I mean—'

'Do I have any unusual and compulsive fears, such as acrophobia or claustrophobia. I don't.'

Her lips pressed tightly together, and for a moment she seemed on the verge of sharp comment.

'Do you use or have you used any hallucinogenic or addictive drugs?'

'No.'

'Do you have any relatives who have been arrested on charges of crimes against the government or against the Network?'

'No.'

'Sign this loyalty oath and this Games Commission release form, Mr, uh, Richards.'

He scratched his signature.

'Show the orderly your card and tell him the number—'

He left her in midsentence and gestured at the buck-toothed orderly with his thumb. 'Number twenty-six, Bugs.' The orderly brought his things. Richards dressed slowly and went over by the elevator. His anus felt hot and embarrassed, violated, a little slippery with the lubricant the doctor had used.

When they were all bunched together, the elevator

door opened. The bulletproof Judas hole was empty this time. The cop was a skinny man with a large wen beside his nose. 'Step to the rear,' he chanted. 'Please step to the rear.'

As the doors closed, Richards could see the S's coming in at the far end of the hall. The doctor with the clipboard was approaching them. Then the doors clicked together, cutting off the view.

They rode up to the third floor, and the doors opened on a huge, semilit dormitory. Rows and rows of narrow iron-and-canvas cots seemed to stretch out to infinity.

Two cops began to check them out of the elevator, giving them bed numbers. Richards's was 940. The cot had one brown blanket and a very flat pillow. Richards lay down on the cot and let his shoes drop to the floor. His feet dangled over the end; there was nothing to be done about it.

He crossed his arms under his head and stared at the ceiling.

... MINUS 094   and COUNTING ...

He was awakened promptly at six the following morning by a very loud buzzer. For a moment he was foggy, disoriented, wondering if Sheila had bought an alarm clock or what. Then it came to him and he sat up.

They were led by groups of fifty into a large industrial bathroom where they showed their cards to a camera guarded by a policeman. Richards went to a blue-tiled booth that contained a mirror, a basin, a shower, a toilet. On the shelf above the basin was a row of toothbrushes wrapped in cellophane, an electric razor, a bar of soap, and a half-used tube of toothpaste. A sign tucked into the

corner of the mirror read: *RESPECT THIS PROP-
ERTY!* Beneath it, someone had scrawled: *I ONLY
RESPECT MY ASS!*

Richards showered, dried with a towel that topped a
pile on the toilet tank, shaved, and brushed.

They were let into a cafeteria where they showed their
ID cards again. Richards took a tray and pushed it down
a stainless steel ledge. He was given a box of cornflakes,
a greasy dish of home fries, a scoop of scrambled eggs, a
piece of toast as cold and hard as a marble gravestone, a
halfpint of milk, a cup of muddy coffee (no cream), an
envelope of sugar, an envelope of salt, and a pat of fake
butter on a tiny square of oily paper.

He wolfed the meal; they all did. For Richards it was
the first real food, other than greasy pizza wedges and
government pill-commodities, that he had eaten in God
knew how long. Yet it was oddly bland, as if some vampire
chef in the kitchen had sucked all the taste out of it and
left only brute nutrients.

What were *they* eating this morning? Kelp pills. Fake
milk for the baby. A sudden feeling of desperation swelled
over him. Christ, when would they start seeing money?
Today? Tomorrow? Next week?

Or maybe that was just a gimmick too, a flashy come-
on. Maybe there wasn't even any rainbow, let alone a pot
of gold.

He sat staring at his empty plate until the seven o'clock
buzzer went and they were moved on to the elevators.

. . . MINUS 093 and COUNTING . . .

On the fourth floor Richards's group of fifty was herded
first into a large, furnitureless room ringed with what

looked like letter slots. They showed their cards again, and the elevator doors whooshed closed behind them.

A gaunt man with receding hair with the Games emblem (the silhouette of a human head superimposed over a torch) on his lab coat came into the room.

'Please undress and remove all valuables from your clothes,' he said. 'Then drop your clothes into one of the incinerator slots. You'll be issued Games coveralls.' He smiled magnanimously. 'You may keep the coveralls no matter what your personal Games resolution may be.'

There was some grumbling, but everyone complied.

'Hurry, please,' the gaunt man said. He clapped his hands together twice, like a first-grade teacher signaling the end of playtime. 'We have lots ahead of us.'

'Are you going to be a contestant, too?' Richards asked.

The gaunt man favored him with a puzzled expression. Somebody in the back snickered.

'Never mind,' Richards said, and stepped out of his trousers.

He removed his unvaluable valuables and dumped his shirt, pants, and skivvies into a letter slot. There was a brief, hungry flash of flame from somewhere far below.

The door at the other end opened (there was *always* a door at the other end; they were like rats in a huge, upward-tending maze: an American maze, Richards reflected), and men trundled in large baskets on wheels, labeled S, M, L, and XL. Richards selected an XL for its length and expected it to hang baggily on his frame, but it fit quite well. The material was soft, clingy, almost like silk, but tougher than silk. A single nylon zipper ran up the front. They were all dark blue, and they all had the Games emblem on the right breast pocket. When the entire group was wearing them, Ben Richards felt as if he had lost his face.

'This way, please,' the gaunt man said, and ushered

them into another waiting room. The inevitable Free-Vee blared and cackled. 'You'll be called in groups of ten.'

The door beyond the Free-Vee was topped by another sign reading THIS WAY, complete with arrow.

They sat down. After a while, Richards got up and went to the window and looked out. They were higher up, but it was still raining. The streets were slick and black and wet. He wondered what Sheila was doing.

... MINUS 092   and COUNTING ...

He went through the door, one of a group of ten now, at quarter past ten. They went through single file. Their cards were scanned. There were ten three-sided booths, but these were more substantial. The sides were constructed of drilled soundproof cork paneling. The overhead lighting was soft and indirect. Muzak was emanating from hidden speakers. There was a plush carpet on the floor; Richards's feet felt startled by something that wasn't cement.

The gaunt man had said something to him.

Richards blinked. 'Huh?'

'Booth 6,' the gaunt man said reprovingly.

'Oh.'

He went to Booth 6. There was a table inside, and a large wall clock mounted at eye level beyond it. On the table was a sharpened G-A/IBM pencil and a pile of unlined paper. Cheap grade, Richards noted.

Standing beside all this was a dazzling computer-age priestess, a tall, Junoesque blonde wearing iridescent short shorts which cleanly outlined the delta-shaped rise of her pudenda. Rouged nipples poked perkily through a silk fishnet blouselet.

'Sit down, please,' she said. 'I am Rinda Ward, your tester.' She held out her hand.

Startled, Richards shook it. 'Benjamin Richards.'

'May I call you Ben?' The smile was seductive but impersonal. He felt exactly the token rise of desire he was supposed to feel for this well-stacked female with her well-fed body on display. It angered him. He wondered if she got her kicks this way, showing it off to the poor slobs on their way to the meat grinder.

'Sure,' he said. 'Nice tits.'

'Thank you,' she said, unruffled. He was seated now, looking up while she looked down, and it added an even more embarrassing angle to the picture. 'This test today is to your mental faculties what your physical yesterday was to your body. It will be a fairly long test, and your luncheon will be around three this afternoon – assuming you pass.' The smile winked on and off.

'The first section is verbal. You have one hour from the time I give you the test booklet. You may ask questions during the examination, and I will answer them if I am allowed to do so. I will not give you any answers to test questions, however. Do you understand?'

'Yes.'

She handed him the booklet. There was a large red hand printed on the cover, palm outward. In large red letters beneath, it said:

STOP!

Beneath this: *Do not turn to the first page until your tester instructs you to proceed.*

'Heavy,' Richards remarked.

'Pardon me?' The perfectly sculpted eyebrows went up a notch.

'Nothing.'

'You will find an answer sheet when you open your booklet,' she recited. 'Please make your marks heavy and black. If you wish to change an answer, please erase completely. If you do not know an answer, do *not* guess. Do you understand?'

'Yes.'

'Then please turn to page one and begin. When I say stop, please put your pencil down. You may begin.'

He didn't begin. He eyed her body slowly, insolently.

After a moment, she flushed. 'Your hour has begun, Ben. You had better—'

'Why,' he asked, 'does everybody assume that when they are dealing with someone from south of the Canal they are dealing with a horny mental incompetent?'

She was completely flustered now. 'I . . . I never . . .'

'No, you never.' He smiled and picked up his pencil. 'My Christ, you people are dumb.'

He bent to the test while she was still trying to find an answer or even a reason for his attack; she probably really didn't understand.

The first section required him to mark the letter of the correct fill-in-the-blank answer.

1. One _____ does not make a summer.

         a. thought
         b. beer
         c. swallow
         d. crime
         e. none of these

He filled in his answer sheet rapidly, rarely stopping to deliberate or consider an answer twice. Fill-ins were followed by vocabulary, then by word-contrasts. When he finished, the hour allotted still had fifteen minutes to run. She made him keep his exam – legally he couldn't give it to her until the hour was up – so Richards leaned back and wordlessly ogled her nearly naked body. The silence grew thick and oppressive, charged. He could see her wishing for an overcoat and it pleased him.

When the time was up, she gave him a second exam. On the first page, there was a drawing of a gasoline carburetor. Below:

You would put this in a

   a. lawnmower
   b. Free-Vee
   c. electric hammock
   d. automobile
   e. none of these

The third exam was a math diagnostic. He was not so good with figures and he began to sweat lightly as he saw the clock getting away from him. In the end, it was nearly a dead heat. He didn't get a chance to finish the last question. Rinda Ward smiled a trifle too widely as she pulled the test and answer sheet away from him. 'Not so fast on that one, Ben.'

'But they'll all be right,' he said, and smiled back at her. He leaned forward and swatted her lightly on the rump. 'Take a shower, kid. You done good.'

She blushed furiously. 'I could have you disqualified.'

'Bullshit. You could get yourself fired, that's all.'

'Get out. Get back in line.' She was snarling, suddenly near tears.

He felt something almost like compassion and choked it back. 'You have a nice night tonight,' he said. 'You go out and have a nice six-course meal with whoever you're sleeping with this week and think about my kid dying of flu in a shitty three-room Development apartment.'

He left her staring after him, white-faced.

His group of ten had been cut to six, and they trooped into the next room. It was one-thirty.

... MINUS 091 and COUNTING ...

The doctor sitting on the other side of the table in the small booth wore glasses with tiny thick lenses. He had a kind of nasty, pleased grin that reminded Richards of a half-wit he had known as a boy. The kid had enjoyed crouching under the high school bleachers and looking up girls' skirts while he flogged his dog. Richards began to grin.

'Something pleasant?' the doctor asked, flipping up the first inkblot. The nasty grin widened the tiniest bit.

'Yes. You remind me of someone I used to know.'

'Oh? Who?'

'Never mind.'

'Very well. What do you see here?'

Richards looked at it. An inflated blood pressure cuff had been cinched to his right arm. A number of electrodes had been pasted to his head, and wires from both his head and arm were jacked into a console beside the doctor. Squiggly lines moved across the face of a computer console.

'Two Negro women. Kissing.'

He flipped up another one. 'This?'

'A sports car. Looks like a Jag.'

'Do you like gascars?'

Richards shrugged. 'I had a model collection when I was a kid.'

The doctor made a note and flipped up another card.

'Sick person. She's lying on her side. The shadows on her face look like prison bars.'

'And this last one?'

Richards burst out laughing. 'Looks like a pile of shit.' He thought of the doctor, complete with his white coat, running around under the bleachers, looking up girls' skirts and jacking off, and he began to laugh again. The doctor sat smiling his nasty smile, making the vision more real, thus funnier. At last his giggles tapered off to a snort or two. Richards hiccupped once and was still.

'I don't suppose you'd care to tell me—'

'No,' Richards said. 'I wouldn't.'

'We'll proceed then. Word association.' He didn't bother to explain it. Richards supposed word was getting around. That was good; it would save time.

'Ready?'

'Yes.'

The doctor produced a stopwatch from an inside pocket, clicked the business end of his ballpoint pen, and considered a list in front of him.

'Doctor.'

'Nigger,' Richards responded.

'Penis.'

'Cock.'

'Red.'

'Black.'

'Silver.'

'Dagger.'

'Rifle.'

'Murder.'

'Win.'

'Money.'

'Sex.'

'Tests.'

'Strike.'

'Out.'

The list continued; they went through over fifty words before the doctor clicked the stem of the stopwatch down and dropped his pen. 'Good,' he said. He folded his hands and looked at Richards seriously. 'I have a final question, Ben. I won't say that I'll know a lie when I hear it, but the machine you're hooked up to will give a very strong indication one way or the other. Have you decided to try for qualification status in the Games out of any suicidal motivation?'

'No.'

'What is your reason?'

'My little girl's sick. She needs a doctor. Medicine. Hospital care.'

The ballpoint scratched. 'Anything else?'

Richards was on the verge of saying no (it was none of their business) and then decided he would give it all. Perhaps because the doctor looked like that nearly forgotten dirty boy of his youth. Maybe only because it needed to be said once, to make it coalesce and take concrete shape, as things do when a man forces himself to translate unformed emotional reactions into spoken words.

'I haven't had work for a long time. I want to work again, even if it's only being the sucker-man in a loaded game. I want to work and support my family. I have pride. Do you have pride, Doctor?'

'It goes before a fall,' the doctor said. He clicked the tip of his ballpoint in. 'If you have nothing to add, Mr Richards—' He stood up. That, and the switch back to his surname, suggested that the interview was over whether Richards had any more to say or not.

'No.'

'The door is down the hall to your right. Good luck.'

'Sure,' Richards said.

. . . MINUS 090 and COUNTING . . .

The group Richards had come in with was now reduced to four. The new waiting room was much smaller, and the whole group had been reduced roughly by the same figure of sixty percent. The last of the *Y*'s and *Z*'s straggled in at four-thirty. At four, an orderly had circulated with a tray of tasteless sandwiches. Richards got two of them and sat munching, listening to a pal named Rettenmund as he regaled Richards and a few others with a seemingly inexhaustible fund of dirty stories.

When the whole group was together, they were shunted into an elevator and lifted to the fifth floor. Their quarters were made up of a large common room, a communal lavatory, and the inevitable sleep-factory with its rows of cots. They were informed that a cafeteria down the hall would serve a hot meal at seven o'clock.

Richards sat still for a few minutes, then got up and walked over to the cop stationed by the door they had come in through. 'Is there a telephone, pal?' He didn't expect they would be allowed to phone out, but the cop merely jerked his thumb toward the hall.

Richards pushed the door open a crack and peered out. Sure enough, there it was. Pay phone.

He looked at the cop again. 'Listen, if you loan me fifty cents for the phone, I'll—'

'Screw off, Jack.'

Richards held his temper. 'I want to call my wife. Our kid is sick. Put yourself in my place, for Christ's sake.'

The cop laughed: a short, chopping, ugly sound. 'You types are all the same. A story for every day of the year.

Technicolor and 3-D on Christmas and Mother's Day.'

'You bastard,' Richards said, and something in his eyes, the stance of his shoulders suddenly made the cop shift his gaze to the wall. 'Aren't you married yourself? Didn't you ever find yourself strapped and have to borrow, even if it tasted like shit in your mouth?'

The cop suddenly jammed a hand into his jumper pocket and came up with a fistful of plastic coins. He thrust two New Quarters at Richards, stuffed the rest of the money back in his pocket, and grabbed a handful of Richards's tunic. 'If you send anybody else over here because Charlie Grady is a soft touch, I'll beat your sonofabitching brains out, maggot.'

'Thank you,' Richards said steadily. 'For the loan.'

Charlie Grady laughed and let him go. Richards went out into the hall, picked up the phone, and dropped his money into the horn. It banged hollowly and for a moment nothing happened – *oh, Jesus, all for nothing* – but then the dial tone came. He punched the number of the fifth floor hall phone slowly, hoping the Jenner bitch down the hall wouldn't answer. She'd just as soon yell wrong number when she recognized his voice and he would lose his money.

It rang six times, and then an unfamiliar voice said: 'Hello?'

'I want to talk to Sheila Richards in 5C.'

'I think she went out,' the voice said. It grew insinuating. 'She walks up an down the block, you know. They got a sick kid. The man there is shifless.'

'Just knock on the door,' he said, cotton mouthed.

'Hold on.'

The phone on the other end crashed against the wall as the unfamiliar voice let it dangle. Far away, dim, as if in a dream, he heard the unfamiliar voice knocking and yelling: 'Phone! Phone for ya, Missus Richards!'

Half a minute later the unfamiliar voice was back on the line. 'She ain't there. I can hear the kid yellin, but she ain't there. Like I say, she keeps an eye out when the fleet's in.' The voice giggled.

Richards wished he could teleport himself through the phone line and pop out on the other end, like an evil genie from a black bottle, and choke the unfamiliar voice until his eyeballs popped out and rolled on the floor.

'Take a message,' he said. 'Write it on the wall if you have to.'

'Ain't got no pencil. I'm hangin up. G'bye.'

'Wait!' Richards yelled, panic in his voice.

'I'm . . . just a second.' Grudgingly the voice said, 'She comin up the stairs now.'

Richards collapsed sweatily against the wall. A moment later Sheila's voice was in his ear, quizzical, wary, a little frightened: 'Hello?'

'Sheila.' He closed his eyes, letting the wall support him.

'Ben. Ben, is that you? Are you all right?'

'Yeah. Fine. Cathy. Is she—'

'The same. The fever isn't so bad but she sounds so *croupy*. Ben, I think there's water in her lungs. What if she has pneumonia?'

'It'll be all right. It'll be all right.'

'I—' She paused, a long pause. 'I hate to leave her, but I had to. Ben, I turned two tricks this morning. I'm sorry. But I got her some medicine at the drug. Some good medicine.' Her voice had taken on a zealous, evangelical lilt.

'That stuff is shit,' he said. 'Listen: No more, Sheila. Please. I think I'm in here. Really. They can't cut many more guys because there's too many shows. There's got to be enough cannon fodder to go around. And they give advances, I think. Mrs Upshaw—'

'She looked awful in black,' Sheila broke in tonelessly.

'Never mind that. You stay with Cathy, Sheila. No more tricks.'

'All right. I won't go out again.' But he didn't believe her voice. *Fingers crossed, Sheila?* 'I love you, Ben.'

'And I lo—'

'Three minutes are up,' the operator broke in. 'If you wish to continue, please deposit one New Quarter or three old quarters.'

'Wait a second!' Richards yelled. 'Get off the goddam line, bitch. You—'

The empty hum of a broken connection.

He threw the receiver. It flew the length of its silver cord, then rebounded, striking the wall and then penduluming slowly back and forth like some strange snake that had bitten once and then died.

Somebody has to pay, Richards thought numbly as he walked back. Somebody *has* to.

. . . MINUS 089   and COUNTING . . .

They were quartered on the fifth floor until ten o'clock the following day, and Richards was nearly out of his mind with anger, worry, and frustration when a young and slightly faggoty-looking pal in a skintight Games uniform asked them to please step into the elevator. They were perhaps three hundred in all: over sixty of their number had been removed soundlessly and painlessly the night before. One of them had been the kid with the inexhaustible fund of dirty jokes.

They were taken to a small auditorium on the sixth floor in groups of fifty. The auditorium was very luxurious, done in great quantities of red plush. There was an ashtray built into the realwood arm of every seat, and Richards hauled out his crumpled pack of Blams. He tapped his ashes on the floor.

There was a small stage at the front, and in the center of that, a lectern. A pitcher of water stood on it.

At about fifteen minutes past ten, the faggoty-looking fellow walked to the lectern and said: 'I'd like you to meet Arthur M. Burns, Assistant Director of Games.'

'Huzzah,' somebody behind Richards said in a sour voice.

A portly man with a tonsure surrounded by gray hair strode to the lectern, pausing and cocking his head as he arrived, as if to appreciate a round of applause which only he could hear. Then he smiled at them, a broad, twinkling smile that seemed to transform him into a pudgy, aging Cupid in a business suit.

'Congratulations,' he said. 'You've made it.'

There was a huge collective sigh, followed by some laughter and back-slapping. More cigarettes were lit up.

'Huzzah,' the sour voice repeated.

'Shortly, your program assignments and seventh floor room numbers will be passed out. The executive producers of your particular programs will explain further exactly what is expected of you. But before that happens, I just want to repeat my congratulations and tell you that I find you to be a courageous, resourceful group, refusing to live on the public dole when you have means at your disposal to acquit yourselves as men, and, may I add personally, as true heroes of our time.'

'Bullshit,' the sour voice remarked.

'Furthermore, I speak for the entire Network when I wish you good luck and Godspeed.' Arthur M. Burns chuckled porkily and rubbed his hands together. 'Well, I know you're anxious to get those assignments, so I'll spare you any more of my jabber.'

A side door popped open, and a dozen Games ushers wearing red tunics came into the auditorium. They began to call out names. White envelopes were passed out, and soon they littered the floor like confetti. Plastic assignment cards were read, exchanged with new acquaintances. There were muffled groans, cheers, catcalls. Arthur M. Burns presided over it all from his podium, smiling benevolently.

—That Christly *How Hot Can You Take It*, Jesus I hate the heat

—the show's a goddam two-bitter, comes on right after the flictoons, for God's sake

—*Treadmill to Bucks*, gosh, I didn't know my heart was—

—I was hoping I'd get it but I didn't really think—

—Hey Jake, you ever seen this *Swim the Crocodiles?* I thought—

—nothing like I expected—

—I don't think you can—

—Miserable goddam—

—This *Run For Your Guns*—

'Benjamin Richards! Ben Richards?'

'Here!'

He was handed a plain white envelope and tore it open. His fingers were shaking slightly and it took him two tries to get the small plastic card out. He frowned down at it, not understanding. No program assignment was punched on it. The card read simply: ELEVATOR SIX.

He put the card in his breast pocket with his ID and left the auditorium. The first five elevators at the end of the hall were doing a brisk business as they ferried the following week's contestants up to the seventh floor. There were four others standing by the closed doors of Elevator 6, and Richards recognized one of them as the owner of the sour voice.

'What's this?' Richards asked. 'Are we getting the gate?'

The man with the sour voice was about twenty-five, not bad looking. One arm was withered, probably by polio, which had come back strong in 2005. It had done especially well in Co-Op.

'No such luck,' he said, and laughed emptily. 'I think we're getting the big-money assignments. The ones where they do more than just land you in the hospital with a stroke or put out an eye or cut off an arm or two. The ones where they kill you. Prime time, baby.'

They were joined by a sixth pal, a good-looking kid who was blinking at everything in a surprised way.

'Hello, sucker,' the man with the sour voice said.

At eleven o'clock, after all the others had been taken away, the doors of Elevator 6 popped open. There was a cop riding in the Judas hole again.

'See?' The man with the sour voice said. 'We're dangerous characters. Public enemies. They're gonna rub us out.' He made a tough gangster face and sprayed the bulletproof compartment with an imaginary Sten gun. The cop stared at him woodenly.

...MINUS 088 and COUNTING...

The waiting room on the eighth floor was very small, very plush, very intimate, very private. Richards had it all to himself.

At the end of the elevator ride, three of them had been promptly whisked away down a plushly carpeted corridor by three cops. Richards, the man with the sour voice, and the kid who blinked a lot had been taken here.

A receptionist who vaguely reminded Richards of one of the old tee-vee sex stars (Liz Kelly? Grace Taylor?) he had watched as a kid smiled at the three of them when they came in. She was sitting at a desk in an alcove, surrounded by so many potted plants that she might have been in an Ecuadorian foxhole. 'Mr Jansky,' she said with a blinding smile. 'Go right in.'

The kid who blinked a lot went into the inner sanctum. Richards and the man with the sour voice, whose name was Jimmy Laughlin, made wary conversation. Richards discovered that Laughlin lived only three blocks away from him, on Dock Street. He had held a part-time job until the year before as an engine wiper for General Atomics, and had then been fired for taking part in a sit-down strike protesting leaky radiation shields.

'Well, I'm alive, anyway,' he said. 'According to those maggots, that's all that counts. I'm sterile, of course. *That* don't matter. That's one of the little risks you run for the princely sum of seven New Bucks a day.'

When G-A had shown him the door, the withered arm had made it even tougher to get a job. His wife had come down with bad asthma two years before, was now bed-ridden. 'Finally I decided to go for the big brass ring,' Laughlin said with a bitter smile. 'Maybe I'll get a chance to push a few creeps out a high window before McCone's boys get me.'

'Do you think it really is—'

'*The Running Man?* Bet your sweet ass. Give me one of those cruddy cigarettes, pal.'

Richards gave him one.

The door opened and the kid who blinked a lot came out on the arm of a beautiful dolly wearing two handkerchiefs and a prayer. The kid gave them a small, nervous smile as they went by.

'Mr Laughlin? Would you go in, please?'

So Richards was alone, unless you counted the receptionist, who had disappeared into her foxhole again.

He got up and went over to the free cigarette machine in the corner. Laughlin must be right, he reflected. The cigarette machine dispensed Dokes. They must have hit the big leagues. He got a package of Blams, sat down, and lit one up.

About twenty minutes later Laughlin came out with an ash-blonde on his arm. 'A friend of mine from the car pool,' he said to Richards, and pointed at the blonde. She dimpled dutifully. Laughlin looked pained. 'At least the bastard talks straight,' he said to Richards. 'See you.'

He went out. The receptionist poked her head out of her foxhole. 'Mr Richards? Would you step in, please?'

He went in.

... MINUS 087 and COUNTING ...

The inner office looked big enough to play killball in. It was dominated by a huge, one-wall picture window that looked west over the homes of the middle class, the dock-side warehouses and oil tanks, and Harding Lake itself. Both sky and water were pearl-gray; it was still raining. A large tanker far out was chugging from right to left.

The man behind the desk was of middle height and very black. So black, in fact, that for a moment Richards was struck with unreality. He might have stepped out of a minstrel show.

'Mr Richards.' He rose and extended his hand over the desk. When Richards did not shake it, he did not seem particularly flustered. He merely took his hand back to himself and sat down.

A sling chair was next to the desk. Richards sat down and butted his smoke in an ashtray with the Games emblem embossed on it.

'I'm Dan Killian, Mr Richards. By now you've probably guessed why you've been brought here. Our records and your test scores both say you're a bright boy.'

Richards folded his hands and waited.

'You've been slated as a contestant on *The Running Man*, Mr Richards. It's our biggest show; it's the most lucrative — and dangerous — for the men involved. I've got your final consent form here on my desk. I've no doubt that you'll sign it, but first I want to tell you why you've been selected and I want you to understand fully what you're getting into.'

Richards said nothing.

Killian pulled a dossier onto the virgin surface of his desk blotter. Richards saw that it had his name typed on the front. Killian flipped it open.

'Benjamin Stuart Richards. Age twenty-eight, born August 8, 1997, city of Harding. Attended South City Manual Trades from September of 2011 until December of 2013. Suspended twice for failure to respect authority. I believe you kicked the assistant principal in the upper thigh once while his back was turned?'

'Crap,' Richards said. 'I kicked him in the ass.'

Killian nodded. 'However you say, Mr Richards. You married Sheila Richards, née Gordon, at the age of sixteen. Old-style lifetime contract. Rebel all the way, uh? No union affiliation due to your refusal to sign the Union Oath of Fealty and the Wage Control Articles. I believe that you referred to Area Governor Johnsbury as "a corn-holing sonofabitch."'

'Yes,' Richards said.

'Your work record has been spotty and you've been fired . . . let's see . . . a total of six times for such things as insubordination, insulting superiors, and abusive criticism of authority.'

Richards shrugged.

'In short, you are regarded as antiauthoritarian and anti-social. You're a deviate who has been intelligent enough to stay out of prison and serious trouble with the government, and you're not hooked on anything. A staff psychologist reports you saw lesbians, excrement, and a pollutive gas vehicle in various inkblots. He also reports a high, unexplained degree of hilarity—'

'He reminded me of a kid I used to know. He liked to hide under the bleachers at school and whack off. The kid, I mean. I don't know what your doctor likes to do.'

'I see.' Killian smiled briefly, white teeth glittering in all that darkness, and went back to his folder. 'You held racial responses outlawed by the Racial Act of 2004. You made several rather violent responses during the word-association test.'

'I'm here on violent business,' Richards said.

'To be sure. And yet we – and here I speak in a larger sense than the Games Authority; I speak in the national sense – view these responses with extreme disquiet.'

'Afraid someone might tape a stick of Irish to your ignition system some night?' Richards asked, grinning.

Killian wet his thumb reflectively and turned to the next sheet. 'Fortunately – for us – you've given a hostage to fortune, Mr Richards. You have a daughter named Catherine, eighteen months. Was that a mistake?' He smiled frostily.

'Planned,' Richards said without rancor. 'I was working for G-A then. Somehow, some of my sperm lived through it. A jest of God, maybe. With the world the way it is, I sometimes think we must have been off our trolley.'

'At any rate, you're here,' Killian said, continuing to smile his cold smile. 'And next Tuesday you will appear on *The Running Man*. You've seen the program?'

'Yes.'

'Then you know it's the biggest thing going on Free-Vee. It's filled with chances for viewer participation, both vicarious and actual. I am executive producer of the program.'

'That's really wonderful,' Richards said.

'The program is one of the surest ways the Network has of getting rid of embryo troublemakers such as yourself, Mr Richards. We've been on for six years. To date, we have no survivals. To be brutally honest, we expect to have none.'

'Then you're running a crooked table,' Richards said flatly.

Killian seemed more amused than horrified. 'But we're not. You keep forgetting you're an anachronism, Mr Richards. People won't be in the bars and hotels or gathering in the cold in front of appliance stores rooting for you to get away. Goodness! no. They want to see you wiped out, and they'll help if they can. The more messy the better. And there is McCone to contend with. Evan McCone and the Hunters.'

'They sound like a neo-group,' Richards said.

'McCone never loses,' Killian said.

Richards grunted.

'You'll appear live Tuesday night. Subsequent programs will be a patch-up of tapes, films, and live tricasts when possible. We've been known to interrupt scheduled broadcasting when a particularly resourceful contestant is on the verge of reaching his . . . personal Waterloo, shall we say.

'The rules are simplicity themselves. You − or your surviving family − will win one hundred New Dollars for each hour you remain free. We stake you to forty-eight hundred dollars running money on the assumption that you will be able to fox the Hunters for forty-eight hours. The unspent balance refundable, of course, if you fall before the forty-eight hours are up. You're given a twelve-hour head start. If you last thirty days, you win the Grand Prize. One billion New Dollars.'

Richards threw back his head and laughed.

'My sentiments exactly,' Killian said with a dry smile. 'Do you have any questions?'

'Just one,' Richards said, leaning forward. The traces of humor had vanished from his face completely. 'How would you like to be the one out there, on the run?'

Killian laughed. He held his belly and huge mahogany laughter rolled richly in the room. 'Oh . . . Mr Richards . . . you must excuse m-me—' and he went off into another gale.

At last, dabbing his eyes with a large white handkerchief, Killian seemed to get himself under control. 'You see, not only are you possessed of a sense of humor, Mr Richards. You . . . I—' He choked new laughter down. 'Please excuse me. You've struck my funnybone.'

'I see I have.'

'Other questions?'

'No.'

'Very good. There will be a staff meeting before the program. If any questions should develop in that fascinating mind of yours, please hold them until then.' Killian pressed a button on his desk.

'Spare me the cheap snatch,' Richards said. 'I'm married.'

Killian's eyebrows went up. 'Are you quite sure? Fidelity is admirable, Mr Richards, but it's a long time from Friday to Tuesday. And considering the fact that you may never see your wife again—'

'I'm married.'

'Very well.' He nodded to the girl in the doorway and she disappeared. 'Anything we *can* do for you, Mr Richards? You'll have a private suite on the ninth floor, and meal requests will be filled within reason.'

'A good bottle of bourbon. And a telephone so I can talk to my w—'

'Ah, no, I'm sorry, Mr Richards. The bourbon we can do. But once you sign this release form,' – he pushed it over to Richards along with a pen – 'you're incommunicado until Tuesday. Would you care to reconsider the girl?'

'No,' Richards said, and scrawled his name on the dotted line. 'But you better make that two bottles of bourbon.'

'Certainly.' Killian stood and offered his hand again.

Richards disregarded it again, and walked out.

Killian looked after him with blank eyes. He was not smiling.

... MINUS 086 and COUNTING ...

The receptionist popped promptly out of her foxhole as Richards walked through and handed him an envelope. On the front:

Mr Richards,

I suspect one of the things that you will not mention during our interview is the fact that you need money badly right now. Is it not true?

Despite rumors to the contrary, Games Authority does *not* give advances. You must not look upon yourself as a contestant with all the glitter that word entails. You are not a Free-Vee star but only a working joe who is being paid extremely well for undertaking a dangerous job.

However, Games Authority has no rule which forbids me from extending you a personal loan. Inside you will find ten percent of your advance salary – not in New

Dollars, I should caution you, but in Games Certificates redeemable for dollars. Should you decide to send these certificates to your wife, as I suspect you will, she will find they have one advantage over New Dollars: a reputable doctor will accept them as legal tender, while a quack will not.

Sincerely,
Dan Killian

Richards opened the envelope and pulled out a thick book of coupons with the Games symbol on the vellum cover. Inside were forty-eight coupons with a face value of ten New Dollars each. Richards felt an absurd wave of gratitude toward Killian sweep him and crushed it. He had no doubt that Killian would attach four hundred and eighty dollars of his advance money, and besides that, four-eighty was a pretty goddam cheap price to pay for insurance on the big show, the continued happiness of the client, and Killian's own big-money job.

'Shit,' he said.

The receptionist poked attentively out of her foxhole. 'Did you say something, Mr Richards?'

'No. Which way to the elevators?'

. . . MINUS 085 and COUNTING . . .

The suite was sumptuous.

Wall-to-wall carpeting almost deep enough to breaststroke in covered the floors of all three rooms: living room, bedroom, and bath. The Free-Vee was turned off; blessed silence prevailed. There were flowers in the vases, and on the wall next to the door was a button discreetly marked SERVICE. The service would be fast, too,

Richards thought cynically. There were two cops stationed outside his ninth-floor suite just to make sure he didn't go wandering.

He pushed the service button, and the door opened. 'Yes, Mr Richards,' one of the cops said. Richards fancied he could see how sour that *Mister* tasted in his mouth. 'The bourbon you asked for will be —'

'It's not that,' Richards said. He showed the cop the book of coupons Killian had left for him. 'I want you to take this somewhere.'

'Just write the name and address, Mr Richards, and I'll see that it's delivered.'

Richards found the cobbler's receipt and wrote his address and Sheila's name on the back of it. He gave the tattered paper and the coupon book to the cop. He was turning away when a new thought struck Richards. 'Hey! Just a second!'

The cop turned back, and Richards plucked the coupon book out of his hand. He opened it to the first coupon, and tore one tenth of it along the perforated line. Equivalent value: One New Dollar.

'Do you know a cop named Charlie Grady?'

'Charlie?' The cop looked at him warily. 'Yeah, I know Charlie. He's got fifth-floor duty.'

'Give him this.' Richards handed him the coupon section. 'Tell him the extra fifty cents is his usurer's fee.'

The cop turned away again, and Richards called him back once more.

'You'll bring me written receipts from my wife and from Grady, won't you?'

Disgust showed openly on the cop's face. 'Ain't you the trusting soul?'

'Sure,' Richards said, smiling thinly. 'You guys taught me that. South of the Canal you taught me all about it.'

'It's gonna be fun,' the cop said, 'watching them go

43

after you. I'm gonna be glued to my Free-Vee with a beer in each hand.'

'Just bring me the receipts,' Richards said, and closed the door gently in the cop's face.

The bourbon came twenty minutes later, and Richards told the surprised deliveryman that he would like a couple of thick novels sent up.

'Novels?'

'Books. You know. Read. Words. Movable press.' Richards pantomimed flipping pages.

'Yes, sir,' he said doubtfully. 'Do you have a dinner order?'

Christ, the shit was getting thick. He was drowning in it. Richards saw a sudden fantasy-cartoon: Man falls into outhouse hole and drowns in pink shit that smells like Chanel No. 5. The kicker: It still tastes like shit.

'Steak. Peas. Mashed potatoes.' God, what was Sheila sitting down to? A protein pill and a cup of fake coffee? 'Milk. Apple cobbler with cream. Got it?'

'Yes, sir. Would you like—'

'No,' Richards said, suddenly distraught. 'No. Get out.' He had no appetite. Absolutely none.

... MINUS 084 and COUNTING ...

With sour amusement Richards thought that the Games bellboy had taken him literally about the novels: He must have picked them out with a ruler as his only guide. Anything over an inch and a half is okay. He had brought Richards three books he had never heard of: two golden oldies titled *God Is an Englishman* and *Not as a Stranger* and a huge tome written three years ago called *The Pleasure of Serving*. Richards peeked into that one first and wrinkled his nose. Poor boy makes good in General Atomics. Rises from engine wiper to gear tradesman. Takes night courses (on what? Richards wondered, Monopoly money?). Falls in love with beautiful girl (apparently syphilis hadn't rotted her nose off yet) at a block orgy. Promoted to junior technico following dazzling aptitude scores. Three-year marriage contract follows, and—

Richards threw the book across the room. *God Is an Englishman* was a little better. He poured himself a bourbon on the rocks and settled into the story.

By the time the discreet knock came, he was three hundred pages in, and pretty well in the bag to boot. One of the bourbon bottles was empty. He went to the door holding the other in his hand. The cop was there. 'Your receipts, Mr Richards,' he said, and pulled the door closed.

Sheila had not written anything, but had sent one of Cathy's baby pictures. He looked at it and felt the easy tears of drunkenness prick his eyes. He put it in his pocket and looked at the other receipt. Charlie Grady had written briefly on the back of a traffic ticket form:

> Thanks, maggot. Get stuffed.
> Charlie Grady

Richards snickered and let the paper flitter to the carpet. 'Thanks, Charlie,' he said to the empty room. 'I needed that.'

He looked at the picture of Cathy again, a tiny, red-faced infant of four days at the time of the photo, screaming her head off, swimming in a white cradle dress that Sheila had made herself. He felt the tears lurking and made himself think of good old Charlie's thank-you note. He wondered if he could kill the entire second bottle before he passed out, and decided to find out.

He almost made it.

. . . MINUS 083 and COUNTING . . .

Richards spent Saturday living through a huge hangover. He was almost over it by Saturday evening, and ordered two more bottles of bourbon with supper. He got through both of them and woke up in the pale early light of Sunday morning seeing large caterpillars with flat, murderous eyes crawling slowly down the far bedroom wall. He decided then it would be against his best interests to wreck his reactions completely before Tuesday, and laid off the booze.

This hangover was slower dissipating. He threw up a good deal, and when there was nothing left to throw up, he had dry heaves. These tapered off around six o'clock Sunday evening, and he ordered soup for dinner. No bourbon. He asked for a dozen neo-rock discers to play on the suite's sound system, and tired of them quickly.

He went to bed early. And slept poorly.

He spent most of Monday on the tiny glassed-in terrace that opened off the bedroom. He was very high above the waterfront now, and the day was a series of sun and showers that was fairly pleasant. He read two novels, went to bed early again, and slept a little better. There was an unpleasant dream: Sheila was dead, and he was at her funeral. Somebody had propped her up in her coffin and stuffed a grotesque corsage of New Dollars in her mouth. He tried to run to her and remove the obscenity; hands grabbed him from behind. He was being held by a dozen cops. One of them was Charlie Grady. He was grinning and saying: 'This is what happens to losers, maggot.' They were putting their pistols to his head when he woke up.

'Tuesday,' he said to no one at all, and rolled out of bed. The fashionable G-A sunburst clock on the far wall said it was nine minutes after seven. The live tricast of *The Running Man* would be going out all over North America in less than eleven hours. He felt a hot drop of fear in his stomach. In twenty-three hours he would be fair game.

He had a long hot shower, dressed in his coverall, ordered ham and eggs for breakfast. He also got the bellboy on duty to send up a carton of Blams.

He spent the rest of the morning and early afternoon reading quietly. It was two o'clock on the nose when a single formal rap came at the door. Three police and Arthur M. Burns, looking potty and more than a bit ridiculous in a Games singlet, walked in. All of the cops were carrying move-alongs.

'It's time for your final briefing, Mr Richards,' Burns said. 'Would you—'

'Sure,' Richards said. He marked his place in the book he had been reading and put it down on the coffee table. He was suddenly terrified, close to panic, and he was very glad there was no perceptible shake in his fingers.

... MINUS 082   and COUNTING ...

The tenth floor of the Games Building was a great deal different from the ones below, and Richards knew that he was meant to go no higher. The fiction of upward mobility which started in the grimy street-level lobby ended here on the tenth floor. This was the broadcast facility.

The hallways were wide, white, and stark. Bright

yellow go-carts powered by G-A solar-cell motors pottered here and there, carrying loads of Free-Vee technicos to studios and control rooms.

A cart was waiting for them when the elevator stopped, and the five of them – Richards, Burns, and cops – climbed aboard. Necks craned and Richards was pointed out several times as they made the trip. One woman in a yellow Games shorts-and-halter outfit winked and blew Richards a kiss. He gave her the finger.

They seemed to travel miles, through dozens of interconnecting corridors. Richards caught glimpses into at least a dozen studios, one of them containing the infamous treadmill seen on *Treadmill to Bucks*. A tour group from uptown was trying it out and giggling.

At last they came to a stop before a door which read *THE RUNNING MAN: ABSOLUTELY NO ADMITTANCE*. Burns waved to the guard in the bulletproof booth beside the door, and then looked at Richards.

'Put your ID in the slot between the guard booth and the door,' Burns said.

Richards did it. His card disappeared into the slot, and a small light went on in the guard booth. The guard pushed a button and the door slid open. Richards got back into the cart and they were trundled into the room beyond.

'Where's my card?' Richards asked.

'You don't need it anymore.'

They were in a control room. The console section was empty except for a bald technico who was sitting in front of a blank monitor screen, reading numbers into a microphone.

Across to the left, Dan Killian and two men Richards hadn't met were sitting around a table with frosty glasses. One of them was vaguely familiar, too pretty to be a technico.

'Hello, Mr Richards. Hello, Arthur. Would you care for a soft drink, Mr Richards?'

Richards found he was thirsty; it was quite warm on ten in spite of the many air-conditioning units he had seen. 'I'll have a Rooty-Toot,' he said.

Killian rose, went to a cold-cabinet, and snapped the lid from a plastic squeeze-bottle. Richards sat down and took the bottle with a nod.

'Mr Richards, this gentleman on my right is Fred Victor, the director of *The Running Man*. This other fellow, as I'm sure you know, is Bobby Thompson.'

Thompson, of course. Host and emcee of *The Running Man*. He wore a natty green tunic, slightly iridescent, and sported a mane of hair that was silvery-attractive enough to be suspect.

'Do you dye it?' Richards asked.

Thompson's impeccable eyebrows went up. 'I beg pardon?'

'Never mind,' Richards said.

'You'll have to make allowances for Mr Richards,' Killian said, smiling. 'He seems afflicted with an extreme case of the rudes.'

'Quite understandable,' Thompson said, and lit a cigarette. Richards felt a wave of unreality surge over him. 'Under the circumstances.'

'Come over here, Mr Richards, if you please,' Victor said, taking charge. He led Richards to the bank of screens on the other side of the room. The technico had finished with his numbers and had left the room.

Victor punched two buttons and left-right views of *The Running Man* set sprang into view.

'We don't do a run-through here,' Victor said. 'We think it detracts from spontaneity. Bobby just wings it, and he does a pretty damn good job. We go on at six o'clock, Harding time. Bobby is center stage on that raised blue dais. He does the lead-in, giving a rundown on you. The monitor will flash a couple of still pictures. You'll be in the wings at stage right, flanked by two Games guards. They'll come on with you, armed with riot guns. Move-alongs would be more practical if you decided to give trouble, but the riot guns are good theater.'

'Sure,' Richards said.

'There will be a lot of booing from the audience. We pack it that way because it's good theater. Just like the killball matches.'

'Are they going to shoot me with fake bullets?' Richards asked. 'You could put a few blood bags on me, to spatter on cue. That would be good theater, too.'

'Pay attention, please,' Victor said. 'You and the guards go on when your name is called. Bobby will, uh, interview you. Feel free to express yourself as colorfully as you please. It's all good theater. Then, around six-ten, just before the first Network promo, you'll be given your stake money and exit – *sans* guards – at stage left. Do you understand?'

'Yes. What about Laughlin?'

Victor frowned and lit a cigarette. 'He comes on after you, at six-fifteen. We run two contests simultaneously because often one of the contestants is, uh, inadept at staying ahead of the Hunters.'

'With the kid as a back-up?'

'Mr Jansky? Yes. But none of this concerns you, Mr Richards. When you exit stage left, you'll be given a tape machine which is about the size of a box of popcorn. It weighs six pounds. With it, you'll be given sixty tape clips which are about four inches long. The equipment will fit inside a coat pocket without a bulge. It's a triumph of modern technology.'

'Swell.'

Victor pressed his lips together. 'As Dan has already told you, Richards, you're a contestant only for the masses.

Actually, you are a working man and you should view your role in that light. The tape cartridges can be dropped into any mailslot and they will be delivered express to us so we can edit them for airing that night. Failure to deposit two clips per day will result in legal default of payment.'

'But I'll still be hunted down.'

'Right. So mail those tapes. They won't give away your location; the Hunters operate independently of the broadcasting section.'

Richards had his doubts about that but said nothing.

'After we give you the equipment, you will be escorted to the street elevator. This gives directly on Rampart Street. Once you're there, you're on your own.' He paused. 'Questions?'

'No.'

'Then Mr Killian has one more money detail to straighten out with you.'

They walked back to where Dan Killian was in conversation with Arthur M. Burns. Richards asked for another Rooty-Toot and got it.

'Mr Richards,' Killian said, twinkling his teeth at him. 'As you know, you leave the studio unarmed. But this is not to say you cannot arm yourself by fair means or foul. Goodness! no. You – or your estate – will be paid an additional one hundred dollars for any Hunter or representative of the law you should happen to dispatch—'

'I know, don't tell me,' Richards said. 'It's good theater.'

Killian smiled delightedly. 'How very astute of you. Yes. However, try not to bag any innocent bystanders. That's not kosher.'

Richards said nothing.

'The other aspect of the program—'

'The stoolies and independent cameramen. I know.'

'They're not stoolies; they're good North American citizens.' It was difficult to tell whether Killian's tone of hurt was real or ironic. 'Anyway, there's an 800 number for anyone who spots you. A verified sighting pays one hundred New Dollars. A sighting which results in a kill pays a thousand. We pay independent cameramen ten dollars a foot and up—'

'Retire to scenic Jamaica on blood money,' Richards cried, spreading his arms wide. 'Get your picture on a hundred 3-D weeklies. Be the idol of millions. Just holograph for details.'

'That's enough,' Killian said quietly. Bobby Thompson was buffing his fingernails; Victor had wandered out and could be faintly heard yelling at someone about camera angles.

Killian pressed a button. 'Miss Jones? Ready for you, sweets.' He stood up and offered his hand again. 'Make-up next, Mr Richards. Then the lighting runs. You'll be quartered offstage and we won't meet again before you go on. So—'

'It's been grand,' Richards said. He declined the hand. Miss Jones led him out. It was 2:30.

. . . MINUS 081 and COUNTING . . .

Richards stood in the wings with a cop on each side, listening to the studio audience as they frantically applauded Bobby Thompson. He was nervous. He jeered at himself for it, but the nervousness was a fact. Jeering would not make it go away. It was 6:01.

'Tonight's first contestant is a shrewd, resourceful man from south of the Canal in our own home city,' Thompson was saying. The monitor faded to a stark portrait of Richards in his baggy gray workshirt, taken by a hidden camera days before. The background looked like the fifth floor waiting room. It had been retouched, Richards thought, to make his eyes deeper, his forehead a little lower, his cheeks more shadowed. His mouth had been given a jeering, curled expression by some technico's airbrush. All in all, the Richards on the monitor was terrifying – the angel of urban death, brutal, not very bright, but possessed of a certain primitive animal cunning. The uptown apartment dweller's boogeyman.

'This man is Benjamin Richards, age twenty-eight. Know the face well! In a half-hour, this man will be on the prowl. A verified sighting brings you one hundred New Dollars! A sighting which results in a kill results in one thousand New Dollars for *you*!'

Richards's mind was wandering; it came back to the point with a mighty snap.

'. . . and *this* is the woman that Benjamin Richards's award will go to, if and when he is brought down!'

The picture dissolved to a still of Sheila . . . but the airbrush had been at work again, this time wielded with a heavier hand. The results were brutal. The sweet, not-so-good-looking face had been transformed into that of a vapid slattern. Full, pouting lips, eyes that seemed to glitter with avarice, a suggestion of a double chin fading down to what appeared to be bare breasts.

'You *bastard*!' Richards grated. He lunged forward, but powerful arms held him back.

'Simmer down, buddy. It's only a picture.'

A moment later he was half led, half dragged onstage.

The audience reaction was immediate. The studio was filled with screamed cries of 'Boo! Cycle bum!' 'Get out, you creep!' 'Kill him! Kill the bastard!' 'You eat it!' 'Get out, get out!'

Bobby Thompson held his arms up and shouted good naturedly for quiet. 'Let's hear what he's got to say.' The audience quieted, but reluctantly.

Richards stood bull-like under the hot lights with his head lowered. He knew he was projecting exactly the aura of hate and defiance that they wanted him to project, but he could not help it.

He stared at Thompson with hard, red-rimmed eyes. 'Somebody is going to eat their own balls for that picture of my wife,' he said.

'Speak up, speak up, Mr Richards!' Thompson cried with just the right note of contempt. 'Nobody will hurt you . . . at least not *yet*.'

More screams and hysterical vituperation from the audience.

Richards suddenly wheeled to face them, and they quieted as if slapped. Women stared at him with frightened, half-sexual expressions. Men grinned up at him with blood-hate in their eyes.

'You bastards!' He cried. 'If you want to see somebody die so bad, why don't you kill each other?'

His final words were drowned in more screams. People from the audience (perhaps paid to do so) were trying to get onstage. The police were holding them back. Richards faced them, knowing how he must look.

'Thank you, Mr Richards, for those words of wisdom.' The contempt was palpable now, and the crowd, nearly silent again, was eating it up. 'Would you like to tell our audience in the studio and at home how long you think you can hold out?'

'I want to tell everybody in the studio and at home that that wasn't my wife! That was a cheap fake—'

The crowd drowned him out. Their screams of hate had reached a near fever pitch. Thompson waited nearly a minute for them to quiet a little, and then repeated: 'How long do you expect to hold out, *Mister* Richards?'

'I expect to go the whole thirty,' Richards said coolly. 'I don't think you've got anybody who can take me.'

More screaming. Shaken fists. Someone threw a tomato.

Bobby Thompson faced the audience again and cried: 'With those last cheap words of bravado, Mr Richards will be led from our stage. Tomorrow at noon, the hunt begins. *Remember his face!* It may be next to you on a pneumo bus . . . in a jet plane . . . at a 3-D rack . . . in your local killball arena. Tonight he's in Harding. Tomorrow in New York? Boise? Albuquerque? Columbus? Skulking outside *your* home? *Will you report him?'*

'*YESS!!!*' They screamed.

Richards suddenly gave them the finger — both fingers. This time the rush for the stage was by no stretch of the imagination simulated. Richards was rushed out the stage-left exit before they could rip him apart on camera, thus depriving the Network of all the juicy upcoming coverage.

. . . MINUS 080   and COUNTING . . .

Killian was in the wings, and convulsed with amusement. 'Fine performance, Mr Richards. Fine! God, I wish I could give you a bonus. Those fingers . . . superb!'

'We aim to please,' Richards said. The monitors were dissolving to a promo. 'Give me the goddam camera and go fuck yourself.'

'That's generically impossible,' Killian said, still grinning, 'but here's the camera.' He took it from the technico who had been cradling it. 'Fully loaded and ready to go. And here are the clips.' He handed Richards a small, surprisingly heavy oblong box wrapped in oilcloth.

Richards dropped the camera into one coat pocket, the clips into the other. 'Okay. Where's the elevator?'

'Not so fast,' Killian said. 'You've got a minute ... twelve of them, actually. Your twelve hours' leeway doesn't start officially until six-thirty.'

The screams of rage had begun again. Looking over his shoulder, Richards saw that Laughlin was on. His heart went out to him.

'I like you, Richards, and I think you'll do well,' Killian said. 'You have a certain crude style that I enjoy immensely. I'm a collector, you know. Cave art and Egyptian artifacts are my areas of specialization. You are more analogous to the cave art than to my Egyptian urns, but no matter. I wish you could be preserved – collected, if you please – just as my Asian cave paintings have been collected and preserved.'

'Grab a recording of my brain waves, you bastard. They're on record.'

'So I'd like to give you a piece of advice,' Killian said, ignoring him. 'You don't really have a chance; nobody does with a whole nation in on the manhunt and with the incredibly sophisticated equipment and training that the Hunters have. But if you stay low, you'll last longer. Use your legs instead of any weapons you happen to pick up. And stay close to your own people.' He leveled a finger at Richards in emphasis. 'Not these good middle-class folks out there; they hate your guts. You symbolize all the fears of this dark and broken time. It wasn't all show and audience-packing out there, Richards. *They hate your guts.* Could you feel it?'

'Yes,' Richards said. 'I felt it. I hate them, too.'

Killian smiled. 'That's why they're killing you.' He took Richards's arm; his grip was surprisingly strong. 'This way.'

Behind them, Laughlin was being ragged by Bobby Thompson to the audience's satisfaction.

Down a white corridor, their footfalls echoing hollowly – alone. All alone. One elevator at the end.

'This is where you and I part company,' Killian said. 'Express to the street. Nine seconds.'

He offered his hand for the fourth time, and Richards refused it again. Yet he lingered a moment.

'What if I could go up?' he asked, and gestured with his head toward the ceiling and the eighty stories above the ceiling. 'Who could I kill up there? Who could I kill if I went right to the top?'

Killian laughed softly and punched the button beside the elevator; the doors popped open. 'That's what I like about you, Richards. You think big.'

Richards stepped into the elevator. The doors slid toward each other.

'Stay low,' Killian repeated, and then Richards was alone.

The bottom dropped out of his stomach as the elevator sank toward the street.

. . . MINUS 079 and COUNTING . . .

The elevator opened directly onto the street. A cop was standing by its frontage on Nixon Memorial Park, but he did not look at Richards as he stepped out; only tapped his move-along reflectively and stared into the soft drizzle that filled the air.

The drizzle had brought early dusk to the city. The lights glowed mystically through the darkness, and the people moving on Rampart Street in the shadow of the Games Building were only insubstantial shadows, as Richards knew he must be himself. He breathed deeply of the wet, sulphur-tainted air. It was good in spite of the taste. It seemed that he had just been let out of prison, rather than from one communicating cell to another. The air was good. The air was fine.

Stay close to your own people, Killian had said. Of course he was right. Richards hadn't needed Killian to tell him that. Or to know that the heat would be heaviest in Co-Op City when the truce broke at noon tomorrow. But by then he would be over the hills and far away.

He walked three blocks and hailed a taxi. He was hoping the cab's Free-Vee would be busted – a lot of them were – but this one was in A-1 working order, and blaring the closing credits of *The Running Man*. Shit.

'Where, buddy?'

'Robard Street.' That was five blocks from his destination; when the cab dropped him, he would go backyard express to Molie's place.

The cab accelerated, ancient gas-powered engine a discordant symphony of pounding pistons and manifold noise. Richards slumped back against the vinyl cushions, into what he hoped was deeper shadow.

'Hey, I just seen you on the Free-Vee!' the cabbie exclaimed. 'You're that guy Pritchard!'

'Pritchard. That's right,' Richards said resignedly. The Games Building was dwindling behind them. A psychological shadow seemed to be dwindling proportionally in his mind, in spite of the bad luck with the cabby.

'Jesus, you got balls, buddy. I'll say that. You really do. Christ, they'll killya. You know that? They'll killya fuckin-eye dead. You must really have balls.'

'That's right. Two of them. Just like you.'

'Two of 'm!' the cabby repeated. He was ecstatic. 'Jesus, that's good. That's hot! You mind if I tell my wife I hadja as a fare? She goes batshit for the Games. I'll hafta reportcha too, but Christ, I won't get no hunnert for it. Cabbies gotta have at least one supportin witness, y'know. Knowin my luck, no one sawya gettin in.'

'That would be tough,' Richards said. 'I'm sorry you

can't help kill me. Should I leave a note saying I was here?'

'Jesus, couldja? That'd be—'

They had just crossed the Canal. 'Let me out here,' Richards said abruptly. He pulled a New Dollar from the envelope Thompson had handed him, and dropped it on the front seat.

'Gee, I didn't say nothin, did I? I dint meanta—'

'No,' Richards said.

'Couldja gimme that note—'

'Get stuffed, maggot.'

He lunged out and began walking toward Drummond Street. Co-Op City rose skeletal in the gathering darkness before him. The cabbie's yell floated after him: *I hope they getya early, you cheap fuck!*

... MINUS 078 and COUNTING ...

Through a backyard; through a ragged hole in a cyclone fence separating one barren asphalt desert from another; across a ghostly, abandoned construction site; pausing far back in shattered shadows as a cycle pack roared by, head-lamps glaring in the dark like the psychopathic eyes of nocturnal werewolves. Then over a final fence (cutting one hand) and he was rapping on Molie Jernigan's back door – which is to say, the main entrance.

Molie ran a Dock Street hockshop where a fellow with enough bucks to spread around could buy a police-special move-along, a full-choke riot gun, a submachine gun, heroin, Push, cocaine, drag disguises, a styroflex pseudo-woman, a real whore if you were too strapped to afford styroflex, the current address of one of three floating crap-games, the current address on a swinging Perverto Club, or a hundred other illegal items. If Molie didn't have what you wanted, he would order it for you.

Including false papers.

When he opened the peephole and saw who was there, he offered a kindly smile and said: 'Why don't you go away, pal? I never saw you.'

'New Dollars,' Richards remarked, as if to the air itself. There was a pause. Richards studied the cuff of his shirt as if he had never seen it before.

Then the bolts and locks were opened, quickly, as if Molie were afraid Richards would change his mind. Richards came in. They were in Molie's place behind the store, which was a rat warren of old newsies, stolen musical instruments, stolen cameras, and boxes of black-market groceries. Molie was by necessity something of a Robin Hood; a pawnbroker south of the Canal did not remain in business long if he became too greedy. Molie took the rich uptown maggots as heavily as he could and sold in the neighborhood at close to cost – sometimes lower than cost if some pal was being squeezed hard. Thus his reputation in Co-Op City was excellent, his protection superb. If a cop asked a South City stoolie (and there were hundreds of them) about Molie Jernigan, the informant let it be known that Molie was a slightly senile old-timer who took a little graft and sold a little black market. Any number of uptown swells with strange sexual tendencies could have told the police differently, but there were no vice busts anymore. Everyone knew vice was bad for any real revolutionary climate. The fact that Molie also ran a moderately profitable trade in forged documents, strictly for local customers, was unknown uptown. Still, Richards knew, tooling papers for someone as hot as he was would be extremely dangerous.

'What papers?' Molie asked, sighing deeply and turning on an ancient gooseneck lamp that flooded the working area of his desk with bright white light. He was an old man, approaching seventy-five, and in the close glow of the light his hair looked like spun silver.

'Driver's license. Military Service Card. Street Identicard. Axial charge card. Social Retirement card.'

'Easy. Sixty-buck job for anyone but you, Bennie.'

'You'll do it?'

'For your wife, I'll do it. For you, no. I don't put my head in the noose for any crazy-ass bastard like Bennie Richards.'

'How long, Molie?'

Molie's eyes flashed sardonically. 'Knowin your situation as I do, I'll hurry it. An hour for each.'

'Christ, five hours . . . can I go—'

'No, you can't. Are you nuts, Bennie? A cop comes pullin up to your Development last week. He's got a envelope for your ol lady. He came in a Black Wagon with about six buddies. Flapper Donnigan was standin on the corner pitchin nicks with Gerry Hanrahan when it transfired. Flapper tells me everythin. The boy's soft, you know.'

'I know Flapper's soft,' Richards said impatiently. 'I sent the money. Is she—'

'Who knows? Who sees?' Molie shrugged and rolled his eyes as he put pens and blank forms in the center of the pool of light thrown by the lamp. 'They're four deep around your building, Bennie. Anyone who sent to offer their condolences would end up in a cellar talkin to a bunch of rubber clubs. Even good friends don't need that scam, not even with your ol lady flush. You got a name you want special on these?'

'Doesn't matter as long as it's Anglo. Jesus, Molie, she must have come out for groceries. And the doctor—'

'She sent Budgie O'Sanchez's kid. What's his name.'

'Walt.'

'Yeah, that's it. I can't keep the goddam spics and micks straight no more. I'm gettin senile, Bennie. Blowin my cool.' He glared up at Richards suddenly. 'I remember when Mick Jagger was a big name. You don't even know who he was, do ya?'

'I know who he was,' Richards said, distraught. He turned to Molie's sidewalk-level window, frightened. It was worse than he thought. Sheila and Cathy were in the cage, too. At least until—

'They're okay, Bennie,' Molie said softly. 'Just stay away. You're poison to them now. Can you dig it?'

'Yes,' Richards said. He was suddenly overwhelmed with despair, black and awful. *I'm homesick*, he thought, amazed, but it was more, it was worse. Everything seemed out of whack, surreal. The very fabric of existence bulging at the seams. Faces, whirling: Laughlin, Burns, Killian, Jansky, Molie, Cathy, Sheila—

He looked out into the blackness, trembling. Molie had gone to work, crooning some old song from his vacant past, something about having Bette Davis eyes, who the hell was *that*?

'He was a drummer,' Richards said suddenly. 'With that English group, the Beetles. Mick McCartney.'

'Yah, you kids,' Molie said, bent over his work. 'That's all you kids know.'

... MINUS 077   and COUNTING ...

He left Molie's at ten past midnight, twelve hundred New Dollars lighter. The pawnbroker had also sold him a limited but fairly effective disguise: gray hair, spectacles, mouth wadding, plastic buck-teeth which subtly trans-figured his lip line. 'Give yourself a little limp, too,' Molie advised. 'Not a big attention-getter. Just a little one. Remember, you have the power to cloud men's minds, if you use it. Don't remember that line, do ya?'

Richards didn't.

According to his new wallet cards, he was John Griffen Springer, a text-tape salesman from Harding. He was a forty-three-year-old widower. No technico status, but that was just as well. Technicos had their own language.

Richards reemerged on Robard Street at 12:30, a good hour to get rolled, mugged, or killed, but a bad hour to make any kind of unnoticed getaway. Still, he had lived south of the Canal all his life.

He crossed the Canal two miles farther west, almost on the edge of the lake. He saw a party of drunken winos huddled around a furtive fire, several rats, but no cops. By 1:15 A.M. he was cutting across the far edge of the no-man's-land of warehouses, cheap beaneries, and shipping offices on the north side of the Canal. At 1:30 he was surrounded by enough uptowners hopping from one sleazy dive to the next to safely hail a cab.

This time the driver didn't give him a second look.

'Jetport,' Richards said.

'I'm your man, pal.'

The airthrusters shoved them up into traffic. They were at the airport by 1:50. Richards limped past several cops and security guards who showed no interest in him. He bought a ticket to New York because it came naturally to mind. The ID check was routine and uneventful. He was on the 2:20 speed shuttle to New York. There were only forty or so passengers, most of them snoozing businessmen and students. The cop in the Judas hole dozed through the entire trip. After a while, Richards dozed, too.

They touched down at 3:06, and Richards deplaned and left the airport without incident.

At 3:15 the cab was spiraling down the Lindsay Overway. They crossed Central Park on a diagonal, and at 3:20, Ben Richards disappeared into the largest city on the face of the earth.

. . . MINUS 076 and COUNTING . . .

He went to earth in the Brant Hotel, a so-so establishment on the East Side. That part of the city had been gradually entering a new cycle of chic. Yet the Brant was less than a mile from Manhattan's own blighted inner city – also the largest in the world. As he checked in, he again thought of Dan Killian's parting words: *Stay close to your own people.*

After leaving the taxi he had walked to Times Square, not wanting to check into any hotel during the small morning hours. He spent the five and a half hours from 3:30 to 9:00 in an all-night perverto show. He had wanted desperately to sleep, but both times he had dozed off, he had been snapped awake by the feel of light fingers crawling up his inner thigh.

'How long will you be staying, sir?' the desk clerk asked, glancing at Richards's registration as John G. Springer.

'Don't know,' Richards said, trying for meek affability. 'All depends on the clients, you understand.' He paid sixty New Dollars, holding the room for two days, and took the elevator up to the twenty-third floor. The room offered a somber view of the squalid East River. It was raining in New York, too.

The room was clean but sterile; there was a connecting bathroom and the toilet made constant, ominous noises that Richards could not rectify even by wiggling the ball in the tank.

He had breakfast sent up – a poached egg on toast,

orange drink, coffee. When the boy appeared with the tray, he tipped lightly and forgettably.

With breakfast out of the way, he took out the video-tape camera and looked at it. A small metal plate labeled INSTRUCTIONS was set just below the viewfinder. Richards read:

1. Push tape cartridge into slot marked **A** until it clicks home.
2. Set viewfinder by means of crosshairs within the sight.
3. Push button marked **B** to record sound and video.
4. When the bell sounds, tape cartridge will pop out automatically. Recording time: 10 minutes.

Good, Richards thought. They can watch me sleep.

He set the camera on the bureau next to the Gideon Bible and sighted the crosshairs on the bed. The wall behind was blank and nondescript; he didn't see how anyone could pinpoint his location from either the bed or the background. Street noise from this height was negligible, but he would leave the shower running just in case.

Even with forethought, he nearly pressed the button and stepped into the camera's field of vision with his naked disguise hanging out. Some of it could have been removed, but the gray hair had to stay. He put the pillowslip over his head. Then he pressed the button, walked over to the bed, and sat down facing the lens.

'Peekaboo,' Ben Richards said hollowly to his immense listening and viewing audience that would watch this tape later tonight with horrified interest. 'You can't see it, but I'm laughing at you shiteaters.'

He lay back, closed his eyes, and tried to think of nothing at all. When the tape clip popped out ten minutes later, he was fast asleep.

...MINUS 075 and COUNTING...

When he woke up it was just after 4 P.M. – the hunt was on, then. Had been for three hours, figuring for the time difference. The thought sent a chill through his middle.

He put a new tape in the camera, took down the Gideon Bible, and read the Ten Commandments over and over for ten minutes with the pillowslip on his head.

There were envelopes in the desk drawer, but the name and address of the hotel was on them. He hesitated, and knew it made no difference. He would have to take Killian's word that his location, as revealed by postmarks or return addresses, would not be revealed to McCone and his bird dogs by the Games Authority. He had to use the postal service. They had supplied him with no carrier pigeons.

There was a mail drop by the elevators, and Richards dropped the clips into the out-of-town slot with huge misgivings. Although postal authorities were not eligible for any Games money for reporting the whereabouts of contestants, it still seemed like a horribly risky thing to do. But the only other thing was default, and he couldn't do that, either.

He went back to his room, shut off the shower (the bathroom was as steamy as a tropical jungle), and lay down on the bed to think.

How to run? What was the best thing to do?

He tried to put himself in the place of an average contestant. The first impulse, of course, was pure animal instinct: Go to earth. Make a den and cower in there.

And so he had done. The Brant Hotel.

Would the Hunters expect that? Yes. They would not be looking for a running man at all. They would be looking for a hiding man.

Could they find him in his den?

He wanted very badly to answer no, but he could not. His disguise was good, but hastily put together. Not many people are observant, but there are always some. Perhaps he had been tabbed already. The desk clerk. The bellboy who had brought his breakfast. Perhaps even by one of the faceless men in the perverto show on Forty-second Street.

Not likely, but possible.

And what about his real protection, the false ID Molie had provided? Good for how long? Well, the taxi driver who had taken him from the Games Building could put him in South City. And the Hunters were fearfully, dreadfully good. They would be leaning hard on everyone he knew, from Jack Crager to that bitch Eileen Jenner down the hall. Heavy heat. How long until somebody, maybe a head-softie like Flapper Donnigan, let it slip that Molie had forged papers on occasion? And if they found Molie, he was blown. The pawnbroker would hold out long enough to take a belting around; he was canny enough to want a few visible battle scars to sport around the neighborhood. Just so his place didn't have a bad case of spontaneous combustion some night. Then? A simple check of Harding's three jetports would uncover John G. Springer's midnight jaunt to Freak City.

If they found Molie.

You assume they will. You have to assume they will.

Then run. Where?

He didn't know. He had spent his entire life in Harding. In the Midwest. He didn't know the East Coast; there was no place here he could run to and feel that he was on familiar turf. So where? Where?

His teased and unhappy mind drifted into a morbid day-dream. They had found Molie with no trouble at all. Pried the Springer name out of him in an easy five minutes, after pulling two fingernails, filling his navel with lighter fluid and threatening to strike a match. They had gotten Richards's flight number with one quick call (handsome, nondescript men in gabardine coats of identical cut and make) and had arrived in New York by 2:30 E.S.T. Advance men had already gotten the address of the Brant by a telex canvass of the New York City hotel-listings, which were computer tabulated day by day. They were outside now, surrounding the place. Busboys and bellboys and clerks and bartenders had been replaced by Hunters. Half a dozen coming up the fire escape. Another fifty packing all three elevators. More and more, pulling up in air cars all around the building. Now they were in the hall, and in a moment the door would crash open and they would lunge in, a tape machine grinding enthusiastically away on a rolling tripod above their muscular shoulders, getting it all down for posterity as they turned him into hamburger.

Richards sat up, sweating. Didn't even have a gun, not yet.

Run. Fast.

Boston would do, to start.

. . . MINUS 074 and COUNTING . . .

He left his room at 5:00 P.M. and went down to the lobby. The desk clerk smiled brightly, probably looking forward to his evening relief.

'Afternoon, Mr, uh—'

'Springer.' Richards smiled back. 'I seem to have struck

oil, my man. Three clients who seem . . . receptive. I'll be occupying your excellent facility for an additional two days. May I pay in advance?'

'Certainly, sir.'

Dollars changed hands. Still beaming, Richards went back up to his room. The hall was empty. Richards hung the DO NOT DISTURB sign on the doorknob and went quickly to the fire stairs.

Luck was with him and he met no one. He went all the way to the ground floor and slipped out the side entrance unobserved.

The rain had stopped, but the clouds still hung and lowered over Manhattan. The air smelled like a rancid battery. Richards walked briskly, discarding the limp, to the Port Authority Electric Bus terminal. A man could still buy a ticket on a Greyhound without signing his name.

'Boston,' he said to the bearded ticket-vendor.

'Twenty-three bucks, pal. Bus pulls out at six-fifteen sharp.'

He passed over the money; it left him with something less than three thousand New Dollars. He had an hour to kill, and the terminal was chock-full of people, many of them Vol-Army, with their blue berets and blank, boyish, brutal faces. He bought a Pervert Mag, sat down, and propped it in front of his face. For the next hour he stared at it, turning a page occasionally to try and avoid looking like a statue.

When the bus rolled up to the pier, he shuffled toward the open doors with the rest of the nondescript assortment.

'Hey! Hey, you!'

Richards stared around; a security cop was approaching on the run. He froze, unable to take flight. A distant part of his brain was screaming that he was about to be cut down right here, right here in this shitty bus terminal with wads of gum on the floor and casual obscenities scrawled on the dirt-caked walls; he was going to be some dumb flatfoot's fluke trophy.

'Stop him! Stop that guy!'

The cop was veering. It wasn't him at all, Richards saw. It was a scruffy-looking kid who was running for the stairs, swinging a lady's purse in one hand and bowling bystanders this way and that like tenpins.

He and his pursuer disappeared from sight, taking the stairs three by three in huge leaps. The knot of embarkers, debarkers, and greeters watched them with vague interest for a moment and then picked up the threads of what they had been doing, as if nothing had happened.

Richards stood in line, trembling and cold.

He collapsed into a seat near the back of the coach, and a few minutes later the bus hummed smoothly up the ramp, paused, and joined the flow of traffic. The cop and his quarry had disappeared into the general mob of humanity.

If I'd had a gun, I would have burned him where he stood, Richards thought. Christ. Oh, Christ.

And on the heels of that: *Next time it won't be a purse snatcher. It'll be you.*

He would get a gun in Boston anyway. Somehow.

He remembered Laughlin saying that he would push a few of them out a high window before they took him.

The bus rolled north in the gathering darkness.

. . . MINUS 073   and COUNTING . . .

The Boston YMCA stood on upper Hunington Avenue. It was huge, black with years, old-fashioned, and boxy. It stood in what used to be one of Boston's better areas in the middle of the last century. It stood there like a guilty reminder of another time, another day, its old-fashioned neon still winking its letters toward the sinful theater district. It looked like the skeleton of a murdered idea.

When Richards walked into the lobby, the desk clerk was arguing with a tiny, scruffy black boy in a killball jersey so big that it reached down over his blue jeans to midshin. The disputed territory seemed to be a gum machine that stood inside the lobby door.

'I loss my nickel, honky. I loss my muh-fuhn nickel!'

'If you don't get out of here, I'll call the house detective, kid. That's all. I'm done talking to you.'

'But that goddam machine took my nickel!'

'You stop swearing at me, you little scumbag!' The clerk, who looked an old, cold thirty, reached down and shook the jersey. It was too huge for him to be able to shake the boy inside, too. 'Now get out of here. I'm through talking.'

Seeing he meant it, the almost comic mask of hate and defiance below the dark sunburst of the kid's afro broke into a hurt, agonized grimace of disbelief. 'Lissen, thass the oney muh-fuhn nickel I got. That gumball machine ate my nickel! That—'

'I'm calling the house dick right now.' The clerk turned toward the switchboard. His jacket, a refugee from some bargain counter, flapped tiredly around his thin butt.

The boy kicked the plaxteel post of the gum machine, then ran. 'Muh-fuhn white honky sum*bitch*!'

The clerk looked after him, the security button, real or mythical, unpressed. He smiled at Richards, showing an old keyboard with a few missing keys. 'You can't talk to niggers anymore. I'd keep them in cages if I ran the Network.'

'He really lose a nickel?' Richards asked, signing the register as John Deegan from Michigan.

'If he did, he stole it,' the clerk said. 'Oh, I suppose he did. But if I gave him a nickel, I'd have two hundred pickaninnies in here by nightfall claiming the same thing. Where do they learn that language? That's what I want to know. Don't their folks care what they do? How long will you be staying, Mr Deegan?'

'I don't know. I'm in town on business.' He tried on a greasy smile, and when it felt right, he widened it. The desk clerk recognized it instantly (perhaps from his own reflection looking up at him from the depths of the fake-marble counter, which had been polished by a million elbows) and gave it back to him.

'That's $15.50, Mr Deegan.' He pushed a key attached to a worn wooden tongue across the counter to Richards. 'Room 512.'

'Thank you.' Richards paid cash. Again, no ID. Thank God for the YMCA.

He crossed to the elevators and looked down the corridor to the Christian Lending Library on the left. It was dimly lit with flyspecked yellow globes, and an old man wearing an overcoat and galoshes was perusing a tract, turning the pages slowly and methodically with a trembling, wetted finger. Richards could hear the clogged whistle of his breathing from where he was by the elevators, and felt a mixture of sorrow and horror.

The elevator clunked to a stop, and the doors opened with wheezy reluctance. As he stepped in, the clerk said loudly: 'It's a sin and a shame. I'd put them all in cages.'

Richards glanced up, thinking the clerk was speaking to him, but the clerk was not looking at anything.

The lobby was very empty and very silent.

...MINUS 072 and COUNTING...

The fifth floor hall stank of pee.

The corridor was narrow enough to make Richards feel claustrophobic, and the carpet, which might have been red, had worn away in the middle to random strings. The doors were industrial gray, and several of them showed the marks of fresh kicks, smashes, or attempts to jimmy. Signs at every twenty paces advised that there would be NO SMOKING IN THIS HALL. BY ORDER OF FIRE MARSHAL. There was a communal bathroom in the center, and the urine stench became suddenly sharp. It was a smell Richards associated automatically with despair. People moved restlessly behind the gray doors like animals in cages — animals too awful, too frightening, to be seen. Someone was chanting what might have been the Hail Mary over and over in a drunken voice. Strange gobbling noises came from behind another door. A country-western tune from behind another ('I ain't got a buck for the phone / and I'm so alone . . .'). Shuffling noises. The solitary squeak of bedsprings that might mean a man in his own hand. Sobbing. Laughter. The hysterical grunts of a drunken argument. And from behind these, silence. And silence. And silence. A man with a hideously sunken chest walked past Richards without looking at him, carry-ing a bar of soap and a towel in one hand, wearing gray pajama bottoms tied with string. He wore paper slippers on his feet.

Richards unlocked his room and stepped in. There was a police bar on the inside, and he used it. There was a bed with almost-white sheets and an Army surplus blanket.

There was a bureau from which the second drawer was missing. There was a picture of Jesus on one wall. There was a steel rod with two coathangers kitty-cornered in the right angle of two walls. There was nothing else but the window, which looked out on blackness. It was 10:15.

Richards hung up his jacket, slipped off his shoes, and lay down on the bed. He realized how miserable and unknown and vulnerable he was in the world. The universe seemed to shriek and clatter and roar around him like a huge and indifferent jalopy rushing down a hill and toward the lip of a bottomless chasm. His lips began to tremble, and then he cried a little.

He didn't put it on tape. He lay looking at the ceiling, which was cracked into a million crazy scrawls, like a bad potter's-glaze. They had been after him for over eight hours now. He had earned eight hundred dollars of his stake money. Christ, not even out of the hole yet.

And he'd missed himself on the Free-Vee. Christ, yes. The bag-over-the-head spectacular.

Where were they? Still in Harding? New York? Or on their way to Boston? No, they couldn't be on their way here, could they? The bus had not passed through any roadblocks. He had left the biggest city in the world anonymously, and he was here under an assumed name. They couldn't be onto him. No way.

The Boston Y might be safe for as long as two days. After that he could move north toward New Hampshire and Vermont, or south toward Hartford or Philadelphia or even Atlanta. Further east was the ocean, and beyond it was Britain and Europe. It was an intriguing idea, but probably out of reach. Passage by plane required ID, what with France under martial law, and while stowing-away might be possible, discovery would mean a quick and final end to the whole thing. And west was out. West was where the heat was the hottest.

If you can't stand the heat, get out of the kitchen. Who had said that? Molie would know. He snickered a little and felt better.

The disembodied sound of a radio came to his ears.

It would be good to get the gun now, tonight, but he was too tired. The ride had tired him. Being a fugitive tired him. And he knew in an animal way that went deeper than the rational that very soon he might be sleeping in an October-cold culvert or in a weed- and cinder-choked gully.

The gun tomorrow night.

He turned off the light and went to bed.

... MINUS 071 and COUNTING ...

It was showtime again.

Richards stood with his buttocks toward the video recorder, humming the theme music to *The Running Man.* A YMCA pillowslip was over his head, turned inside out so the name stamped on its hem wouldn't show.

The camera had inspired Richards to a kind of creative humor that he never would have believed he possessed. The self-image he'd always held was that of a rather dour man, with little or no humor in his outlook. The prospect of his approaching death had uncovered a solitary comedian hiding inside.

When the clip popped out, he decided to save the second for afternoon. The solitary room was boring, and perhaps something else would occur to him.

He dressed slowly and then went to the window and looked out.

Thursday morning traffic hustled busily up and down Hunington Avenue. Both sidewalks were crowded with slowly moving pedestrians. Some of them were scanning bright-yellow Help-Wanted Fax. Most of them just walked. There was a cop, it seemed, on every corner. Richards could hear them in his mind: *Move along. Ain't you got someplace to go? Pick it up, maggot.*

So you moved on to the next corner, which was just like the last corner, and were moved along again. You could try to get mad about it, but mostly your feet hurt too much.

Richards debated the risk of going down the hall and showering. He finally decided it would be okay. He went down with a towel over his shoulder, met no one, and walked into the bathroom.

Essence of urine, shit, puke, and disinfectant mingled. All the crapper doors had been yanked off, of course. Someone had scrawled FUK THE NETWORK in foot-high letters above the urinal. It looked as though he might have been angry when he did it. There was a pile of feces in one of the urinals. Someone must have been really drunk, Richards thought. A few sluggish autumn flies were crawling over it. He was not disgusted; the sight was too common; but he was matter-of-factly glad he had worn his shoes.

He also had the shower room to himself. The floor was cracked porcelain, the walls gouged tile with thick runnels of decay near the bottoms. He turned on a rust-clogged showerhead, full hot, and waited patiently for five minutes until the water ran tepid, and then showered quickly. He used a scrap of soap he found on the floor; the Y had either neglected to supply it or the chambermaid had walked off with his.

On his way back to his room, a man with a harelip gave him a tract.

Richards tucked his shirt in, sat on his bed, and lit a cigarette. He was hungry but would wait until dusk to go out and eat.

Boredom drove him to the window again. He counted

different makes of cars – Fords, Chevies, Wints, VW's, Plymouths, Studebakers, Rambler-Supremes. First one to a hundred wins. A dull game, but better than no game.

Further up Hunington Avenue was Northeastern University, and directly across the street from the Y was a large automated bookshop. While he counted cars, Richards watched the students come and go. They were in sharp contrast to the Wanted-Fax idlers; their hair was shorter, and they all seemed to be wearing tartan jumpers, which were this year's kampus kraze. They walked through the milling ruck and inside to make their purchases with an air of uncomfortable patronization and hail-fellow that left a curdled amusement in Richards's mouth. The five-minute spaces in front of the store filled and emptied with sporty, flashy cars, often of exotic make. Most of them had college decals in the back windows: Northeastern, MIT, Boston College, Harvard. Most of the news-fax bums treated the sporty cars as part of the scenery, but a few looked at them with dumb and wretched longing.

A Wint pulled out of the space directly in front of the store and a Ford pulled in, settling to an inch above the pavement as the driver, a crewcut fellow smoking a foot-long cigar, put it in idle. The car dipped slightly as his passenger, a dude in a brown and white hunting jacket, got out and zipped inside.

Richards sighed. Counting cars was a very poor game. Fords were ahead of their nearest contender by a score of 78 to 40. The outcome going to be predictable as the next election.

Someone pounded on the door and Richards stiffened like a bolt.

'Frankie? You in there, Frankie?'

Richards said nothing. Frozen with fear, he played a statue.

'You eat shit, Frankie-baby.' There was a chortle of

drunken laughter and the footsteps moved on. Pounding on the next door up. 'You in there, Frankie?'

Richards's heart slipped slowly down from his throat.

The Ford was pulling out, and another Ford took its place. Number 79. Shit.

The day slipped into afternoon, and then it was one o'clock. Richards knew this by the ringing of various chimes in churches far away. Ironically, the man living by the clock had no watch.

He was playing a variation of the car game now. Fords worth two points, Studebakers three, Wints four. First one to five hundred wins.

It was perhaps fifteen minutes later that he noticed the young man in the brown and white hunting jacket leaning against a lamppost beyond the bookstore and reading a concert poster. He was not being moved along; in fact, the police seemed to be ignoring him.

You're jumping at shadows, maggot. Next you'll see them in the corners.

He counted a Wint with a dented fender. A yellow Ford. An old Studebaker with a wheezing air cylinder, dipping in slight cycles. A VW – no good, they're out of the running. Another Wint. A Studebaker.

A man smoking a foot-long cigar was standing non-chalantly at the bus stop on the corner. He was the only person there. With good reason. Richards had seen the buses come and go, and knew there wouldn't be another one along for forty-five minutes.

Richards felt a coolness creep into his testicles . . .

An old man in a threadbare black overcoat sauntered down the side of the street and leaned casually against the building.

Two fellows in tartan jumpers got out of a taxi, talking animatedly, and began to study the menu in the window of the Stockholm Restaurant.

A cop walked over and conversed with the man at the bus stop. Then the cop walked away again.

Richards noted with a numb, distant terror that a good many of the newspaper bums were idling along much more slowly. Their clothes and styles of walking seemed oddly familiar, as if they had been around a great many times before and Richards was just becoming aware of it – in the tentative, uneasy way you recognize the voices of the dead in dreams.

There were more cops, too.

I'm being bracketed, he thought. The idea brought a helpless, rabbit terror.

No, his mind corrected. *You've already* been *bracketed.*

...MINUS 070   and COUNTING...

Richards walked rapidly to the bathroom, being calm, ignoring his terror the way a man on a high ledge ignores the drop. If he was going to get out of this, it would be by keeping his head. If he panicked, he would die quickly.

Someone was in the shower, singing a popular song in a cracked and pitchless voice. No one was at the urinals or the washstands.

The trick had popped effortlessly into his mind as he had stood by the window, watching them gather in their offhand, sinister way. If it hadn't occurred to him, he thought he would be there yet, like Aladdin watching smoke from the lamp coalesce into an omnipotent djinn. They had used the trick as boys to steal newspapers from Development basements. Molie bought them; two cents a pound.

He took one of the wire toothbrush holders off the wall with a hard snap of his wrist. It was a little rusted, but that wouldn't matter. He walked down to the elevator, bending the toothbrush holder out straight.

He pushed the call button, and the cage took a slow eternity to come down from eight. It was empty. Thank Christ it was empty.

He stepped in, looked briefly down the halls, and then turned to the control panel. There was a key slot beside the button marked for the basement. The janitor would have a special card to shove in there. An electric eye scanned the card and then the janitor could push the button and ride down to the basement.

What if it doesn't work?

Never mind that. Never mind that now.

Grimacing in anticipation of a possible electric shock, Richards jammed the toothbrush wire into the slot and pushed the basement button simultaneously.

There was a noise from inside the control panel that sounded like a brief electronic curse. There was a light, tingling jolt up his arm. For a moment, nothing else. Then the folding brass gate slid across, the doors closed, and the elevator lurched unhappily downward. A small tendril of blue smoke curled out of the slot in the panel.

Richards stood away from the elevator door and watched the numbers flash backwards. When the *L* lit, the motor high above made a grinding sound, and the car seemed about to stop. Then, after a moment (perhaps after it thought it had scared Richards enough), it descended again. Twenty seconds later the doors slid open and Richards stepped out into the huge dim basement. There was water dripping somewhere, and the scurry of a disturbed rat. But otherwise, the basement was his. For now.

... MINUS 069   and COUNTING ...

Huge, rusted heating pipes festooned with cobwebs crawled crazily all over the ceiling. When the furnace kicked on suddenly, Richards almost screamed in terror. The surge of adrenaline to his limbs and heart was painful, for a moment almost incapacitating.

There were newspapers here, too, Richards saw. Thousands of them, stacked up and tied with string. The rats had nested in them by the thousands. Whole families stared out at the interloper with ruby distrustful eyes.

He began to walk away from the elevator, pausing halfway across the cracked cement floor. There was a large fuse box bolted to a supporting post, and behind it, leaning against the other side, a litter of tools. Richards took the crowbar and continued to walk, keeping his eyes on the floor.

Near the far wall he spied the main storm drain, to his left. He walked over and looked at it, wondering in the back of his mind if they knew he was down here yet.

The storm drain was constructed of vented steel. It was about three feet across, and on the far side there was a slot for the crowbar. Richards slipped it in, levered up the cover, and then put one foot on the crowbar to hold it. He got his hands under the lip of the cover and pushed it over. It fell to the cement with a clang that made the rats squeak with dismay.

The pipe beneath slanted down at a forty-five-degree angle, and Richards guessed that its bore could be no more than two and a half feet. It was very dark. Claustrophobia suddenly filled his mouth with flannel. Too small to maneuver in, almost too small to breathe in. But it had to be.

He turned the storm-drain cover back over and edged it toward the pipe entrance just enough so he could grip it from beneath once he was down there. Then he walked over to the fuse box, hammered the padlock off with the crowbar, and shoved it open. He was about to begin pulling fuses when another idea occurred to him.

He walked over to the newspapers which lay in dirty yellow drifts against the whole eastern length of the cellar. Then he ferreted out the folded and dog-eared book of matches he had been lighting his smokes with. There were three left. He yanked out a sheet of paper and formed it into a spill; held it under his arm like a dunce cap and lit a match. The first one guttered out in a draft. The second fell out of his trembling hand and hissed out on the damp concrete.

The third stayed alight. He held it to his paper spill and yellow flame bloomed. A rat, perhaps sensing what was to come, ran across his foot and into the darkness.

A terrible sense of urgency filled him now, and yet he waited until the spill was flaming a foot high. He had no more matches. Carefully, he tucked it into a fissure in the chest-high paper wall and waited until he saw that the fire was spreading.

The huge oil tank which serviced the Y was built into the adjoining wall. Perhaps it would blow. Richards thought it would.

Trotting now, he went back to the fuse box and began ripping out the long tubular fuses. He got most of them before the basement lights went out. He felt his way across to the storm drain, aided by the growing, flickering light of the burning papers.

He sat down with his feet dangling, and then slowly eased in. When his head was below the level of the floor, he pressed his knees against the sides of the pipe to hold himself steady, and worked his arms up above his head. It was slow work. There was very little room to move. The light of the fire was brilliant yellow now, and the crackling sound of burning filled his ears. Then his groping fingers found the lip of the drain, and he slid them up until they gripped the vented cover. He yanked it forward slowly, supporting more and more of the weight with the muscles of his back and neck. When he judged that the far edge of the cover was on the edge of dropping into place, he gave one last fierce tug.

The cover dropped into place with a clang, bending both wrists back cruelly. Richards let his knees relax, and he slid downward like a boy shooting the chutes. The pipe was coated with slime, and he slid effortlessly about twelve feet to where the pipe elbow bent into a straight line. His feet struck smartly, and he stood there like a drunk leaning against a lamppost.

But he couldn't get into the horizontal pipe. The elbow bend was too sharp.

The taste of the claustrophobia became huge, gagging. *Trapped*, his mind babbled. *Trapped in here, trapped, trapped—*

A steel scream rose in his throat and he choked it down.

Calm down. Sure, it's very hackneyed, very trite, but we must be very calm down here. Very calm. Because we are at the bottom of this pipe and we can't get up and we can't get down and if the fucking oil tank goes boom, we are going to be fricasseed very neatly and—

Slowly he began to wriggle around until his chest was against the pipe instead of his back. The slime coating acted as a lubricant, helping his movement. It was very bright in the pipe now, and getting warmer. The vented cover threw prison-bar shadows on his struggling face.

Once leaning against his chest and belly and groin,

with his knees bending the right way, he could slip down further, letting his calves and feet slide into the horizontal pipe until he was in the praying position. Still no good. His buttocks were pushing against the solid ceramic facing above the entrance to the horizontal pipe.

Faintly, it seemed that he could hear shouted commands above the heavy crackle of the fire, but it might have been his imagination, which was now strained and fevered beyond the point of trust.

He began to flex the muscles of his thighs and calves in a tiring seesaw rhythm, and little by little his knees began to slide out from under him. He worked his hands up over his head again to give himself more room, and now his face lay solidly against the slime of the pipe. He was very close to fitting now. He swayed his back as much as he could and began to push with his arms and head, the only things left in any position to give him leverage.

When he had begun to think there was not enough room, that he was going to simply hang here, unable to move either way, his hips and buttocks suddenly popped through the horizontal pipe's opening like a champagne cork from a tight bottleneck. The small of his back scraped excruciatingly as his knees slid out from under him, and his shirt rucked up to his shoulderblades. Then he was in the horizontal pipe – except for his head and arms, which were bent back at a joint-twisting angle. He wriggled the rest of the way in and then paused there, panting, his face streaked with slime and rat droppings, the skin of his lower back abraded and oozing blood.

This pipe was narrower still; his shoulders scraped lightly on both sides each time his chest rose in respiration.

Thank God I'm underfed.

Panting, he began to back into the unknown darkness of the pipe.

. . . MINUS 068   and COUNTING . . .

He made slow, molelike progress for about fifty yards through the horizontal pipe, backing up blindly. Then the oil tank in the Y's basement suddenly blew with a roar that set up enough sympathetic vibrations in the pipes to nearly rupture his eardrums. There was a yellow-white flash, as if a pile of phosphorus had ignited. It faded to a rosy, shifting glow. A few moments later a blast of thermal air struck him in the face, making him grin painfully.

The tape camera in his jacket pocket swung and bounced as he tried to back up faster. The pipe was picking up heat from the fierce explosion and fire that was raging somewhere above him, the way the handle of a skillet picks up heat from a gas-ring. Richards had no urge to be baked down here like a potato in a Dutch oven.

Sweat rolled down his face, mixing with the black streaks of ordure already there, making him look, in the waxing and waning glow of the reflected fire, like an Indian painted for war. The sides of the pipe were hot to the touch now.

Lobsterlike, Richards humped backwards on his knees and forearms, his buttocks rising to smack the top of the pipe at every movement. His breath came in sharp, doglike gasps. The air was hot, full of the slick taste of oil, uncomfortable to breathe. A headache surfaced within his skull and began to push daggers into the backs of his eyes.

I'm going to fry in here. I'm going to fry.

Then his feet were suddenly dangling in the air. Richards tried to peer through his legs and see what was there, but it was too dark behind and his eyes were too dazzled by the light in front. He would have to take his chance. He backed up until his knees were on the edge of the pipe's ending, and then slid them cautiously over.

His shoes were suddenly in water, cold and shocking after the heat of the pipe.

The new pipe ran at right angles to the one Richards had just come through, and it was much larger – big enough to stand in bent over. The thick, slowly moving water came up over his ankles. He paused for just a moment to stare back into the tiny pipe with its soft circle of reflected fireglow. The fact that he could see any glow at all from this distance meant that it must have been a very big bang indeed.

Richards reluctantly forced himself to know it would be their job to assume him alive rather than dead in the inferno of the YMCA basement, but perhaps they would not discover the way he had taken until the fire was under control. That seemed a safe assumption. But it had seemed safe to assume that they could not trace him to Boston, too.

Maybe they didn't. After all, what did you really see?

No. It had been them. He knew it. The Hunters. They had even carried the odor of evil. It had wafted up to his fifth floor room on invisible psychic thermals.

A rat dog-paddled past him, pausing to look up briefly with glittering eyes.

Richards splashed clumsily off after it, in the direction the water was flowing.

. . . MINUS 067   and COUNTING . . .

Richards stood by the ladder, looking up, dumbfounded by the light. No regular traffic, which was something, but light—

The light was surprising because it had seemed that he had been walking in the sewers for hours piled upon hours. In the darkness, with no visual input and no sound but the gurgle of water, the occasional soft splash of a rat, and the ghostly thumpings in other pipes (what happens if someone flushes a john over my head, Richards wondered morbidly), his time sense had been utterly destroyed.

Now, looking up at the manhole cover some fifteen feet above him, he saw that the light had not yet faded out of the day. There were several circular breather holes in the cover, and pencil-sized rays of light pressed coins of sun on his chest and shoulders.

No air-cars had passed over the cover since he had gotten here; only an occasional heavy ground-vehicle and a fleet of Hondacycles. It made him suspect that, more by good luck and the law of averages than by inner sense of direction, he had managed to find his way to the core of the city – to his own people.

Still, he didn't dare go up until dark. To pass the time, he took out the tape camera, popped in a clip, and began recording his chest. He knew the tapes were 'fast-light,' able to take advantage of the least available light, and he did not want to give away too much of his surroundings. He did no talking or capering this time. He was too tired.

When the tape was done, he put it with the other exposed clip. He wished he could rid himself of the nagging suspicion – almost a certainty – that the tapes were pinpointing him. There had to be a way to beat that. *Had* to.

He sat down stolidly on the third rung of the ladder to wait for dark. He had been running for nearly thirty hours.

...MINUS 066 and COUNTING...

The boy, seven years old, black, smoking a cigarette, leaned closer to the mouth of the alley, watching the street.

There had been a sudden, slight movement in the street where there had been none before. Shadows moved, rested, moved again. The manhole cover was rising. It paused and something – eyes? – glimmered. The cover suddenly slid aside with a clang.

Someone (or *something*, the boy thought with a trace of fear) was moving out there. Maybe the devil was coming out of hell to get Cassie, he thought. Ma said Cassie was going to heaven to be with Dicky and the other angels. The boy thought that was bullshit. Everybody went to hell when they died, and the devil jabbed them in the ass with a pitchfork. He had seen a picture of the devil in the books Bradley had snuck out of the Boston Public Library. Heaven was for Push freaks. The devil was the Man.

It could be the devil, he thought as Richards suddenly boosted himself out of the manhole and leaned for a second on the seamed and split cement to get his breath back. No tail and no horns, not red like in that book, but the mother looked crazy and mean enough.

Now he was pushing the cover back, and now—

—now holy Jesus he was running toward the alley.

The boy grunted, tried to run, and fell over his own feet.

He was trying to get up, scrambling and dropping things, and the devil suddenly grabbed him.

'Doan stick me wif it!' He screamed in a throat-closed whisper. 'Doan stick me wif no fork, you sumbitch—'

'Shhh! Shut up! Shut up!' The devil shook him, making his teeth rattle like marbles in his head, and the boy shut up. The devil peered around in an ecstasy of apprehension. The expression on his face was almost farcical in its extreme fear. The boy was reminded of the comical fellows on that game show *Swim the Crocodiles*. He would have laughed if he hadn't been so frightened himself.

'You ain't the devil,' the boy said.

'You'll think I am if you yell.'

'I ain't gonna,' the boy said contemptuously. 'What you think, I wanna get my balls cut off? Jesus, I ain't even big enough to come yet.'

'You know a quiet place we can go?'

'Doan kill me, man. I ain't got nothin.' The boy's eyes, white in the darkness, rolled up at him.

'I'm not going to kill you.'

Holding his hand, the boy led Richards down the twisting, littered alley and into another. At the end, just before the alley opened onto an airshaft between two faceless highrise buildings, the boy led him into a lean-to built of scrounged boards and bricks. It was built for four feet, and Richards banged his head going in.

The boy pulled a dirty swatch of black cloth across the opening and fiddled with something. A moment later a weak glow lit their faces; the boy had hooked a small lightbulb to an old cracked car battery.

'I kifed that battery myself,' the boy said. 'Bradley tole me how to fix it up. He's got books. I got a nickel bag, too. I'll give it to you if you don't kill me. You better not. Bradley's in the Stabbers. You kill me an he'll make you shit in your boot an eat it.'

'I'm not doing any killings,' Richards said impatiently. 'At least not little kids.'

'I ain't no little kid! I kifed that fuckin battery myself!'

The look of injury forced a dented grin to Richards's face. 'All right. What's your name, kid?'

'Ain't no kid.' Then, sulkily: 'Stacey.'

'Okay. Stacey. Good. I'm on the run. You believe that?'

'Yeah, you on the run. You dint come outta that manhole to buy dirty pos'cards.' He stared speculatively at Richards. 'You a honky? Kinda hard to tell wif all that dirt.'

'Stacey, I—' He broke off and ran a hand through his hair. When he spoke again, he seemed to be talking to himself. 'I got to trust somebody and it turns out to be a kid. A *kid*. Hot Jesus, you ain't even six, boy.'

'I'm eight in March,' the boy said angrily. 'My sister Cassie's got cancer,' he added. 'She screams a lot. Thass why I like it here. Kifed that fuckin battery myself. You wanna toke up, mister?'

'No, and you don't either. You want two bucks, Stacey?'

'Chris' yes!' Distrust slid over his eyes. 'You dint come outta no manhole with two fuckin bucks. Thass bullshit.'

Richards produced a New Dollar and gave it to the boy. He stared at it with awe that was close to horror.

'There's another one if you bring your brother,' Richards said, and seeing his expression, added swiftly: 'I'll give it to you on the side so he won't see it. Bring him alone.'

'Won't do no good to try an kill Bradley, man. He'll make you shit in your boot—'

'And eat it. I know. You run and get him. Wait until he's alone.'

'Three bucks.'

'No.'

'Lissen man, for three bucks I can get Cassie some stuff

at the drug. Then she won't scream so fuckin much.'

The man's face suddenly worked as if someone the boy couldn't see had punched him. 'All right. Three.'

'New Dollars,' the boy persisted.

'Yes, for Christ's sake, *yes*. Get him. And if you bring the cops you won't get anything.'

The boy paused, half in and half out of his little cubbyhole. 'You stupid if you think I do that. I hate them fuckin oinkers worse than anyone. Even the devil.'

He left, a seven-year-old boy with Richards's life in his grubby, scabbed hands. Richards was too tired to be really afraid. He turned off the light, leaned back, and dozed off.

... MINUS 065 and COUNTING ...

Dreaming sleep had just begun when his tight-strung senses ripped him back to wakefulness. Confused, in a dark place, the beginning of the nightmare held him for a moment and he thought that some huge police dog was coming for him, a terrifying organic weapon seven feet high. He almost cried aloud before Stacey made the real world fall into place by hissing:

'If he broke my fuckin light I'm gonna—'

The boy was violently shushed. The cloth across the entrance rippled, and Richards turned on the light. He was looking at Stacey and another black. The new fellow was maybe eighteen, Richards guessed, wearing a cycle jacket, looking at Richards with a mixture of hate and interest.

A switchblade clicked out and glittered in Bradley's hand. 'If you're heeled, drop it down.'

'I'm not.'

'I don't believe that sh—' he broke off, and his eyes widened. 'Hey. You're that guy on the Free-Vee. You offed the YMCA on Hunington Avenue.' The lowering blackness of his face was split by an involuntary grin. 'They said you fried five cops. That probably means fifteen.'

'He come outta the manhole,' Stacey said importantly. 'I knew it wasn't the devil right away. I knew it was some honky sumbitch. You gonna cut him, Bradley?'

'Just shut up an let men talk.' Bradley came the rest of the way inside, squatting awkwardly, and sat across from Richards on a splintery orange crate. He looked at the blade in his hand, seemed surprised to see it still there, and closed it up.

'You're hotter than the sun, man,' he said finally.

'That's true.'

'Where you gonna get to?'

'I don't know. I've got to get out of Boston.'

Bradley sat in silent thought. 'You gotta come home with me an Stacey. We gotta talk, an we can't do it here. Too open.'

'All right,' Richards said wearily. 'I don't care.'

'We go the back way. The pigs are cruising tonight. Now I know why.'

When Bradley led the way out, Stacey kicked Richards sharply in the shin. For a moment Richards stared at him, not understanding, and then remembered. He slipped the boy three New Dollars, and Stacey made it disappear.

. . . MINUS 064 and COUNTING . . .

The woman was very old; Richards thought he had never seen anyone as old. She was wearing a cotton print housedress with a large rip under one arm; an ancient, wrinkled dug swayed back and forth against the rip as she went about making the meal that Richards's New Dollars had purchased. The nicotine-yellowed fingers diced and pared and peeled. Her feet, splayed into grotesque boat shapes by years of standing, were clad in pink terrycloth slippers. Her hair looked as if it might have been self-waved by an iron held in a trembling hand; it was pushed back into a kind of pyramid by the twisted hairnet which had gone askew at the back of her head. Her face was a delta of time, no longer brown or black, but grayish, stitched with a radiating galaxy of wrinkles, pouches, and sags. Her toothless mouth worked craftily at the cigarette held there, blowing out puffs of blue smoke that seemed to hang above and behind her in little bunched blue balls. She puffed back and forth, describing a triangle between counter, skillet, and table. Her cotton stockings were rolled at the knee, and above them and the flapping hem of her dress varicose veins bunched in clocksprings.

The apartment was haunted by the ghost of long-departed cabbage.

In the far bedroom, Cassie screamed, whooped, and was silent. Bradley had told Richards with a kind of angry shame that he should not mind her. She had cancer in both lungs and recently it had spread upward into her throat and down into her belly. She was five.

Stacey had gone back out somewhere.

As he and Bradley spoke together, the maddening aroma of simmering ground beef, vegetables, and tomato sauce began to fill the room, driving the cabbage back into the corners and making Richards realize how hungry he was.

'I could turn you in, man. I could kill you an steal all that money. Turn in the body. Get a thousand more bucks and be on easy street.'

'I don't think you could do it,' Richards said. 'I know I couldn't.'

'Why're you doing it, anyway?' Bradley asked irritably. 'Why you being their sucker? You that greedy?'

'My little girl's name is Cathy,' Richards said. 'Younger than Cassie. Pneumonia. She cries all the time, too.'

Bradley said nothing.

'She could get better. Not like . . . her in there. Pneumonia's no worse than a cold. But you have to have medicine and a doctor. That costs money. I went for the money the only way I could.'

'You still a sucker,' Bradley said with flat and somehow uncanny emphasis. 'You suckin off half the world and they comin in your mouth every night at six-thirty. Your little girl would be better off like Cassie in this world.'

'I don't believe that.'

'Then you ballsier than me, man. I put a guy in the hospital once with a rupture. Some rich guy. Cops chased me three days. But you ballsier than me.' He took a cigarette and lit it. 'Maybe you'll go the whole month. A billion dollars. You'd have to buy a fuckin freight train to haul it off.'

'Don't swear, praise Gawd,' the old woman said from across the room where she was slicing carrots.

Bradley paid no attention. 'You an your wife an little girl would be on easy street then. You got two days already.'

'No,' Richards said. 'The game's rigged. You know those two things I gave Stacey to mail when he and your ma went out for groceries? I have to mail two of those every day before midnight.' He explained to Bradley about the forfeit clause, and his suspicion that they had traced him to Boston by postmark.

'Easy to beat that.'

'How?'

'Never mind. Later. How you gonna get out of Boston? You awful hot. Made 'em mad, blowin up their oinkers at the YMCA. They had Free-Vee on that tonight. An those ones you took with the bag over your head. That was pretty sharp. Ma!' he finished irritably, 'when's that stuff gonna be ready? We're fallin away to shadows right before ya!'

'She comin on,' Ma said. She plopped a cover over the rich, slowly bubbling mass and walked slowly into the bedroom to sit by the girl.

'I don't know,' Richards said. 'I'll try to get a car, I guess. I've got fake papers, but I don't dare use them. I'll do something – wear dark glasses – and get out of the city. I've been thinking about going to Vermont and then crossing over into Canada.'

Bradley grunted and got up to put plates on the table. 'By now they got every highway goin out of Beantown blocked. A man wearin dark glasses calls tention to himself. They'll turn you into monkeymeat before you get six miles.'

'Then I don't know,' Richards said. 'If I stay here, they'll get you for an accessory.'

Bradley began spreading dishes. 'Suppose we get a car. You got the squeezin green. I got a name that isn't hot. There's a spic on Milk Street that'll sell me a Wint for three hundred. I'll get one of my buddies to drive it up to Manchester. It'll be cool as a fool in Manchester because you're bottled up in Boston. You eatin, Ma?'

'Yes an praise Gawd.' She waddled out of the bedroom. 'Your sister is sleepin a little.'

'Good.' He ladled up three dishes of hamburger gumbo and then paused. 'Where's Stacey?'

'Said he was goin to the drug,' Ma said complacently, shoveling gumbo into her toothless maw at a blinding speed. 'Said he goan to get medicine.'

'If he gets busted, I'll break his ass,' Bradley said, sitting heavily.

'He won't,' Richards said. 'He's got money.'

'Yeah, maybe we don't need no charity money, graymeat.'

Richards laughed and salted his meal. 'I'd probably be slabbed now if it wasn't for him,' he said. 'I guess it was earned money.'

Bradley leaned forward, concentrating on his plate. None of them said anything more until the meal was done. Richards and Bradley had two helpings; the old woman had three. As they were lighting cigarettes, a key scratched in the lock and all of them stiffened until Stacey came in, looking guilty, frightened, and excited. He was carrying a brown bag in one hand and he gave Ma a bottle of medicine.

'Thass prime dope,' he said. 'That ol man Curry ast me where I got two dollars an semney-fi cents to buy prime dope an I tole him to go shit in his boot and eat it.'

'Doan swear or the devil will poke you,' Ma said. 'Here's dinner.'

The boy's eyes widened. 'Jesus, there's meat in it!'

'Naw, we jus shat in it to make it thicker,' Bradley said. The boy looked up sharply, saw his brother was joking, giggled, and fell to.

'Will that druggist go to the cops?' Richards asked quietly.

'Curry? Naw. Not if there might be some more squee-zin green in this fambly. He knows Cassie's got to have heavy dope.'

'What about this Manchester thing?'

'Yeah. Well, Vermont's no good. Not enough of our kind of people. Tough cops. I get some good fella like Rich Goleon to drive that Wint to Manchester and park it in an automatic garage. Then I drive you up in another car.' He crushed out his cigarette. 'In the trunk. They're

only using Jiffy Sniffers on the back roads. We'll go right
up 495.'

'Pretty dangerous for you,' Richards said.

'Oh, I wasn't gonna do it free. When Cassie goes, she's
gonna go out wrecked.'

'Praise Gawd,' Ma said.

'Still pretty dangerous for you.'

'Any pig grunts at Bradley, he make 'em shit in their
boot an eat it,' Stacey said, wiping his mouth. When he
looked at Bradley, his eyes glittered with the flat shine of
hero worship.

'You're dribblin on your shirt, Skinner,' Bradley said.
He knuckled Stacey's head. 'You beatin your meat yet,
Skinner? Ain't big enough, are ya?'

'If they catch us, you'll go in for the long bomb,'
Richards said. 'Who's going to take care of the boy?'

'He'll take care of himself if something happens,' Bradley said. 'Himself and Ma here. He's not hooked on
nothin. Are you, Stace?'

Stacey shook his head emphatically.

'An he knows if I find any pricks in his arms I'll beat
his brains out. Ain't that right, Stacey?'

Stacey nodded.

'Besides, we can use the money. This is a hurtin family.
So don't say no more about it. I guess I know what I'm
doin.'

Richards finished his cigarette in silence while Bradley
went in to give Cassie some medicine.

. . . MINUS 063   and COUNTING . . .

When he awoke, it was still dark and the inner tide of his
body put the time at about four-thirty. The girl, Cassie,

had been screaming, and Bradley got up. The three of them were sleeping in the small, drafty back bedroom, Stacey and Richards on the floor. Ma slept with the girl.

Over the steady wheeze of Stacey's deep-sleep respiration, Richards heard Bradley come out of the room. There was a clink of a spoon in the sink. The girl's screams became isolated moans which trailed into silence. Richards could sense Bradley standing somewhere in the kitchen, immobile, waiting for the silence to come. He returned, sat down, farted, and then the bedsprings shifted creakily as he lay down.

'Bradley?'

'What?'

'Stacey said she was only five. Is that so?'

'Yes.' The urban dialectic was gone from his voice, making him sound unreal and dreamlike.

'What's a five-year-old kid doing with lung cancer? I didn't know they got it. Leukemia, maybe. Not lung cancer.'

There was a bitter, whispered chuckle from the bed. 'You're from Harding, right? What's the air-pollution count in Harding?'

'I don't know,' Richards said. 'They don't give them with the weather anymore. They haven't for ... gee, I don't know. A long time.'

'Not since 2020 in Boston,' Bradley whispered back. 'They're scared to. You ain't got a nose filter, do you?'

'Don't be stupid,' Richards said irritably. 'The goddam things cost two hundred bucks, even in the cut-rate stores. I didn't see two hundred bucks all last year. Did you?'

'No,' Bradley said softly. He paused. 'Stacey's got one. I made it. Ma and Rich Goleon an some other people got em, too.'

'You're shitting me,' Richards said.

'No, man.' He stopped. Richards was suddenly sure

that Bradley was weighing what he had said already against a great many more things which he might say. Wondering how much was too much. When the words came again, they came with difficulty. 'We've been reading. That Free-Vee shit is for empty-heads.'

Richards grunted agreement.

'The gang, you know. Some of the guys are just cruisers, you know? All they're interested in is honky-stomping on Saturday night. But some of us have been going down to the library since we were twelve or so.'

'They let you in without a card in Boston?'

'No. You can't get a card unless there's someone with a guaranteed income of five thousand dollars a year in your family. We got some plump-ass kid an kifed his card. We take turns going. We got a gang suit we wear when we go.' Bradley paused. 'You laugh at me and I'll cut you, man.'

'I'm not laughing.'

'At first we only read sexbooks. Then when Cassie first started getting sick, I got into this pollution stuff. They've got all the books on impurity counts and smog levels and nose filters in the reserve section. We got a key made from a wax blank. Man, did you know that everybody in Tokyo had to wear a nose filter by 2012?'

'No.'

'Rich and Dink Moran built a pollution counter. Dink drew the picture out of the book, and they did it from coffee cans and some stuff they boosted out of cars. It's hid out in an alley. Back in 1978 they had an air pollution scale that went from one to twenty. You understand?'

'Yes.'

'When it got up to twelve, the factories and all the pollution-producing shit had to shut down till the weather changed. It was a federal law until 1987, when the Revised Congress rolled it back.' The shadow on the bed rose up on its elbow. 'I bet you know a lot of people with asthma, that right?'

'Sure,' Richards said cautiously. 'I've got a touch myself. You get *that* from the air. Christ, everybody knows you stay in the house when it's hot and cloudy and the air doesn't move—'

'Temperature inversion,' Bradley said grimly.

'—and lots of people get asthma, sure. The air gets like cough syrup in August and September. But lung cancer—'

'You ain't talkin about asthma,' Bradley said. 'You talkin bout emphysema.'

'Emphysema?' Richards turned the word over in his mind. He could not assign a meaning to it, although the word was faintly familiar.

'All the tissues in your lungs swell up. You heave an heave an heave, but you're still out of breath. You know a lot of people who get like that?'

Richards thought. He did. He knew a lot of people who had died like that.

'They don't talk about that one,' Bradley said, as if he had read Richards's thought. 'Now the pollution count in Boston is twenty on a good day. That's like smoking four packs of cigarettes a day just breathing. On a bad day it gets up as high as forty-two. Old dudes drop dead all over town. Asthma goes on the death certificate. But it's the air, the air, the air. And they're pouring it out just as fast as they can, big smokestacks going twenty-four hours a day. The big boys like it that way.

'Those two-hundred-dollar nose filters aren't worth shit. They're just two pieces of screen with a little piece of mentholated cotton between them. That's all. The only good ones are from General Atomics. The only ones who can afford them are the big boys. They gave us the Free-Vee to keep us off the streets so we can breathe ourselves to death without making any trouble. How do you like that? The cheapest G-A nose filter on the market goes for six thousand New Dollars. We made one for Stacey for ten bucks from that book. We used an atomic nugget the size of the moon on your fingernail. Got it out of a hearing aid we bought in a hockshop for seven bucks. How do you like that?'

Richards said nothing. He was speechless.

'When Cassie boots off, you think they'll put cancer on the death certificate? Shit. They'll put asthma. Else somebody might get scared. Somebody might kife a library card and find out lung cancer is up seven hundred percent since 2015.'

'Is that true? Or are you making it up?'

'I read it in a book. Man, they're killing us. The Free-Vee is killing us. It's like a magician getting you to watch the cakes falling outta his helper's blouse while he pulls rabbits out of his pants and puts 'em in his hat.' He paused and then said dreamily: 'Sometimes I think that I could blow the whole thing outta the water with ten minutes talk-time on the Free-Vee. Tell em. Show em. Everybody could have a nose filter if the Network wanted em to have em.'

'And I'm helping them,' Richards said.

'That ain't your fault. You got to run.'

Killian's face, and the face of Arthur M. Burns rose up in front of Richards. He wanted to smash them, stomp them, walk on them. Better still, rip out their nose filters and turn them into the street.

'People's mad,' Bradley said. 'They've been mad at the honkies for thirty years. All they need is a reason. A reason . . . one reason . . .'

Richards drifted off to sleep with the repetition in his ears.

... MINUS 062   and COUNTING ...

Richards stayed in all day while Bradley was out seeing about the car and arranging with another member of the gang to drive it to Manchester.

Bradley and Stacey came back at six, and Bradley thumbed on the Free-Vee. 'All set, man. We go tonight.'

'Now?'

Bradley smiled humorlessly. 'Don't you want to see yourself coast-to-coast?'

Richards discovered he did, and when *The Running Man* lead-in came on, he watched, fascinated.

Bobby Thompson stared deadpan at the camera from the middle of a brilliant post in a sea of darkness. 'Watch,' he said. 'This is one of the wolves that walks among you.'

A huge blowup of Richards's face appeared on the screen. It held for a moment, then dissolved to a second photo of Richards, this time in the John Griffen Springer disguise.

Dissolve back to Thompson, looking grave. 'I speak particularly to the people of Boston tonight. Yesterday afternoon, five policemen went to a blazing, agonized death in the basement of the Boston YMCA at the hands of this wolf, who had set a clever, merciless trap. Who is he tonight? *Where* is he tonight? Look! Look at him!'

Thompson faded into the first of the two clips which Richards had filmed that morning. Stacey had dropped them in a mailbox on Commonwealth Avenue, across the city. He had let Ma hold the camera in the back bedroom, after he had draped the window and all the furniture.

'All of you watching this,' Richards's image said slowly.

'Not the technicos, not the people in the penthouses – I don't mean you shits. You people in the Developments and the ghettos and the cheap highrises. You people in the cycle gangs. You people without jobs. You kids getting busted for dope you don't have and crimes you didn't commit because the Network wants to make sure you aren't meeting together and talking together. I want to tell you about a monstrous conspiracy to deprive you of the very breath in y —'

The audio suddenly became a mixture of squeaks, pops, and gargles. A moment later it died altogether. Richards's mouth was moving, but no sound was coming out.

'We seem to have lost our audio,' Bobby Thompson's voice came smoothly, 'but we don't need to listen to any more of this murderer's radical ravings to understand what we're dealing with, do we?'

'No!' The audience screamed.

'What will you do if you see him on *your* street?'

'TURN HIM IN!'

'And what are we going to do when we find him?'

'KILL HIM!'

Richards pounded his fist against the tired arm of the only easy chair in the apartment's kitchen-living room. 'Those bastards,' he said helplessly.

'Did you think they'd let you go on the air with it?' Bradley asked mockingly. 'Oh no, man. I'm s'prised they let you get away with as much as they did.'

'I didn't think,' Richards said sickly.

'No, I guess you didn't,' Bradley said.

The first clip faded into the second. In this one, Richards had asked the people watching to storm the libraries, demand cards, find out the truth. He had read off a list of books dealing with air pollution and water pollution that Bradley had given him.

Richards's image opened its mouth. 'Fuck every one

of you,' his image said. The lips seemed to be moving around different words, but how many of the two hundred million people watching were going to notice that? 'Fuck all pigs. Fuck the Games Commission. I'm gonna kill every pig I see. I'm gonna—' There was more, enough so that Richards wanted to plug his ears and run out of the room. He couldn't tell if it was the voice of a mimic, or a harangue made up of spliced bits of audio tape.

The clip faded to a split-screen of Thompson's face and the still photo of Richards. 'Behold the man,' Thompson said. 'The man who would kill. The man who would mobilize an army of malcontents like himself to run riot through your streets, raping and burning and overturning. The man would lie, cheat, kill. He has done all these things.

'Benjamin Richards!' The voice cried out with a cold, commanding Old Testament anger. 'Are you watching? If so, you have been paid your dirty blood money. A hundred dollars for each hour – now number fifty-four – that you have remained free. And an extra five hundred dollars. One hundred for each of these five men.'

The faces of young, clear-featured policemen began appearing on the screen. The still had apparently been taken at a Police Academy graduation exercise. They looked fresh, full of sap and hope, heart-breakingly vulnerable. Softly, a single trumpet began to play Taps.

'And these . . .' Thompson's voice was now low and hoarse with emotion, '. . . these were their families.'

Wives, hopefully smiling. Children that had been coaxed to smile into the camera. A lot of children. Richards, cold and sick and nauseated, lowered his head and pressed the back of his hand over his mouth.

Bradley's hand, warm and muscular, pressed his neck. 'Hey, no. No, man. That's put on. That's all fake. They were probably a bunch of old harness bulls who—'

'Shut up,' Richards said. 'Oh shut up. Just. Please. Shut up.'

'Five hundred dollars,' Thompson was saying, and infinite hate and contempt filled his voice. Richards's face on the screen again, cold, hard, devoid of all emotion save an expression of bloodlust that seemed chiefly to be in the eyes. 'Five police, five wives, nineteen children. It comes to just about seventeen dollars and twenty-five cents for each of the dead, the bereaved, the heartbroken. Oh yes, you work cheap, Ben Richards. Even Judas got thirty pieces of silver, but you don't even demand that. Somewhere, even now, a mother is telling her little boy that daddy won't be home ever again because a desperate, greedy man with a gun—'

'Killer!' A woman was sobbing. 'Vile, dirty murderer! God will strike you dead!'

'Strike him dead!' The audience over the chant: 'Behold the man! He has been paid his blood money – but the man who lives by violence shall die by it. And let every man's hand be raised against Benjamin Richards!'

Hate and fear in every voice, rising in a steady, throbbing roar. No, they wouldn't turn him in. They would rip him to shreds on sight.

Bradley turned off the screen and faced him. 'Thass what you're dealing with, man. How about it.'

'Maybe I'll kill them,' Richards said in a thoughtful voice. 'Maybe, before I'm done, I'll get up to the ninetieth floor of that place and just hunt up the maggots who wrote that. Maybe I'll just kill them all.'

'Don't talk no more!' Stacey burst out wildly. 'Don't talk no more about it!'

In the other room, Cassie slept her drugged, dying sleep.

... MINUS 061 and COUNTING ...

Bradley had not dared drill any holes in the floor of the trunk, so Richards curled in a miserable ball with his mouth and nose pressed toward the tiny notch of light which was the trunk's keyhole. Bradley had also pulled out some of the inner trunk insulation around the lid, and that let in a small draft.

The car lifted with a jerk, and he knocked his head against the upper deck. Bradley had told him the ride would be at least an hour and a half, with two stops for roadblocks, perhaps more. Before he closed the trunk, he gave Richards a large revolver.

'Every tenth or twelfth car, they give it a heavy lookin-over,' he said. 'They open the trunk to poke around. Those are good odds, eleven to one. If it don't come up, plug you some pork.'

The car lurched and heaved over the potholed, crack-crazed streets of the inner city. Once a kid jeered and there was the thump of a thrown piece of paving. Then the sounds of increasing traffic all around them and more frequent stops for lights.

Richards lay passively, holding the pistol lightly in his right hand, thinking how different Bradley had looked in the gang suit. It was a sober Dillon Street double-breasted, as gray as bank walls. It was rounded off with a maroon tie and a small gold NAACP pin. Bradley had made the leap from scruffy gang-member (pregnant ladies stay away; some of us'ns eat fetuses) to a sober black business fellow who would know exactly who to Tom.

'You look good,' Richards said admiringly. 'In fact, it's damn incredible.'

'Praise Gawd,' Ma said.

'I thought you'd enjoy the transformation, my good man,' Bradley said with quiet dignity. 'I'm the district manager for Raygon Chemicals, you know. We do a thriving business in this area. Fine city, Boston. Immensely convivial.'

Stacey burst into giggles.

'You best shut up, nigger,' Bradley said. 'Else I make you shit in yo boot an eat it.'

'You Tom so good, Bradley,' Stacey giggled, not intimidated in the least. 'You really fuckin funky.'

Now the car swung right, onto a smoother surface, and descended in a spiraling arc. They were on an entrance ramp. Going onto 495 or a feeder expressway. Copper wires of tension were stuffed into his legs.

One in eleven. That's not bad odds.

The car picked up speed and height, kicked into drive, then slowed abruptly and kicked out. A voice, terrifyingly close, yelling with monotonous regularity: 'Pull over . . . have your license and registration ready . . . pull over . . . have your—'

Already. Starting already.

You so hot, man.

Hot enough to check the trunk on one car in eight? Or six? Or maybe every one?

The car came to a full stop. Richards's eyes moved like trapped rabbits in their sockets. He gripped the revolver.

. . . MINUS 060 and COUNTING . . .

'Step out of your vehicle, sir,' the bored, authoritative voice was saying. 'License and registration, please.'

A door opened and closed. The engine thrummed softly, holding the car an inch off the paving.

'—district manager for Raygon Chemicals—'

Bradley going into his song and dance. Dear God, what if he didn't have the papers to back it up? What if there was no Raygon Chemicals?

The back door opened, and someone began rummaging in the back seat. It sounded as if the cop (or was it the Government Guard that did this, Richards wondered half coherently) was about to crawl right into the trunk with him.

The door slammed. Feet walked around to the back of the car. Richards licked his lips and held the gun tighter. Visions of dead policemen gibbered before him, angelic faces on twisted, porcine bodies. He wondered if the cop would hose him with machine-gun bullets when he opened the trunk and saw Richards lying here like a curled-up salamander. He wondered if Bradley would take off, try to run. He was going to piss himself. He hadn't done that since he was a kid and his brother would tickle him until his bladder let go. Yes, all those muscles down there were loosening. He would put the bullet right at the juncture of the cop's nose and forehead, splattering brains and splintered skull-fragments in startled streamers to the sky. Make a few more orphans. Yes. Good. Jesus loves me, this I know, for my bladder tells me so. Christ Jesus, what's he doing, ripping the seat out? Sheila, I love you so much and how far will six grand take you? A year, maybe, if they don't kill you for it. Then on the street again, up and down, cross on the corner, swinging the hips, flirting with the empty pocketbook. Hey mister, I go down, this is clean kitty, kid, teach you how—

A hand whacked the top of the trunk casually in passing. Richards bit back a scream. Dust in his nostrils, throat tickling. High school biology, sitting in the back row, scratching his initials and Sheila's on the ancient desk-top: *The sneeze is a function of the involuntary muscles.* I'm going to sneeze my goddam head off but it's pointblank and I can still put that bullet right through his squash and—

'What's in the trunk, mister?'

Bradley's voice, jocular, a little bored: 'A spare cylinder that doesn't work half right. I got the key on my ring. Wait, I'll get it.'

'If I wanted it, I'd ask.'

Other back door opened; closed.

'Drive on.'

'Hang tight, fella. Hope you get him.'

'Drive on, mister. Move your ass.'

The cylinders cranked up. The car lifted and accelerated. It slowed once and must have been waved on. Richards jolted a little as the car rose, sailed a little, and kicked into drive. His breath came in tired little moans. He didn't have to sneeze anymore.

. . . MINUS 059   and COUNTING . . .

The ride seemed much longer than an hour and a half, and they were stopped twice more. One of them seemed to be a routine license check. At the next one a drawling cop with a dull-witted voice talked to Bradley for some time about how the goddam commie bikers were helping that guy Richards and probably the other one, too. Laughlin had not killed anyone, but it was rumored that he had raped a woman in Topeka.

After that there was nothing but the monotonous whine of the wind and the scream of his own cramped and frozen muscles. Richards did not sleep, but his punished mind did finally push him into a dazed semiconsciousness. There was no carbon monoxide with the air cars, thank God for that.

Centuries after the last roadblock, the car kicked into a lower gear and banked up a spiraling exit ramp. Richards blinked sluggishly and wondered if he was going to throw up. For the first time in his life he felt carsick.

They went through a sickening series of loops and dives that Richards supposed was a traffic interchange. Another five minutes and city sounds took over again. Richards tried repeatedly to shift his body into a new position, but it was impossible. He finally subsided, waiting numbly for it to be over. His right arm, which was curled under him, had gone to sleep an hour ago. Now it felt like a block of wood. He could touch it with the tip of his nose and feel only the pressure on his nose.

They took a right, went straight for a little, then turned again. The bottom dropped out of Richards's stomach as the car dipped down a sharp incline. The echoing of the cylinders told him that they were inside. They had gotten to the garage.

A little helpless sound of relief escaped him.

'Got your check, buddy?' A voice asked.

'Right here, pal.'

'Rampway 5.'

'Thanks.'

They bore right. The car went up, paused, turned right again, then left. They settled into idle, then the car dropped with a soft bump as the engine died. Journey's end.

There was a pause, then the hollow sound of Bradley's door opening and closing. His footsteps clicked toward the trunk, then the chink of light in front of Richards's eyes disappeared as the key slid home.

'You there, Bennie?'

'No,' he croaked. 'You left me back at the state line. Open this goddam thing.'

'Just a second. Place is empty right now. Your car's parked next to us. On the right. Can you get out quick?'

'I don't know.'

'Try hard. Here we go.'

The trunk lid popped up, letting in dim garage light. Richards got up on one arm, got one leg over the edge, and could go no farther. His cramped body screamed. Bradley took one arm and hauled him out. His legs wanted to buckle. Bradley hooked him under the armpit and half led, half pushed him to the battered green Wint on the right. He propped open the driver's side door, shoved Richards in, and slammed it shut. A moment later Bradley also slid in.

'Jesus,' he said softly. 'We got here, man. We got here.'

'Yeah,' Richards said. 'Back to Go. Collect two hundred dollars.'

They smoked in the shadows, their cigarettes gleaming like eyes. For a little while, neither of them said anything.

... MINUS 058   and COUNTING ...

'We almost got it at that first roadblock,' Bradley was saying as Richards tried to massage feeling back into his arm. It felt as if phantom nails had been pushed into it. 'That cop almost opened it. Almost.' He blew out smoke in a huge huff. Richards said nothing.

'How do you feel?' Bradley asked presently.

'It's getting better. Take my wallet out for me. I can't make my arm work just right yet.'

Bradley shooed the words away with one hand. 'Later. I want to tell you how Rich and I set it up.'

Richards lit another cigarette from the stub of the first. A dozen charley horses were loosening slowly.

'There's a hotel room reserved for you on Winthrop Street. The Winthrop House is the name of the place. Sounds fancy. It ain't. The name is Ogden Grassner. Can you remember that?'

'Yes. I'll be recognized immediately.'

Bradley reached into the back seat, got a box and dropped it in Richards's lap. It was long, brown, tied with string. To Richards it looked like the kind of box that rented graduation gowns come in. He looked at Bradley questioningly.

'Open it.'

He did. There was a pair of thick, blue-tinted glasses lying on top of a drift of black cloth. Richards put the glasses on the dashboard and took out the garment. It was a priest's robe. Beneath it, lying on the bottom of the box, was a rosary, a Bible, and a purple stole.

'A priest?' Richards asked.

'Right. You change right here. I'll help you. There's a cane in the back seat. Your act ain't blind, but it's pretty close. Bump into things. You're in Manchester to attend a Council of Churches meeting on drug abuse. Got it?'

'Yes,' Richards said. He hesitated, fingers on the buttons of his shirt. 'Do I wear my pants under this rig?'

Bradley burst out laughing.

... MINUS 057   and COUNTING ...

Bradley talked rapidly as he drove Richards across town.

'There's a box of gummed mailing labels in your suit-case,' he said. 'That's in the trunk. The stickers say: After five days return to Brickhill Manufacturing Company, Manchester, NH. Rich and another guy ran em off. They got a press at the Stabbers' headquarters on Boylston Street.

Every day you send your two tapes to me in a box with one of those stickers. I'll mail 'em to Games from Boston. Send the stuff Speed Delivery. That's one they'll never figure out.'

The car cozied up to the curb in front of the Winthrop House. 'This car will be back in the U-Park-It. Don't try to drive out of Manchester unless you change your disguise. You got to be a chameleon, man.'

'How long do you think it will be safe here?' Richards asked. He thought: I've put myself in his hands. It didn't seem that he could think rationally for himself anymore. He could smell mental exhaustion on himself like body odor.

'Your reservation's for a week. That might be okay. It might not. Play it by ear. There's a name and an address in the suitcase. Fella in Portland, Maine. They'll hide you for a day or two. It'll cost, but they're safe. I gotta go, man. This is a five-minute zone. Money time.'

'How much?' Richards asked.

'Six hundred.'

'Bullshit. That doesn't even cover expenses.'

'Yes it does. With a few bucks left over for the family.'

'Take a thousand.'

'You need your dough, pal. Uh-uh.'

Richards looked at him helplessly. 'Christ, Bradley—'

'Send us more if you make it. Send us a million. Put us on easy street.'

'Do you think I will?'

Bradley smiled a soft, sad smile and said nothing.

'Then why?' Richards asked flatly. 'Why are you doing so much? I can understand you hiding me out. I'd do that. But you must have busted your club's arm.'

'They didn't mind. They know the score.'

'What score?'

'Ought to naught. That score. If we doan stick out our

necks for our own, they got us. No need to wait for the air. We could just as well run a pipe from the stove to the livin room, turn on the Free-Vee and wait.'

'Someone'll kill you,' Richards said. 'Someone will stool on you and you'll end up on a basement floor with your guts beat out. Or Stacey. Or Ma.'

Bradley's eyes flashed dimly. 'A bad day is comin, though. A bad day for the maggots with their guts full of roast beef. I see blood on the moon for them. Guns and torches. A mojo that walks and talks.'

'People have been seeing those things for two thousand years.'

The five-minute buzzer went off and Richards fumbled for the door handle. 'Thank you,' he said. 'I don't know how to say it any other way—'

'Go on,' Bradley said, 'before I get a ticket.' A strong brown hand clutched the robe. 'An when they get you, take a few along.'

Richards opened the rear door and popped the trunk to get the black satchel inside. Bradley handed him a cordovan-colored cane wordlessly.

The car pulled out into traffic smoothly. Richards stood on the curb for a moment, watching him go – watching him myopically, he hoped. The taillights flashed once at the corner, then the car swung out of sight, back to the parking lot where Bradley would leave it and pick up the other to go back to Boston.

Richards had a weird sensation of relief and realized that he was feeling empathy for Bradley – *how glad he must be to have me off his back, finally!*

Richards made himself miss the first step up to the Winthrop House's entrance, and the doorman assisted him.

... MINUS 056   and COUNTING ...

Two days passed.

Richards played his part well – that is to say, as if his life depended on it. He took dinner at the hotel both nights in his room. He rose at seven, read his Bible in the lobby, and then went out to his 'meeting.' The hotel staff treated him with easy, contemptuous cordiality – the kind reserved for half-blind, fumbling clerics (who paid their bills) in this day of limited legalized murder, germ warfare in Egypt and South America, and the notorious have-one-kill-one Nevada abortion law. The Pope was a muttering old man of ninety-six whose driveling edicts concerning such current events were reported as the closing humorous items on the seven o'clock newsies.

Richards held his one-man 'meetings' in a rented library cubicle where, with the door locked, he was reading about pollution. There was very little information later than 2002, and what there was seemed to jell very badly with what had been written before. The government, as usual, was doing a tardy but efficient job of double thinking.

At noon he made his way down to a luncheonette on the corner of a street not far from the hotel, bumping into people and excusing himself as he went. Some people told him it was quite all right, Father. Most simply cursed in an uninterested way and pushed him aside.

He spent the afternoons in his room and ate dinner watching *The Running Man*. He had mailed four filmclips while enroute to the library during the mornings. The forwarding from Boston seemed to be going smoothly.

The producers of the program had adopted a new tactic

for killing Richards's pollution message (he persisted with it in a kind of grinning frenzy – he had to be getting through to the lip-readers anyway): now the crowd drowned out the voice with a rising storm of jeers, screams, obscenities, and vituperation. Their sound grew increasingly more frenzied; ugly to the point of dementia.

In his long afternoons, Richards reflected that an unwilling change had come over him during his five days on the run. Bradley had done it – Bradley and the little girl. There was no longer just himself, a lone man fighting for his family, bound to be cut down. Now there were all of them out there, strangling on their own respiration – his family included.

He had never been a social man. He had shunned causes with contempt and disgust. They were for pig-simple suckers and people with too much time and money on their hands, like those half-assed college kids with their cute buttons and their neo-rock groups.

Richards's father had slunk into the night when Richards was five. Richards had been too young to remember him in anything but flashes. He had never hated him for it. He understood well enough how a man with a choice between pride and responsibility will almost always choose pride – if responsibility robs him of his manhood. A man can't stick around and watch his wife earning supper on her back. If a man can't do any more than pimp for the woman he married, Richards judged, he might as well walk out of a high window.

He had spent the years between five and sixteen hustling, he and his brother Todd. His mother had died of syphilis when he was ten and Todd was seven. Todd had been killed five years later when a newsy airtruck had lost its emergency brake on a hill while Todd was loading it. The city had fed both mother and son into the Municipal Crematorium. The kids on the street called it either the

Ash Factory or the Creamery; they were bitter but helpless, knowing that they themselves would most likely end up being belched out of the stacks and into the city's air. At sixteen Richards was alone, working a full eight-hour shift as an engine wiper after school. And in spite of his back-breaking schedule, he had felt a constant panic that came from knowing he was alone and unknown, drifting free. He awoke sometimes at three in the morning to the rotted-cabbage smell of the one-room tenement flat with terror lodged in the deepest chamber of his soul. He was his own man.

And so he had married, and Sheila had spent the first year in proud silence while their friends (and Richards's enemies; he had made many by his refusal to go along on mass-vandalizing expeditions and join a local gang) waited for the Uterus Express to arrive. When it didn't, interest flagged. They were left in that particular limbo that was reserved for newlyweds in Co-Op City. Few friends and a circle of acquaintances that reached only as far as the stoop of their own building. Richards did not mind this; it suited him. He threw himself into his work wholly, with grinning intensity, getting overtime when he could. The wages were bad, there was no chance of advancement, and inflation was running wild – but they were in love. They remained in love, and why not? Richards was that kind of solitary man who can afford to expend gigantic charges of love, affection, and, perhaps, psychic domination on the woman of his choice. Up until that point his emotions had been almost entirely untouched. In the eleven years of their marriage, they had never argued significantly.

He quit his job in 2018 because the chances of ever having children decreased with every shift he spent behind the leaky G-A old-style lead shields. He might have been all right if he answered the foreman's aggrieved 'Why are you quitting?' with a lie. But Richards had told him, simply and clearly, what he thought of General Atomics, concluding with an invitation to the foreman to take all his gamma shields and perform a reverse bowel movement with them. It ended in a short, savage scuffle. The foreman was brawny and looked tough, but Richards made him scream like a woman.

The blackball began to roll. He's dangerous. Steer clear. If you need a man bad, put him on for a week and then get rid of him. In G-A parlance, Richards had Shown Red.

During the next five years he had spent a lot of time rolling and loading newsies, but the work thinned to a trickle and then died. The Free-Vee killed the printed word very effectively. Richards pounded the pavement. Richards was moved along. Richards worked intermittently for day-labor outfits.

The great movements of the decade passed by him ignored, like ghosts to an unbeliever. He knew nothing of the Housewife Massacre in '24 until his wife told him about it three weeks later – two hundred police armed with tommy guns and high-powered move-alongs had turned back an army of women marching on the Southwest Food Depository. Sixty had been killed. He was vaguely aware that nerve gas was being used in the Mideast. But none of it affected him. Protest did not work. Violence did not work. The world was what it was, and Ben Richards moved through it like a thin scythe, asking for nothing, looking for work. He ferreted out a hundred miserable day and half-day jobs. He worked cleaning jelly-like slime from under piers and in sump ditches when others on the street, who honestly believed they were looking for work, did nothing.

Move along, maggot. Get lost. No job. Get out. Put on your boogie shoes. I'll blow your effing head off, daddy. Move.

Then the jobs dried up. Impossible to find anything. A rich man in a silk singlet, drunk, accosted him on the street one evening as Richards shambled home after a fruitless day, and told him he would give Richards ten New Dollars if Richards would pull down his pants so he could see if the street freaks really did have peckers a foot long. Richards knocked him down and ran.

It was then, after nine years of trying, that Sheila conceived. He was a wiper, the people in the building said. Can you believe he was a wiper for six years and knocked her up? It'll be a monster, the people in the building said. It'll have two heads and no eyes. *Radiation, radiation, your children will be monsters—*

But instead, it was Cathy. Round, perfect, squalling. Delivered by a midwife from down the block who took fifty cents and four cans of beans.

And now, for the first time since his brother had died, he was drifting again. Every pressure (even, temporarily, the pressure of the chase) had been removed.

His mind and his anger turned toward the Games Federation, with their huge and potent communications link to the whole world. Fat people with nose filters, spending their evenings with dollies in silk underpants. Let the guillotine fall. And fall. And fall. Yet there was no way to get them. They towered above all of them dimly, like the Games Building itself.

Yet, because he was who he was, and because he was alone and changing, he thought about it. He was unaware, alone in his room, that while he thought about it he grinned a huge white-wolf grin that in itself seemed powerful enough to buckle streets and melt buildings. The same grin he had worn on that almost-forgotten day when he had knocked a rich man down and then fled with his pockets empty and his mind burning.

... MINUS 055 and COUNTING ...

Monday was exactly the same as Sunday – the working world took no one particular day off anymore – until six-thirty.

Father Ogden Grassner had Meatloaf Supreme sent up (the hotel's cuisine, which would have seemed execrable to a man who had been weaned on anything better than fast-food hamburgers and concentrate pills, tasted great to Richards) with a bottle of Thunderbird wine and settled down to watch *The Running Man*. The first segment, dealing with Richards himself, went much as it had on the two nights previous. The audio on his clips was drowned out by the studio audience. Bobby Thompson was urbane and virulent. A house-to-house search was taking place in Boston. Anyone found harboring the fugitive would be put to death. Richards smiled without humor as they faded to a Network promo. It wasn't so bad; it was even funny, in a limited way. He could stand anything if they didn't broadcast the cops again.

The second half of the program was markedly different. Thompson was smiling broadly. 'After the latest tapes sent to us by the monster that goes under the name of Ben Richards, I'm pleased to give you some good news—'

They had gotten Laughlin.

He had been spotted in Topeka on Friday, but an intensive search of the city on Saturday and Sunday had not turned him up. Richards had assumed that Laughlin had slipped through the cordon as he had himself. But this afternoon, Laughlin had been observed by two kids. He had been cowering in a Highway Department road shed. He had broken his right wrist at some point.

The kids, Bobby and Mary Cowles, were shown grinning broadly into the camera. Bobby Cowles had a tooth missing. *I wonder if the tooth fairy brought him a quarter,* Richards thought sickly.

Thompson announced proudly that Bobby and Mary, 'Topeka's number one citizens,' would be on *The Running Man* tomorrow night to be presented Certificates of Merit, a lifetime supply of FunTwinks cereal, and checks for a thousand New Dollars each, by Hizzoner the Governor of Kansas. This brought wild cheers from the audience.

Following were tapes of Laughlin's riddled, sagging body being carried out of the shed, which had been reduced to matchwood by concentrated fire. There were mingled cheers, boos, and hisses from the studio audience.

Richards turned away sickly, nauseated. Thin, invisible fingers seemed to press against his temples.

From a distance, the words rolled on. The body was being displayed in the rotunda of the Kansas statehouse. Already long lines of citizens were filing past the body. An interviewed policeman who had been in at the kill said Laughlin hadn't put up much of a fight.

Ah, how nice for you, Richards thought, remembering Laughlin, his sour voice, the straight-ahead, jeering look in his eyes.

A friend of mine from the car pool.

Now there was only one big show. The big show was Ben Richards. He didn't want any more of his Meatloaf Supreme.

... MINUS 054   and COUNTING ...

He had a very bad dream that night, which was unusual. The old Ben Richards had never dreamed.

What was even more peculiar was the fact that he did not exist as a character in the dream. He only watched, invisible.

The room was vague, dimming off to blackness at the edges of vision. It seemed that water was dripping dankly. Richards had an impression of being deep underground.

In the center of the room, Bradley was sitting in a straight wooden chair with leather straps over his arms and legs. His head had been shaved like that of a penitent. Surrounding him were figures in black hoods. The Hunters, Richards thought with budding dread. Oh dear God, these are the Hunters.

'I ain't the man,' Bradley said.

'Yes you are, little brother,' one of the hooded figures said gently, and pushed a pin through Bradley's cheek. Bradley screamed.

'Are you the man?'

'Suck it.'

A pin slid easily into Bradley's eyeball and was withdrawn dribbling colorless fluid. Bradley's eye took on a punched, flattened look.

'Are you the man?'

'Poke it up your ass.'

An electric move-along touched Bradley's neck. He screamed again, and his hair stood on end. He looked like a comical caricature black, a futuristic Stepinfetchit.

'Are you the man, little brother?'

'Nose filters give you cancer,' Bradley said. 'You're all rotted inside, honkies.'

His other eyeball was pierced. 'Are you the man?'

Bradley, blind, laughed at them.

One of the hooded figures gestured, and from the shadows Bobby and Mary Cowles came tripping gaily. They began to skip around Bradley, singing: 'Who's afraid of the big bad wolf, the big bad wolf, the big bad wolf?'

Bradley began to scream and twist in the chair. He seemed to be trying to hold his hands up in a warding-off gesture. The song grew louder and louder, more echoing. The children were changing. Their heads were elongating, growing dark with blood. Their mouths were open and in the caves within, fangs twinkled like razor-blades.

'I'll tell!' Bradley screamed. 'I'll tell! I'll tell! I ain't the man! Ben Richards is the man! I'll tell! God . . . oh . . . G-G-God . . .'

'Where is the man, little brother?'

'I'll tell! I'll tell! He's in—'

But the words were drowned by the singing voices. They were lunging toward Bradley's straining, corded neck when Richards woke up, sweating.

. . . MINUS 053   and COUNTING . . .

It was no good in Manchester anymore.

He didn't know if it was the news of Laughlin's brutal midwestern end, or the dream, or only a premonition.

But on Tuesday morning he stayed in, not going to the library. It seemed to him that every minute he stayed in this place was an invitation to quick doom. Looking out the window, he saw a Hunter with a black hood inside every old beaner and slumped taxi driver. Fantasies of gunmen creeping soundlessly up the hall toward his door tormented him. He felt a huge clock was ticking in his head.

He passed the point of indecision shortly after eleven o'clock on Tuesday morning. It was impossible to stay. He knew they knew.

He got his cane and tapped clumsily to the elevators and went down to the lobby.

'Going out, Father Grassner?' The day clerk asked with his usual pleasant, contemptuous smile.

'Day off,' Richards said, speaking at the day clerk's shoulder. 'Is there a picture show in this town?'

He knew there were at least ten, eight of them showing 3-D perverto shows.

'Well,' the clerk said cautiously, 'there's the Center. I think they show Disneys—'

'That will be fine,' Richards said briskly, and bumped into a potted plant on his way out.

Two blocks from the hotel he went into a drugstore and bought a huge roll of bandage and a pair of cheap aluminum crutches. The clerk put his purchases in a long fiberboard box, and Richards caught a taxi on the next corner.

The car was exactly where it had been, and if there was a stakeout at the U-Park-It, Richards could not spot it. He got in and started up. He had a bad moment when he realized he lacked a driver's license in any name that wasn't hot, and then dismissed it. He didn't think his new disguise would get him past close scrutiny anyway. If there were roadblocks, he would try to crash them. It would get him killed, but he was going to get killed anyway if they tabbed him.

He tossed the Ogden Grassner glasses in the glove box and drove out, waving noncommittally at the boy on duty at the gate. The boy barely looked up from the skin magazine he was reading.

He stopped for a full compressed-air charge on the high-speed urban sprawl on the northern outskirts of the city. The air jockey was in the midst of a volcanic eruption of acne, and seemed pathetically anxious to avoid looking at Richards. So far, so good.

He switched from 91 to Route 17, and from there to a blacktop road with no name or number. Three miles farther along he pulled onto a rutted dirt turnaround and killed the engine.

Tilting the rearview mirror to the right angle, he wrapped the bandage around his skull as quickly as he could, holding the end and clipping it. A bird twitted restlessly in a tired-looking elm.

Not too bad. If he got breathing time in Portland, he could add a neck brace.

He put the crutches beside him on the seat and started the car. Forty minutes later he was entering the traffic circle at Portsmouth. Headed up Route 95, he reached into his pocket and pulled out the crumpled piece of ruled paper that Bradley had left him. He had written on it in the careful script of the self-educated, using a soft lead pencil:

94 State Street, Portland
THE BLUE DOOR, GUESTS
Elton Parrakis (& Virginia Parrakis)

Richards frowned at it a moment, then glanced up. A black-and-yellow police unit was cruising slowly above the traffic on the turnpike, in tandem with a heavy ground-unit below. They bracketed him for a moment and then were gone, zig-zagging across the six lanes in a graceful ballet. Routine traffic patrol.

As the miles passed, a queasy, almost reluctant sense of relief formed in his chest. It made him feel like laughing and throwing up at the same time.

... MINUS 052   and COUNTING ...

The drive to Portland was without incident.

But by the time he reached the edge of the city, driving through the built-up suburbs of Scarborough (rich homes, rich streets, rich private schools surrounded by electrified fences), the sense of relief had begun to fade again. They could be anywhere. They could be all around him. Or they could be nowhere.

State Street was an area of blasted, ancient brownstones not far from an overgrown, junglelike park – a hangout, Richards thought, for this small city's muggers, lovers, hypes, and thieves. No one would venture out on State Street after dark without a police dog on a leash, or a score of fellow gang-members.

Number 94 was a crumbling, soot-encrusted building with ancient green shades pulled down over its windows. To Richards the house looked like a very old man who had died with cataracts on his eyes.

He pulled to the curb and got out. The street was dotted with abandoned air cars, some of them rusted down to almost formless hulks. On the edge of the park, a Studebaker lay on its side like a dead dog. This was not police country, obviously. If you left your car unattended, it would gain a clot of leaning, spitting, slate-eyed boys in fifteen minutes. In half an hour some of the leaning boys would have produced crowbars and wrenches and screwdrivers. They would tap them, compare them, twirl them, have mock swordfights with them. They would hold them up into the air thoughtfully, as if testing the weather or receiving mysterious radio transmission through them. In an hour the car would be a stripped carcass, from aircaps and cylinders to the steering wheel itself.

A small boy ran up to Richards as he was setting his crutches under himself. Puckered, shiny burn scars had turned one side of the boy's face into a hairless Frankenstein horror.

'Scag, mister? Good stuff. Put you on the moon.' He giggled secretly, the lumped and knobbed flesh of his burnt face bobbing and writhing grotesquely.

'Fuck off,' Richards said briefly.

The boy tried to kick one of his crutches out from under him, and Richards swung one of them in a low arc, swatting the boy's bottom. He ran off, cursing.

He made his way up the pitted stone steps slowly and looked at the door. It had once been blue, but now the paint had faded and peeled to a tired desert sky color. There had once been a doorbell, but some vandal had taken care of that with a cold chisel.

Richards knocked and waited. Nothing. He knocked again.

It was late afternoon now, and cold was creeping slowly up the street. Faintly, from the park beyond the end of the block, came the bitter clacking of October branches losing their leaves.

There was no one here. It was time to go.

Yet he knocked again, curiously convinced that there *was* someone in there.

And this time he was rewarded with the slow shuffling of house slippers. A pause at the door. Then: 'Who's out there? I don't buy nothin. Go away.'

'I was told to visit you,' Richards said.

A peephole swung open with a minute squeak and a

brown eye peeked through. Then the peephole closed with a snap.

'I don't know you.' Flat dismissal.

'I was told to ask for Elton Parrakis.'

Grudgingly: 'Oh. You're one of those—'

Behind the door locks began to turn, bolts began to be unbolted, one by one. Chains dropped. There was the click of revolving tumblers in one Yale lock and then another. The *chunk-slap* of a police bar being freed. Finally, the *snick-snick-slamm* of the heavy-duty TrapBolt being withdrawn.

The door swung open and Richards looked at a scrawny woman with no breasts and huge, knotted hands. Her face was unlined, almost cherubic, but it looked as if it had taken hundreds of invisible hooks and jabs and uppercuts in a no-holds-barred brawl with time itself. Perhaps time was winning, but she was not an easy bleeder. She was almost six feet tall, even in her flat, splayed slippers, and her knees were swollen into treestumps with arthritis. Her hair was wrapped in a bath turban. Her brown eyes, staring at him from under a deep ledge of brow (the eyebrows themselves clung to the precipice like desperate mountain bushes, struggling against the aridity and the altitude), were intelligent and wild with what might have been fear or fury. Later he understood she was simply muddled, afraid, tottering on the edge of insanity.

'I'm Virginia Parrakis,' she said flatly. 'I'm Elton's mother. Come in.'

... MINUS 051 and COUNTING ...

She did not recognize him until she had led him into the kitchen to brew tea.

128

The house was old and crumbling and dark, furnished in a decor he recognized immediately from his own environment: Modern junkshop.

'Elton isn't here now,' she said, brooding over the battered aluminum teapot on the gas ring. The light was stronger here, revealing the brown waterstains that blotched the wallpaper, the dead flies, souvenirs of summer past, on the windowsills, the old linoleum creased with black lines, the pile of wet wrapping paper under the leaking drain pipe. There was an odor of disinfectant that made Richards think of last nights in sickrooms.

She crossed the room, and her swollen fingers made a painful search through the heaped junk on the countertop until they found two tea bags, one of them previously used. Richards got the used one. He was not surprised.

'He works,' she said, faintly accentuating the first word and making the statement an accusation. 'You're from that fellow in Boston, the one Eltie writes to about pollution, aintcha?'

'Yes, Mrs Parrakis.'

'They met in Boston. My Elton services automatic vending machines.' She preened for a moment and then began her slow trek back across the dunes of linoleum to the stove. 'I told Eltie that what that Bradley was doing was against the law. I told him it would mean prison or even worse. He doesn't listen to *me*. Not to his old mom, he doesn't.' She smiled with dark sweetness at this calumny. 'Elton was always building things, you know . . . He built a treehouse with four rooms out back when he was a boy. That was before they cut the elm down, you know. But it was that darky's idea that he should build a pollution station in Portland.'

She popped the bags into cups and stood with her back to Richards, slowly warming her hands over the gas ring. 'They write each other. I told him the mails aren't safe.

You'll go to prison or even worse, I said. He said but Mom, we do it in code. He asks for a dozen apples, I tell him my uncle is a little worse. I said: Eltie, do you think they can't figure that Secret Spy stuff out? He doesn't listen. Oh, he used to. I used to be his best friend. But things have changed. Since he got to pooberty, things have changed. Dirty magazines under his bed and all *that* business. Now this darky. I suppose They caught you testing smogs or carcinogens or something and now you're on the run.'

'I—'

'It don't matter!' She said fiercely at the window. It looked out on a backyard filled with rusting pieces of junk and tire rims and some little boy's sandbox that now, many years later, was filled with scruffy October woods.

'It don't matter!' she repeated. 'It's the darkies.' She turned to Richards and her eyes were hooded and furious and bewildered. 'I'm sixty-five, but I was only a fresh young girl of nineteen when it began to happen. It was nineteen seventy-nine and the darkies were everywhere! Everywhere! Yes they were!' she nearly screamed, as if Richards had taken issue with her. 'Everywhere! They sent those darkies to school with the whites. They set em high in the government. Radicals, rabble-rousing, and rebellion. I ain't so—'

She broke off as if the words had been splintered from her mouth. She stared at Richards, seeing him for the first time.

'OhGodhavemercy,' she whispered.

'Mrs Parrakis—'

'Nope!' she said in a fear-hoarsened voice. 'Nope! Nope! Oh, nope!' She began advancing on him, pausing at the counter to pick up a long, gleaming butcher knife out of the general clutter. 'Out! Out! Out!' He got up and began to back away slowly, first through the short hall between the kitchen and shadowy living room, then through the living room itself.

He noticed that an ancient pay telephone hung on the wall from the days when this had been a bona fide inn. The Blue Door, Guests. When was that? Richards wondered. Twenty years ago? Forty? Before the darkies had gotten out of hand, or after?

He was just beginning to back down the hall between the living room and the front door when a key rattled in the lock. They both froze as if some celestial hand had stopped the film while deciding what to do next.

The door opened, and Elton Parrakis walked in. He was immensely fat, and his lackluster blond hair was combed back in preposterous waves from his forehead to show a round baby face that held an element of perpetual puzzlement. He was wearing the blue and gold uniform of the Vendo-Spendo Company. He looked thoughtfully at Virginia Parrakis.

'Put that knife down, Mom.'

'Nope!' she cried, but already the crumbling of defeat had begun to putty her face.

Parrakis closed the door and began walking toward her. He jiggled.

She shrank away. 'You have to make him go, son. He's that badman. That Richards. It'll mean prison or worse. *I don't want you to go!*' She began to wail, dropped the knife, and collapsed into his arms.

He enfolded her and began to rock her gently as she wept. 'I'm not going to jail,' he said. 'Come on, Mom, don't cry. Please don't cry.' He smiled at Richards over one of her hunched and shaking shoulders, an embarrassed awfully-sorry-about-this smile. Richards waited.

'Now,' Parrakis said, when the sobs had died to sniffles. 'Mr Richards is Bradley Throckmorton's good friend, and he is going to be with us for a couple of days, Mom.'

She began to shriek, and he clapped a hand over her mouth, wincing as he did so.

'Yes, Mom. Yes he is. I'm going to drive his car into the park and wire it. And you'll go out tomorrow morning with a package to mail to Cleveland.'

'Boston,' Richards said automatically. 'The tapes go to Boston.'

'They go to Cleveland now,' Elton Parrakis said, with a patient smile. 'Bradley's on the run.'

'Oh. Jesus.'

'You'll be on the run, too!' Mrs Parrakis howled at her son. 'And they'll catch you, too! You're too fat!'

'I'm going to take Mr Richards upstairs and show him his room, Mom.'

'Mr Richards? Mr Richards? Why don't you call him by his right name? Poison!'

He disengaged her with great gentleness, and Richards followed him obediently up the shadowy staircase. 'There are a great many rooms up here,' he said, panting slightly as his huge buttocks flexed and clenched. 'This used to be a rooming house many years ago – when I was a baby. You'll be able to watch the street.'

'Maybe I better go,' Richards said. 'If Bradley's blown, your mother may be right.'

'This is your room,' he said, and threw open a door on a dusty damp room that held the weight of years. He did not seem to have heard Richards's comment. 'It's not much of an accommodation, I'm afraid, but—' He turned to face Richards with his patient I-want-to-please smile. 'You may stay as long as you want. Bradley Throckmorton is the best friend I've ever had.' The smile faltered a bit. 'The *only* friend I've ever had. I'll watch after my Mom. Don't worry.'

Richards only repeated: 'I better go.'

'You can't, you know. That head bandage didn't even

fool Mom for long. I'm going to drive your car to a safe place, Mr Richards. We'll talk later.'

He left quickly, lumberingly. Richards noted that the seat of his uniform pants was shiny. He seemed to leave a faint odor of apologia in the room.

Pulling the ancient green shade aside a little, Richards saw him emerge on the cracked front walk below and get into the car. Then he got out again. He hurried back toward the house, and Richards felt a stab of fear.

Ponderously climbing tread on the stairs. The door opened, and Elton smiled at Richards. 'Mom's right,' he said. 'I don't make a very good secret agent. I forgot the keys.'

Richards gave them to him and then essayed a joke: 'Half a secret agent is better than none.'

It struck a sour chord or no chord at all; Elton Parrakis carried his torments with him too clearly, and Richards could almost hear the phantom, jeering voices of the children that would follow him forever, like small tugs behind a huge liner.

'Thank you,' Richards said softly.

Parrakis left, and the little car that Richards had come from New Hampshire in was driven away toward the park.

Richards pulled the dust cover from the bed and lay down slowly, breathing shallowly and looking at nothing but the ceiling. The bed seemed to clutch him in a perversely damp embrace, even through the coverlet and his clothes. An odor of mildew drifted through the channels of his nose like a senseless rhyme.

Downstairs, Elton's mother was weeping.

...MINUS 050   and COUNTING...

He dozed a little but could not sleep. Darkness was almost full when he heard Elton's heavy tread on the stairs again, and Richards swung his feet onto the floor with relief.

When he knocked and stepped in, Richards saw that Parrakis had changed into a tentlike sports shirt and a pair of jeans.

'I did it,' he said. 'It's in the park.'

'Will it be stripped?'

'No,' Elton said. 'I have a gadget. A battery and two alligator clips. If anyone puts his hand or a crowbar on it, they'll get a shock and a short blast on a siren. Works good. I built it myself.' He seated himself with a heavy sigh.

'What's this about Cleveland?' Richards demanded (it was easy, he found, to demand of Elton).

Parrakis shrugged. 'Oh, he's a fellow like me. I met him once in Boston, at the library with Bradley. Our little pollution club. I suppose Mom said something about that.' He rubbed his hands together and smiled unhappily.

'She said something,' Richards agreed.

'She's.... a little dim,' Parrakis said. 'She doesn't understand much of what's been happening for the last twenty years or so. She's frightened all the time. I'm all she has.'

'Will they catch Bradley?'

'I don't know. He's got quite a ... uh, intelligence network.' But his eyes slipped away from Richards's.

'You—'

The door opened and Mrs Parrakis stood there. Her

arms were crossed and she was smiling, but her eyes were haunted. 'I've called the police,' she said. 'Now you'll have to go.'

Elton's face drained to a pearly yellowish-white. 'You're lying.'

Richards lurched to his feet and then paused, his head cocked in a listening gesture.

Faintly, rising, the sound of sirens.

'She's not lying,' he said. A sickening sense of futility swept him. Back to square one. 'Take me to my car.'

'She's lying,' Elton insisted. He rose, almost touched Richards's arm, then withdrew his hand as if the other man might be hot to the touch. 'They're fire trucks.'

'Take me to my car. Quick.'

The sirens were becoming louder, rising and falling, wailing. The sound filled Richards with a dreamlike horror, locked in here with these two crazies while—

'Mother—' His face was twisted, beseeching.

'I called them!' She blatted, and seized one of her son's bloated arms as if to shake him. 'I had to! For you! That darky has got you all mixed up! We'll say he broke in and we'll get the reward money—'

'Come on,' Elton grunted to Richards, and tried to shake free of her.

But she clung stubbornly, like a small dog bedeviling a Percheron. 'I had to. You've got to stop this radical business, Eltie! You've got to—'

'Eltie!' He screamed. '*Eltie!*' And he flung her away. She skidded across the room and fell across the bed.

'Quick,' Elton said, his face full of terror and misery. 'Oh, come quick.'

They crashed and blundered down the stairs and out the front door, Elton breaking into gigantic, quivering trot. He was beginning to pant again.

And upstairs, filtering both through the closed window

and the open door downstairs, Mrs Parrakis's scream rose to a shriek which met and mixed and blended with the approaching sirens: 'I DID IT FOR YOOOOOOOOOOOO —'

. . . MINUS 049   and COUNTING . . .

Their shadows chased them down the hill toward the park, waxing and waning as they approached and passed each of the mesh-enclosed G.A. streetlamps. Elton Parrakis breathed like a locomotive, in huge and windy gulps and hisses.

They crossed the street and suddenly headlights picked them out on the far sidewalk in hard relief. Blue flashing lights blazed on as the police car came to a screeching, jamming halt a hundred yards away.

'*RICHARDS! BEN RICHARDS!*'

Gigantic, megaphone-booming voice.

'Your car . . . up ahead . . . see?' Elton panted.

Richards could just make the car out. Elton had parked it well, under a copse of run-to-seed birch trees near the pond.

The cruiser suddenly screamed into life again, rear tires bonding hot rubber to the pavement in lines of acceleration, its gasoline-powered engine wailing in climbing revolutions. It slammed up over the curb, headlights skyrocketing, and came down pointing directly at them.

Richards turned toward it, suddenly feeling very cool, feeling almost numb. He dragged Bradley's pistol out of his pocket, still backing up. The rest of the cops weren't in sight. Just this one. The car screamed at them across the October-bare ground of the park, self-sealing rear tires digging out great clods of ripped black earth.

He squeezed off two shots at the windshield. It starred but did not shatter. He leaped aside at the last second and rolled. Dry grass against his face. Up on his knees, he fired twice more at the back of the car and then it was coming around in a hard, slewing power turn, blue lights turning the night into a crazy, shadow-leaping nightmare. The cruiser was between him and the car, but Elton had leaped the other way, and was now working frantically to remove his electrical device from the car door.

Someone was halfway out of the passenger side of the police car, which was on its way again. A thick stuttering sound filled the dark. Sten gun. Bullets dug through the turf around him in a senseless pattern. Dirt struck his cheeks, pattered against his forehead.

He knelt as if praying, and fired again into the windshield. This time, the bullet punched a hole through the glass.

The car was on top of him—

He sprang to the left and the reinforced steel bumper struck his left foot, snapping his ankle and sending him sprawling on his face.

The cruiser's engine rose to a supercharged scream, digging through another power turn. Now the headlights were on him again, turning everything stark monochrome. Richards tried to get up, but his broken ankle wouldn't support him.

Sobbing in great gulps of air, he watched the police car loom again. Everything became heightened, surreal. He was living in an adrenaline delirium and everything seemed slow, deliberate, orchestrated. The approaching police car was like a huge, blind buffalo.

The Sten gun rattled again, and this time a bullet punched through his left arm, knocking him sideways. The heavy car tried to veer and get him, and for a moment he had a clear shot at the figure behind the wheel. He fired once and the window blew inward. The car screamed into a slow, digging, sidewards roll, then went up and over, crashing down on the roof and then onto its side. The motor stalled, and in sudden, shocking silence, the police radio crackled clearly.

Richards still could not get to his feet and so he began to crawl toward the car. Parrakis was in it now, trying to start it, but in his blind panic he must have forgotten to lever the safety vents open; each time he turned the key there was only a hollow, coughing boom of air in the chambers.

The night began to fill up with converging sirens.

He was still fifty yards from the car when Elton realized what was wrong and yanked down the vent lever. The next time he turned the key the engine chopped erratically into life and the air car swept toward Richards.

He got to a half-standing position and tore the passenger door open and fell inside. Parrakis banked left onto Route 77 which intersected State Street above the park, the lower deck of the car no more than an inch from the paving, almost low enough to drag and spill them.

Elton gulped in huge swatches of air and let them out with force enough to flap his lips like window blinds.

Two more police cars screamed around the corner behind them, the blue lights flashed on, and they gave chase.

'We're not fast enough!' Elton screamed. 'We're not fast—'

'They're on wheels!' Richards yelled back. 'Cut through that vacant lot!'

The air car banked left and they were slammed upward violently as they crossed the curb. The battering air pressure shoved them into drive.

The police cars swelled behind them, and then they were shooting. Richards heard steel fingers punching holes in the body of their car. The rear window blew in with a tremendous crash, and they were sprinkled with fragments of safety glass.

Screaming, Elton whipped the air car left and right.

One of the police cars, doing sixty-plus, lost it coming up over the curb. The car veered wildly, revolving blue dome-lights splitting the darkness with lunatic bolts of light, and then it crashed over on its side, digging a hot groove through the littered moraine of the empty lot, until a spark struck its peeled-back gas tank. It exploded whitely, like a road flare.

The second car was following the road again, but Elton beat them. They had cut the cruiser off, but it would gain back the lost distance very shortly. The gas-driven ground cars were nearly three times faster than air drive. And if an air car tried to go too far off the road, the uneven surface beneath the thrusters would flip the car over, as Parrakis had nearly flipped them crossing the curb.

'Turn right!' Richards cried.

Parrakis pulled them around in another grinding, stomach-lurching turn. They were on Route 1; ahead, Richards could see that they would soon be forced up the entranceway to the Coast Turnpike. No evasive action would be possible there; only death would be possible there.

'Turn off! Turn off, goddammit! That alley!' For a moment, the police car was one turn behind them, lost from view.

'NO! No!' Parrakis was gibbering now. 'We'll be like rats in a trap!'

Richards leaned over and hauled the wheel around, knocking Elton's hand from the throttle with the same gesture. The air car skidded around in a nearly ninety-degree turn. They bounced off the concrete of the building on the left of the alley's mouth, sending them in at a crooked angle. The blunt nose of the car struck a pile of heaped trash, garbage cans, and splintered crates. Behind these, solid brick.

Richards was pitched violently into the dashboard as they crashed, and his nose broke with a sudden snap, gushing blood with violent force.

The air car lay askew in the alley, one cylinder still coughing a little. Parrakis was a silent lump lolling over the steering wheel. There was no time for him yet.

Richards slammed his shoulder against the crimped passenger door. It popped open, and he hopped on one leg to the mouth of the alley. He reloaded his gun from the crumpled box of shells Bradley had supplied him with. They were greasy-cool to the touch. He dropped some of them around his feet. His arm had begun to throb like an ulcerated tooth, making him feel sick and nauseated with pain.

Headlights turned the deserted city expressway from night to sunless day. The cruiser skidded around the turn, rear tires fighting for traction, sending up the fragrant smell of seared rubber. Looping black marks scored the expansion-joint macadam in parabolas. Then it was leaping forward again. Richards held the gun in both hands, leaning against the building to his left. In a moment they would realize they could see no taillights ahead. The cop riding shotgun would see the alley, know—

Snuffling blood through his broken nose, he began to fire. The range was nearly pointblank, and at this distance, the highpowered slugs smashed through the bullet-proof glass as if it had been paper. Each recoil of the heavy pistol pulsed through his wounded arm, making him scream.

The car roared up over the curb, flew a short, wingless distance, and crashed into the blank brick wall across the street. ECHO FREE-VEE REPAIR, a faded sign on this wall read. BECAUSE YOU WATCH IT, WE WON'T BOTCH IT.

The police car, still a foot above the ground, met the brick wall at high speed and exploded.

But others were coming; always others.

Panting, Richards made his way back to the air car. His good leg was very tired.

'I'm hurt,' Parrakis was groaning hollowly. 'I'm hurt so bad. Where's Mom? Where's my Momma?'

Richards fell on his knees, wriggled under the air car on his back, and began to pull trash and debris from the air chambers like a madman. Blood ran down his cheeks from his ruptured nose and pooled beside his ears.

. . . MINUS 048   and COUNTING . . .

The car would only run on five of its six cylinders, and it would go no faster than forty, leaning drunkenly to one side.

Parrakis directed him from the passenger seat, where Richards had manhandled him. The steering column had gone into his abdomen like a railspike, and Richards thought he was dying. The blood on the dented steering wheel was warm and sticky on Richards's palms.

'I'm very sorry,' Parrakis said. 'Turn left here . . . It's really my fault. I should have known better. She . . . she doesn't think straight. She doesn't . . .' He coughed up a glut of black blood and spat it listlessly into his lap. The sirens filled the night, but they were far behind and off to the west. They had gone out Marginal Way, and from there Parrakis had directed him onto back roads. Now they were on Route 9 going north, and the Portland suburbs were petering out into October-barren scrub countryside. The strip lumberers had been through like locusts, and the end result was a bewildering tangle of second growth and marsh.

'Do you know where you're telling me to go?' Richards asked. He was a huge brand of pain from one end to the other. He was quite sure his ankle was broken; there was no doubt at all about his nose. His breath came through it in flattened gasps.

'To a place I know,' Elton Parrakis said, and coughed up more blood. 'She used to tell me a boy's best friend is his Mom. Can you believe that? I used to believe it. Will they hurt her? Take her to jail?'

'No,' Richards said shortly, not knowing if they would or not. It was twenty minutes of eight. He and Elton had left the Blue Door at ten minutes past seven. It seemed as if decades had passed.

A far distance off, more sirens were joining in the general chorus. *The unspeakable in pursuit of the inedible*, Richards thought disjointedly. *If you can't stand the heat, get out of the kitchen*. He had dispatched two police cars singlehanded. Another bonus for Sheila. Blood money. And Cathy. Would Cathy sicken and die on milk paid for with bounty cash? *How are you, my darlings? I love you. Here on this twisting, crazy back road fit only for deer jackers and couples looking for a good make-out spot, I love you and wish that your dreams be sweet. I wish—*

'Turn left,' Elton croaked.

Richards swung left up a smooth tarred road that cut through a tangle of denuded sumac and elm, pine and spruce, scrubby nightmare second growth. A river, ripe and sulphurous with industrial waste, smote his nose. Low-hanging branches scraped the roof of the car with skeleton screeches. They passed a sign which read: SUPER PINE TREE MALL – UNDER CONSTRUCTION – KEEP OUT! – TRESPASSERS WILL BE PROSECUTED!!

They topped a final rise and there was the Super Pine Tree Mall. Work must have stopped at least two years ago, Richards thought, and things hadn't been too advanced when it did. The place was a maze, a rat warren of half-built stores and shops, discarded lengths of pipe, piles of cinderblock and boards, shacks and rusted Quonset huts, all overgrown with scrubby junipers and laurels and witchgrass and blue spruce, blackberry and blackthorn, devil's paintbrush and denuded goldenrod. And it stretched on for miles. Gaping oblong foundation holes like graves dug for Roman gods. Rusted skeleton steel. Cement walls with steel core-rods protruding like shadowy cryptograms. Bulldozed oblongs that were to be parking lots now grassed over.

Somewhere overhead, an owl flew on stiff and noiseless wings, hunting.

'Help me . . . into the driver's seat.'

'You're in no condition to drive,' Richards said, pushing hard on his door to open it.

'It's the least I can do,' Elton Parrakis said with grave and bloody absurdity. 'I'll play hare . . . drive as long as I can.'

'No,' Richards said.

'Let me go!' He screamed at Richards, his fat baby face terrible and grotesque. 'I'm dying and you just better let me guh – guh – guh—' He trailed off into hideous silent coughs that brought up fresh gouts of blood. It smelled very moist in the car; like a slaughterhouse. 'Help me,' he whispered. 'I'm too fat to do it by myself. Oh God please help me do this.'

Richards helped him. He pushed and heaved and his hands slipped and squelched in Elton's blood. The front seat was an abbatoir. And Elton (who would have thought anyone could have so much blood in him?) continued to bleed.

Then he was wedged behind the wheel and the air car was rising jaggedly, turning. The brake lights blinked on and off, on and off, and the car bunted at trees lightly before Elton found the road out.

Richards thought he would hear the crash, but there was none. The erratic *thumpa-thumpa-thumpa* of the air cylinders grew fainter, beating in the deadly one-cylinder-flat rhythm that would burn out the others in an hour or so. The sound faded. Then there was no sound at all but the faraway buzz of a plane. Richards realized belatedly that he had left the crutches he had purchased for disguise purposes in the back of the car.

The constellations whirled indifferently overhead.

He could see his breath in small, frozen puffs; it was colder tonight.

He turned from the road and plunged into the jungle of the construction site.

. . . MINUS 047   and COUNTING . . .

He spied a pile of cast-off insulation lying in the bottom of a cellar hole and climbed down, using the protruding core rods for handholds. He found a stick and pounded the insulation to scare out the rats. He was rewarded with nothing but a thick, fibrous dust that made him sneeze and yelp with the pain-burst in his badly used nose. No rats. All the rats were in the city. He uttered a harsh bray of laughter that sounded jagged and splintered in the big dark.

He wrapped himself in strips of the insulation until he looked like a human igloo – but it was warm. He leaned back against the wall and fell into a half-doze.

When he roused fully, a late moon, no more than a

cold scrap of light, hung over the eastern horizon. He was still alone. There were no sirens. It might have been three o'clock.

His arm throbbed uneasily, but the flow of blood had stopped on its own; he saw this after pulling the arm out of the insulation and brushing the fibers gently away from the clot. The Sten gun bullet had apparently ripped a fairly large triangular hunk of meat from the side of his arm just above the elbow. He supposed he was lucky that the bullet hadn't smashed the bone. But his ankle throbbed with a steady, deep ache. The foot itself felt strange and ethereal, barely attached. He supposed the break should be splinted.

Supposing, he dozed again.

When he woke, his head was clearer. The moon had risen halfway up in the sky, but there was still no sign of dawn, true or false. *He was forgetting something—*

It came to him in a nasty, jolting realization.

He had to mail two tape clips before noon, if they were to get to the Games Building by the six-thirty air time. That meant traveling or defaulting the money.

But Bradley was on the run, or captured.

And Elton Parrakis had never given him the Cleveland name.

And his ankle was broken.

Something large (a deer? weren't they extinct in the east?) suddenly crashed through the underbrush off to his right, making him jump. Insulation slid off him like snakes, and he pulled it back around himself miserably, snuffling through his broken nose.

He was a city-dweller sitting in a deserted Development gone back to the wild in the middle of nowhere. The night suddenly seemed alive and malevolent, frightening of its own self, full of crazed bumps and creaks.

Richards breathed through his mouth, considering his options and their consequences.

1. *Do nothing.* Just sit here and wait for things to cool off. Consequence: The money he was piling up, a hundred dollars an hour, would be cut off at six tonight. He would be running for free, but the hunt wouldn't stop, not even if he managed to avoid them for the whole thirty days. The hunt would continue until he was carried off on a board.

2. *Mail the clips to Boston.* It couldn't hurt Bradley or the family, because their cover was already blown. Consequences: (1) The tapes would undoubtedly be sent to Harding by the Hunters watching Bradley's mail, but (2) they would still be able to trace him directly to wherever he mailed the tapes from, with no intervening Boston postmark.

3. *Mail the tapes directly to the Games Building in Harding.* Consequences: The hunt would go on, but he would probably be recognized in any town big enough to command a mailbox.

They were all lousy choices.

Thank you, Mrs Parrakis. Thank you.

He got up, brushing the insulation away, and tossed the useless head bandage on top of it. As an afterthought, he buried it in the insulation.

He began hunting around for something to use as a crutch (the irony of leaving the real crutches in the car struck him again), and when he found a board that reached approximately to armpit height, he threw it over the lip of the cellar foundation and began to climb laboriously back up the core rods.

When he got to the top, sweating and shivering simultaneously, he realized that he could see his hands. The first faint gray light of dawn had begun to probe the darkness. He looked longingly at the deserted Development, thinking: *It would have made such a fine hiding place—*

No good. He wasn't supposed to be a hiding man; he

was a running man. Wasn't that what kept the ratings up?

A cloudy, cataractlike ground mist was creeping slowly through the denuded trees. Richards paused to get his directions and then struck off toward the woods that bordered the abandoned Super Mall on the north.

He paused only once to wrap his coat around the top of his crutch and then continued.

. . . MINUS 046   and COUNTING . . .

It had been full daylight for two hours and Richards had almost convinced himself he was going around in large circles when he heard, through the rank brambles and ground bushes up ahead, the whine of air cars.

He pushed on cautiously and then peered out on a two-lane macadam highway. Cars rushed to and fro with fair regularity. About a half a mile up, Richards could make out a cluster of houses and what was either an air station or an old general store with pumps in front.

He pushed on, paralleling the highway, falling over occasionally. His face and hands were a needlepoint of blood from briars and brambles, and his clothes were studded with brown sticker-balls. He had given up trying to brush them away. Burst milkweed pods floated lightly from both shoulders, making him look as if he had been in a pillow fight. He was wet from top to toe; he had made it through the first two brooks, but in the third his 'crutch' had slipped on the treacherous bottom and he had fallen headlong. The camera, of course, was undamaged. It was waterproof and shockproof. Of course.

The bushes and trees were thinning. Richards got down on his hands and knees and crawled. When he had gone as far as he thought he safely could, he studied the situation.

He was on a slight rise of land, a peninsula of the scrubby second-growth weeds he had been walking through. Below him was the highway, a number of ranch-type houses, and a store with air pumps. A car was in there now, being attended to while the driver, a man in a suede windbreaker, chatted with the air jockey. Beside the store, along with three or four gumball machines and a Maryjane vendor, stood a blue and red mailbox. It was only two hundred yards away. Looking at it, Richards realized bitterly that if he had arrived before first light he could have probably done his business unseen.

Well, spilt milk and all that. The best laid plans of mice and men.

He withdrew until he could set up his camera and do his taping without being seen.

'Hello, all you wonderful people out there in Free-Vee land,' he began. 'This is jovial Ben Richards, taking you on my annual nature hike. If you look closely you may see the fearless scarlet tanager or a great speckled cowbird. Perhaps even a yellow-bellied pig bird or two.' He paused. 'They may let that part through, but not the rest. If you're deaf and read lips, remember what I'm saying. Tell a neighbor or a friend. Spread the word. The Network is poisoning the air you breathe and denying you cheap protection because—'

He recorded both tapes and put them in his pants pocket. Okay. What next? The only possible way to do it was to go down with the gun drawn, deposit the tapes, and run. He could steal a car. It wasn't as if they weren't going to know where he was anyway.

Randomly, he wondered how far Parrakis had gotten before they cut him down. He had the gun out and in his fist when he heard the voice, startlingly close, seemingly in his left ear: 'Come on, Rolf!'

There was a sudden volley of barks that made Richards

jump violently and he had just time to think: *Police dogs, Christ, they've got police dogs*, when something huge and black broke cover and arrowed at him.

The gun was knocked into the brush and Richards was on his back. The dog was on top of him, a big German shepherd with a generous streak of mongrel, lapping his face and drooling on his shirt. His tail flagged back and forth in vigorous semaphores of joy.

'Rolf! Hey Rolf! Ro! – oh Gawd!' Richards caught an obscured glimpse of running legs in blue jeans, and then a small boy was dragging the dog away. 'Jeez, I'm sorry, mister. Jeez, he don't bite, he's too dumb to bite, he's just friendly, he ain't . . . Gawd, ain't you a mess! You get lost?'

The boy was holding Rolf by the collar and staring at Richards with frank interest. He was a good-looking boy, well made, perhaps eleven, and there was none of the pale and patched inner-city look on his face. There was something suspicious and alien in his features, yet familiar also. After a moment Richards placed it. It was innocence.

'Yes,' he said dryly. 'I got lost.'

'Gee, you sure must have fallen around some.'

'That I did, pal. You want to take a close look at my face and see if it's scratched up very badly? I can't see it, you know.'

The boy leaned forward obediently and scanned Richards's face. No sign of recognition flickered there. Richards was satisfied.

'It's all burr-caught,' the boy said (there was a delicate New England twang in his voice; not exactly Down East, but lightly springy, sardonic), 'but you'll live.' His brow furrowed. 'You escaped from Thomaston? I know you ain't from Pineland cause you don't look like a retard.'

'I'm not escaped from anywhere,' Richards said,

wondering if that was a lie or the truth. 'I was hitchhiking. Bad habit, pal. You never do it, do you?'

'No way,' the boy said earnestly. 'There's crazy dudes running the roads these days. That's what my dad says.'

'He's right,' Richards said. 'But I just had to get to ... uh ...' He snapped his fingers in a pantomime of it-just-slipped-my-mind. 'You know, jetport.'

'You must mean Voigt Field.'

'That's it.'

'Jeez, that's over a hundred miles from here, mister. In Derry.'

'I know,' Richards said ruefully, and ran a hand over Rolf's fur. The dog rolled over obligingly and played dead. Richards fought an urge to utter a morbid chuckle. 'I picked up a ride at the New Hampshire border with these three maggots. Real tough guys. They beat me up, stole my wallet and dumped me at some deserted shopping center—'

'Yeah, I know that place. Cripes, you wanna come down to the house and have some breakfast?'

'I'd like to, bucko, but time's wasting. I have to get to that jetport by tonight.'

'You going to hitch another lift?' The boy's eyes were round.

'Got to.' Richards started to get up, then settled back as if a great idea had struck him. 'Listen, do me a favor?'

'I guess so,' the boy said cautiously.

Richards took out the two exposed tape-clips. 'These are charge-plate cash vouchers,' he said glibly. 'If you drop them in a mailbox for me, my company will have a lump of cash waiting for me in Derry. Then I'll be on my merry way.'

'Even without an address?'

'These go direct,' Richards said.

'Sure. Okay. There's a mailbox down at Jarrold's Store.'
He got up, his inexperienced face unable to disguise the
fact that he thought Richards was lying in his teeth. 'Come
on, Rolf.'

He let the boy get fifteen feet and then said: 'No. Come
here again.'

The boy turned and came back with his feet dragging.
There was dread on his face. Of course, there were enough
holes in Richards's story to drive a truck through.

'I've got to tell you everything, I guess,' Richards said.
'I was telling you the truth about most of it, pal. But I
didn't want to risk the chance that you might blab.'

The morning October sun was wonderfully warm on
his back and neck and he wished he could stay on the hill
all day, and sleep sweetly in fall's fugitive warmth. He
pulled the gun from where it had fallen and let it lie loosely
on the grass. The boy's eyes went wide.

'Government,' Richards said quietly.

'*Jee-zus!*' The boy whispered. Rolf sat beside him, his
pink tongue lolling rakishly from the side of his mouth.

'I'm after some pretty hard guys, kid. You can see that
they worked me over pretty well. Those clips you got
there have *got* to get through.'

'I'll mail em,' the boy said breathlessly. 'Jeez, wait'll I
tell—'

'Nobody,' Richards said. 'Tell nobody for twenty-four
hours. There might be reprisals,' he added ominously. 'So
until tomorrow this time, you never saw me. Understand?'

'Yeah! Sure!'

'Then get on it. And thanks, pal.' He held out his hand
and the boy shook it awefully.

Richards watched them trot down the hill, a boy in a
red plaid shirt with his dog crashing joyfully through the
golden-rod beside him. *Why can't my Cathy have something
like that?*

His face twisted into a terrifying and wholly unconscious grimace of rage and hate, and he might have cursed
God Himself if a better target had not interposed itself on
the dark screen of his mind: the Games Federation. And
behind that, like the shadow of a darker god, the Network.

He watched until he saw the boy, made tiny with
distance, drop the tapes into the mailbox.

Then he got up stiffly, propping his crutch under him,
and crashed back into the brush, angling toward the road.

The jetport, then. And maybe someone else would pay
some dues before it was all over.

... MINUS 045   and COUNTING ...

He had seen an intersection a mile back and Richards left
the woods there, making his way awkwardly down the
gravel bank between the woods and the road.

He sat there like a man who has given up trying to
hook a ride and has decided to enjoy the warm autumn
sun instead. He let the first two cars go by; both of them
held two men, and he figured the odds were too high.

But when the third one approached the stop sign, he
got up. The closing-in feeling was back. This whole area
had to be hot, no matter how far Parrakis had gotten. The
next car could be police, and that would be the ballgame.

It was a woman in the car, and she was alone. She
would not look at him; hitchhikers were distasteful and
thus to be ignored. He ripped the passenger door open
and was in even as the car was accelerating again. He
was picked up and thrown sideways, one hand holding
desperately onto the doorjamb, his good foot dragging.

The thumping hiss of brakes; the air car swerved wildly.
'What — who — you can't—'

Richards pointed the gun at her, knowing he must look grotesque close up, like a man who had been run through a meat grinder. The fierce image would work for him. He dragged his foot in and slammed the door, gun never swerving. She was dressed for town, and wore blue wraparound sunglasses. Good looking from what he could see.

'Wheel it,' Richards said.

She did the predictable; slammed both feet on the brake and screamed. Richards was thrown forward, his bad ankle scraping excruciatingly. The air car juddered to a stop on the shoulder, fifty feet beyond the intersection.

'You're that . . . you're . . . R-R-R—'

'Ben Richards. Take your hands off the wheel. Put them in your lap.'

She did it, shuddering convulsively. She would not look at him. Afraid, Richards supposed, that she would be turned to stone.

'What's your name, ma'am?'

'A-Amelia Williams. Don't shoot me. Don't kill me. I . . . I . . . you can have my money only *for God sake don't kill meeeeeeee*—'

'Shhhhh,' Richards said soothingly. 'Shhhhh, shhhhhh.' When she had quieted a little he said: 'I won't try to change your mind about me, Mrs Williams. Is it Mrs?'

'Yes,' she said automatically.

'But I have no intention of harming you. Do you understand that?'

'Yes,' she said, suddenly eager. 'You want the car. They got your friend and now you need a car. You can take it – it's insured – I won't even tell. I swear I won't. I'll say someone stole it in the parking lot—'

'We'll talk about it,' Richards said. 'Begin to drive. Go up Route 1 and we'll talk about it. Are there roadblocks?'

'N – yes. Hundreds of them. They'll catch you.'

'Don't lie, Mrs Williams. Okay?'

She began to drive, erratically at first, then more smoothly. The motion seemed to soothe her. Richards repeated his question about roadblocks.

'Around Lewiston,' she said with frightened unhappiness. 'That's where they got that other mag— fellow.'

'How far is that?'

'Thirty miles or more.'

Parrakis had gotten farther than Richards would have dreamed.

'Will you rape me?' Amelia Williams asked so suddenly that Richards almost barked with laughter.

'No,' he said; then, matter-of-factly: 'I'm married.'

'I saw her,' she said with a kind of smirking doubtfulness that made Richards want to smash her. *Eat garbage, bitch. Kill a rat that was hiding in the breadbox, kill it with a whiskbroom and then see how you talk about my wife.*

'Can I get off here?' She asked pleadingly, and he felt a trifle sorry for her again.

'No,' he said. 'You're my protection, Mrs Williams. I have to get to Voigt Field, in a place called Derry. You're going to see that I get there.'

'That's a hundred and fifty miles!' She wailed.

'Someone else told me a hundred.'

'They were wrong. You'll never get through to there.'

'I might,' Richards said, and then looked at her. 'And so might you, if you play it right.'

She began to tremble again but said nothing. Her attitude was that of a woman waiting to wake up.

. . . MINUS 044 and COUNTING . . .

They traveled north through autumn burning like a torch. The trees were not dead this far north, murdered by the big, poisonous smokes of Portland, Manchester, and Boston; they were all hues of yellow, red, brilliant starburst purple. They awoke in Richards an aching feeling of melancholy. It was a feeling he never would have suspected his emotions could have harbored only two weeks before. In another month the snow would fly and cover all of it.

Things ended in fall.

She seemed to sense his mood and said nothing. The driving filled the silence between them, lulled them. They passed over the water at Yarmouth, then there were only woods and trailers and miserable poverty shacks with outhouses tacked on the sides (yet one could always spot the Free-Vee cable attachment, bolted on below a sagging, paintless windowsill or beside a hinge-smashed door, winking and heliographing in the sun) until they entered Freeport.

There were three police cruisers parked just outside of town, the cops meeting in a kind of roadside conference. The woman stiffened like a wire, her face desperately pale, but Richards felt calm.

They passed the police without notice, and she slumped.

'If they had been monitoring traffic, they would have been on us like a shot,' Richards said casually. 'You might as well paint BEN RICHARDS IS IN THIS CAR on your forehead in Day-Glo.'

'Why can't you let me go?' She burst out, and in the same breath: 'Have you got a jay?'

Rich folks blow Dokes. The thought brought a bubble of ironic laughter and he shook his head.

'You're laughing at me?' She asked, stung. 'You've got some nerve, don't you, you cowardly little murderer! Scaring me half out of my life, probably planning to kill me the way you killed those poor boys in Boston—'

'There was a full gross of those poor boys,' Richards said. 'Ready to kill me. That's their job.'

'Killing for pay. Ready to do anything for money. Wanting to overturn the country. Why don't you find decent work? Because you're too lazy! Your kind spit in the face of anything decent.'

'Are you decent?' Richards asked.

'Yes!' She stormed. 'Isn't that why you picked on me? Because I was defenseless and . . . and decent? So you could use me, drag me down to your level and then laugh about it?'

'If you're so decent, how come you have six thousand New Dollars to buy this fancy car while my little girl dies of the flu?'

'What—' She looked startled. Her mouth started to open and she closed it with a snap. 'You're an enemy of the Network,' she said. 'It says so on the Free-Vee. I saw some of those disgusting things you did.'

'You know what's disgusting?' Richards asked, lighting a cigarette from the pack on the dashboard. 'I'll tell you. It's disgusting to get blackballed because you don't want to work in a General Atomics job that's going to make you sterile. It's disgusting to sit home and watch your wife earning the grocery money on her back. It's disgusting to know the Network is killing millions of people each year with air pollutants when they could be manufacturing nose filters for six bucks a throw.'

'You lie,' she said. Her knuckles had gone white on the wheel.

'When this is over,' Richards said, 'you can go back to your nice split-level duplex and light up a Doke and get stoned and love the way your new silverware sparkles in the highboy. No one fighting rats with broomhandles in your neighborhood or shitting by the back stoop because the toilet doesn't work. I met a little girl five years old with lung cancer. How's that for disgusting? What do—'

'Stop!' She screamed at him. '*You talk dirty!*'

'That's right,' he said, watching as the countryside flowed by. Hopelessness filled him like cold water. There was no base of communication with these beautiful chosen ones. They existed up where the air was rare. He had a sudden, raging urge to make this woman pull over: knock her sunglasses onto the gravel, drag her through the dirt, make her eat a stone, rape her, jump on her, knock her teeth into the air like startled digits, strip her nude and ask her if she was beginning to see the big picture, the one that runs twenty-four hours a day on channel one, where the national anthem never plays before the sign-off.

'That's right,' he muttered. 'Dirty-talking old me.'

. . . MINUS 043   and COUNTING . . .

They got farther than they had any right to, Richards figured. They got all the way to a pretty town by the sea called Camden over a hundred miles from where he had hitched a ride with Amelia Williams.

'Listen,' he said as they were entering Augusta, the state capital. 'There's a good chance they'll sniff us here. I have no interest in killing you. Dig it?'

'Yes,' she said. Then, with bright hate: 'You need a hostage.'

'Right. So if a cop pulls out behind us, you pull over. Immediately. You open your door and lean out. Just *lean*. Your fanny is not to leave that seat. Understand?'

'Yes.'

'You holler: Benjamin Richards is holding me hostage. If you don't give him free passage he'll kill me.'

'And you think *that* will work?'

'It better,' he said with tense mockery. 'It's your ass.'

She bit her lip and said nothing.

'It'll work. I think. There will be a dozen freelance cameramen around in no time, hoping to get some Games money or even the Zapruder Award itself. With that kind of publicity, they'll have to play it straight. Sorry you won't get to see us go out in a hail of bullets so they can talk about you sanctimoniously as Ben Richards's last victim.'

'Why do you *say* these things?' she burst out.

He didn't reply; only slid down in his seat until just the top of his head showed and waited for the blue lights in the rear-view mirror.

But there were no blue lights in Augusta. They continued on for another hour and a half, skirting the ocean as the sun began to wester, catching little glints and peaks of the water, across fields and beyond bridges and through heavy firs.

It was past two o'clock when they rounded a bend not far from the Camden town line and saw a roadblock; two police cars parked on either side of the road. Two cops were checking a farmer in an old pick-up and waving it through.

'Go another two hundred feet and then stop,' Richards said. 'Do it just the way I told you.'

She was pallid but seemingly in control. Resigned, maybe. She applied the brakes evenly and the air car came to a neat stop in the middle of the road fifty feet from the checkpoint.

The trooper holding the clipboard waved her forward imperiously. When she didn't come, he glanced inquiringly at his companion. A third cop, who had been sitting inside one of the cruisers with his feet up, suddenly grabbed the hand mike under the dash and began to speak rapidly.

Here we go, Richards thought. *Oh God, here we go.*

... MINUS 042   and COUNTING ...

The day was very bright (the constant rain of Harding seemed light-years away) and everything was very sharp and clearly defined. The troopers' shadows might have been drawn with black Crayolas. They were unhooking the narrow straps that crossed their gunbutts.

Mrs Williams swung open the door and leaned out. 'Don't shoot, please,' she said, and for the first time Richards realized how cultured her voice was, how rich. She might have been in a drawing room except for the pallid knuckles and the fluttering, birdlike pulse in her throat. With the door open he could smell the fresh, invigorating odor of pine and timothy grass.

'Come out of the car with your hands over your head,' the cop with the clipboard said. He sounded like a well-programmed machine. General Atomics Model 6925-A9, Richards thought. The Hicksville Trooper. 16-psm Iridium Batteries included. Comes in White Only. 'You and your passenger, ma'am. We see him.'

'My name is Amelia Williams,' she said very clearly. 'I can't get out as you ask. Benjamin Richards is holding me hostage. If you don't give him free passage, he says he'll kill me.'

The two cops looked at each other, and something barely perceptible passed between them. Richards, with his nerves strung up to a point where he seemed to be operating with a seventh sense, caught it.

'*Drive!*' He screamed.

She stared around at him, bewildered. 'But they won't—'

The clipboard clattered to the road. The two cops fell into the kneeling posture almost simultaneously, guns out, gripped in right hands, left hands holding right wrists. One on each side of the solid white line.

The sheets of flimsy on the clipboard fluttered errantly.

Richards tromped his bad foot on Amelia Williams's right shoe, his lips drawing back into a tragedy mask of pain as the broken ankle grated. The air car ripped forward.

The next moment two hollow punching noises struck the car, making it vibrate. A moment later the windshield blew in, splattering them both with bits of safety glass. She threw both hands up to protect her face and Richards leaned savagely against her, swinging the wheel.

They shot through the gap between the veed cars with scarcely a flirt of the rear deck. He caught a crazy glimpse of the troopers whirling to fire again and then his whole attention was on the road.

They mounted a rise, and then there was one more hollow *thunnn!* as a bullet smashed a hole in the trunk. The car began to fishtail and Richards hung on, whipping the wheel in diminishing arcs. He realized dimly that Williams was screaming.

'Steer!' he shouted at her. 'Steer, goddammit! Steer! Steer!'

Her hands groped reflexively for the wheel and found it. He let go and batted the dark glasses away from her eyes with an open-handed blow. They hung on one ear for a moment and then dropped off.

'Pull over!'

'They shot at us.' Her voice began to rise. 'They shot at us. *They shot at—*'

'Pull over!'

The scream of sirens rose behind them.

She pulled over clumsily, sending the car around in a shuddering half-turn that spumed gravel into the air.

'I told them and they tried to kill us,' she said wonderingly. 'They tried to kill us.'

But he was out already, out and hopping clumsily back the way they had come, gun out. He lost his balance and fell heavily, scraping both knees.

When the first cruiser came over the rise he was in a sitting position on the shoulder of the road, the pistol held firmly at shoulder level. The car was doing eighty easily, and still accelerating; some backroad cowboy at the wheel with too much engine up front and visions of glory in his eyes. They perhaps saw him, perhaps tried to stop. It didn't matter. There were no bulletproof tires on these. The one closest to Richards exploded as if there had been dynamite inside. The cruiser took off like a big-ass bird, gunning across the shoulder in howling, uncontrolled flight. It crashed into the bole of a huge elm. The driver's side door flew off. The driver rammed through the windshield like a torpedo and flew thirty yards before crashing into the puckerbrush.

The second car came almost as fast and it took Richards four shots to find a tire. Two slugs splattered sand next to his spot. This one slid around in a smoking half-turn and rolled three times, spraying glass and metal.

Richards struggled to his feet, looked down and saw his shirt darkening slowly just above the belt. He hopped back toward the air car, and then dropped on his face as the second cruiser exploded, spewing shrapnel above and around him.

He got up, panting and making strange whimpering noises in his mouth. His side had begun to throb in slow, aching cycles.

She could have gotten away, perhaps, but she had made no effort. She was staring, transfixed, at the burning police car in the road. When Richards got in, she shrank from him.

'You killed them. You killed those men.'

'They tried to kill me. You too. Drive. Fast.'

'THEY DID NOT TRY TO KILL ME!'

'Drive!'

She drove.

The mask of the well-to-do young *hausfrau* on her way back from the market now hung in tatters and shreds. Beneath it was something from the cave, something with twitching lips and rolling eyes. Perhaps it had been there all along.

They drove about five miles and came to a roadside store and air station.

'Pull in,' Richards said.

... MINUS 041   and COUNTING ...

'Get out.'

'No.'

He jammed the gun against her right breast and she whimpered. 'Don't. Please.'

'I'm sorry. But there's no more time for you to play prima donna. Get out.'

She got out and he slid after her.

'Let me lean on you.'

He slung an arm around her shoulders and pointed with the gun at the telephone booth beside the ice dispenser. They began shuffling toward it, a grotesque two-man vaudeville team. Richards hopped on his good foot. He felt tired. In his mind he saw the cars crashing, the body flying like a torpedo, the leaping explosion. These scenes played over and over again, like a continuous loop of tape.

The store's proprietor, an old pal with white hair and

scrawny legs hidden by a dirty butcher's apron, came out and stared at them with worried eyes.

'Hey,' he said mildly. 'I don't want you here. I got a fam'ly. Go down the road. Please. I don't want no trouble.'

'Go inside, pop,' Richards said. The man went.

Richards slid loosely into the booth, breathing through his mouth, and fumbled fifty cents into the coin horn. Holding the gun and receiver in one hand, he punched O.

'What exchange is this, operator?'

'Rockland, sir.'

'Put me through to the local newsie hookup, please.'

'You may dial that, sir. The number is—'

'You dial it.'

'Do you wish—'

Just dial it!

'Yes, sir,' she said, unruffled. There were clicks and pops in Richards's ear. Blood had darkened his shirt to a dirty purple color. He looked away from it. It made him feel ill.

'Rockland Newsie,' a voice said in Richards's ear. 'Free-Vee Tabloid Number 6943.'

'This is Ben Richards.'

There was a long silence. Then: 'Look, maggot, I like a joke as well as the next guy, but this has been a long, hard d—'

'Shut up. You're going to get confirmation of this in ten minutes at the outside. You can get it now if you've got a police-band radio.'

'I . . . just a second.' There was the clunk of a dropping phone on the other end, and a faint wailing sound. When the phone was picked up, the voice was hard and business-like, with an undercurrent of excitement.

'Where are you, fella? Half the cops in eastern Maine just went through Rockland . . . at about a hundred and ten.'

Richards craned his neck at the sign over the store. 'A place called Gilly's Town Line Store & Airstop on US 1. You know it?'

'Yeah. Just—'

'Listen to me, maggot. I didn't call to give you my life story. Get some photogs out here. Quick. And get this on the air. Red Newsbreak Top. I've got a hostage. Her name is Amelia Williams. From—' He looked at her.

'Falmouth,' she said miserably.

'From Falmouth. Safe conduct or I'll kill her.'

'Jesus, I smell the Pulitzer Prize!'

'No, you just shit your pants, that's all,' Richards said. He felt lightheaded. 'You get the word out. I want the State Pigs to find out everyone knows I'm not alone. Three of them at a roadblock tried to blow us up.'

'What happened to the cops!'

'I killed them.'

'All three? Hot damn!' The voice, pulled away from the phone, yelled distantly: 'Dicky, open the national cable!'

'I'm going to kill her if they shoot,' Richards said, simultaneously trying to inject sincerity into his voice and to remember all the old gangster movies he had seen on tee-vee as a kid. 'If they want to save the girl, they better let me through.'

'When—'

Richards hung up and hopped clumsily out of the booth. 'Help me.'

She put an arm around him, grimacing at the blood. 'See what you're getting yourself into?'

'Yes.'

'This is madness. You're going to be killed.'

'Drive north,' he mumbled. 'Just drive north.'

He slid into the car, breathing hard. The world insisted on going in and out. High, atonal music jangled in his ears. She pulled out and onto the road. His blood had smeared on her smart green and black-striped blouse. The old man, Gilly, cracked the screen door open and poked out a very old Polaroid camera. He clicked the shutter, pulled the tape, and waited. His face was painted with horror and excitement and delight.

In this distance, rising and converging, sirens.

... MINUS 040 and COUNTING ...

They traveled five miles before people began running out onto their lawns to watch them pass. Many had cameras and Richards relaxed.

'They were shooting at the aircaps at that roadblock,' she said quietly. 'It was a mistake. That's what it was. A mistake.'

'If that maggot was aiming for an aircap when he put out the windshield, there must have been a sight on that pistol three feet high.'

'It was a mistake!'

They were entering the residential district of what Richards assumed was Rockland. Summer homes. Dirt roads leading down to beachfront cottages. Breeze Inn. *Private Road.* Just Me 'n Patty. *Keep Out.* Elizabeth's Rest. *Trespassers Will Be Shot.* Cloud-Hi. *5000 Volts.* Set-A-Spell. *Guard Dogs on Patrol.*

Unhealthy eyes and avid faces peering at them from behind trees, like Cheshire cats. The blare of battery-powered Free-Vees came through the shattered windshield.

A crazy, weird air of carnival about everything.

'These people,' Richards said, 'only want to see someone bleed. The more the better. They would just as soon it was both of us. Can you believe that?'

'No.'

'Then I salute you.'

An older man with silvery barbershop hair, wearing madras shorts that came down over his knees, ran out to the edge of the road. He was carrying a huge camera with a cobra-like telephoto lens. He began snapping pictures wildly, bending and dipping. His legs were fish-belly white. Richards burst into a sudden bray of laughter that made Amelia jump.

'What—'

'He's still got the lens cover on,' Richards said. 'He's still got—' But laughter overcame him.

Cars crowded the shoulders as they topped a long, slowly rising hill and began to descend toward the clustered town of Rockland itself. Perhaps it had once been a picturesque seacoast fishing village, full of Winslow Homer men in yellow rain-slickers who went out in small boats to trap the wily lobster. If so, it was long gone. There was a huge shopping center on either side of the road. A main street strip of honky-tonks, bars, and AutoSlot emporiums. There were neat middle-class homes overlooking the main drag from the heights, and a growing slum looking up from the rancid edge of the water. The sea at the horizon was yet unchanged. It glittered blue and ageless, full of dancing points and nets of light in the late afternoon sun.

They began the descent, and there were two police cars parked across the road. The blue lights flick-flick-flicked jaggedly, crazy and out of sync with each other. Parked at an angle on the left embankment was an armored car with a short, stubby cannon barrel tracking them.

'You're done,' she said softly, almost regretfully. 'Do I have to die, too?'

'Stop fifty yards from the roadblock and do your stuff,' Richards said. He slid down in the seat. A nervous tic stitched his face.

She stopped and opened the car door, but did not lean out. The air was dead silent. *A hush falls over the crowd,* Richards thought ironically.

'I'm scared,' she said. 'Please. I'm so scared.'

'They won't shoot you,' he said. 'There are too many people. You can't kill hostages unless no one is watching. Those are the rules of the game.'

She looked at him for a moment, and he suddenly wished they could have a cup of coffee together. He would listen carefully to her conversation and stir real cream into his hot drink — her treat, of course. Then they could discuss the possibilities of social inequity, the way your socks always fall down when you're wearing rubber boots, and the importance of being earnest.

'Go on, Mrs Williams,' he said with soft, tense mockery. 'The eyes of the world are upon you.'

She leaned out.

Six police cars and another armored van had pulled up thirty feet behind them, blocking their retreat.

He thought: *Now the only way out is straight up to heaven.*

...MINUS 039   and COUNTING...

'My name is Amelia Williams. Benjamin Richards is holding me hostage. If you don't give us safe conduct, he says he'll kill me.'

Silence for a moment, so complete that Richards could hear the faraway honk of some distant yacht's air horn.

Then, asexual, blaring, amplified: 'WE WANT TO TALK TO BEN RICHARDS.'

'No,' Richards said swiftly.

'He says he won't.'

'COME OUT OF THE CAR, MADAM.'

'He'll kill me!' She cried wildly. 'Don't you listen? Some men almost killed us back *there!* He says you don't care who you kill. *My God, is he right?*'

A hoarse voice in the crowd yelled 'Let her through!'

'COME OUT OF THE CAR OR WE'LL SHOOT.'

'Let her through! Let her through!' The crowd had taken up the chant like eager fans at a killball match.

'COME OUT—'

The crowd drowned it out. From somewhere, a rock flew. A police car windshield starred into a matrix of cracks.

There was suddenly a rev of motors, and the two cruisers began to pull apart, opening a narrow slot of pavement. The crowd cheered happily and then fell silent, waiting for the next act.

'ALL CIVILIANS LEAVE THE AREA,' the bullhorn chanted. 'THERE MAY BE SHOOTING. ALL CIVILIANS LEAVE THE AREA OR YOU MAY BE CHARGED WITH OBSTRUCTION AND UNLAWFUL ASSEMBLY. THE PENALTY FOR OBSTRUCTION AND UNLAWFUL ASSEMBLY IS TEN YEARS IN THE STATE PENITENTIARY OR A FINE OF TEN THOUSAND DOLLARS OR BOTH. CLEAR THE AREA. CLEAR THE AREA.'

'Yeah, so no one'll see you shoot the girl!' a hysterical voice yelled. 'Screw all pigs!'

The crowd didn't move. A yellow and black newsie-mobile had pulled up with a flashy screech. Two men jumped out and began setting up a camera.

Two cops rushed over and there was a short, savage scuffle for the possession of the camera. Then one of the cops yanked it free, picked it up by the tripod, and smashed it on the road. One of the newsmen tried to reach the cop that had done it and was clubbed.

A small boy darted out of the crowd and fired a rock at the back of a cop's head. Blood splattered the road as the cop fell over. A half-dozen more descended on the boy, bearing him off. Incredibly, small and savage fistfights had begun on the sidelines between the well-dressed townfolk and the rattier slum-dwellers. A woman in a ripped and faded housedress suddenly descended on a plump matron and began to pull her hair. They fell heavily to the road and began to roll on the macadam, kicking and screaming.

'My God,' Amelia said sickly.

'What's happening?' Richards asked. He dared look no higher than the clock on the dashboard.

'Fights. Police hitting people. Someone broke a newsie's camera.'

'GIVE UP, RICHARDS. COME OUT.'

'Drive on,' Richards said softly.

The air car jerked forward erratically. 'They'll shoot for the air caps,' she said. 'Then wait until you have to come out.'

'They won't,' Richards said.

'Why?'

'They're too dumb.'

They didn't.

They proceeded slowly past the ranked police cars and the bug-eyed spectators. They had split themselves into two groups in unconscious segregation. On one side of the road were the middle- and upper-class citizens, the ladies who had their hair done at the beauty parlor, the men who wore Arrow shirts and loafers. Fellows wearing coveralls with company names on the back and their own names stitched in gold thread over the breast pockets. Women like Amelia Williams herself, dressed for the market and the shops. Their faces were different in all ways but similar in one: They looked oddly incomplete, like pictures with holes for eyes or a jigsaw puzzle with a minor piece missing. It was a lack of desperation, Richards thought. No wolves howled in these bellies. These minds were not filled with rotted, crazed dreams or mad hopes.

These people were on the right side of the road, the side that faced the combination marina and country club they were just passing.

On the other side, the left, were the poor people. Red noses with burst veins. Flattened, sagging breasts. Stringy hair. White socks. Cold sores. Pimples. The blank and hanging mouths of idiocy.

The police were deployed more heavily here, and more were coming all the time. Richards was not surprised at the swiftness and the heaviness of their crunch, despite the suddenness of his appearance. Even here, in Boondocks, USA, the club and the gun were kept near to hand. The dogs were kept hungry in the kennel. The poor break into summer cottages closed for autumn and winter. The poor crash supermarts in subteen gangs. The poor have been known to soap badly spelled obscenities on shop windows. The poor always have itchy assholes and the sight of Naugahyde and chrome and two-hundred-dollar suits and fat bellies have been known to make the mouths of the poor fill with angry spit. And the poor must have their Jack Johnson, their Muhammad Ali, their Clyde Barrow. They stood and watched.

Here on the right, folks, we have the summer people, Richards thought. Fat and sloppy but heavy with armor. On the left, weighing in at only a hundred and thirty – but a scrappy contender with a mean and rolling eyeball – we have the Hungry Honkies. Theirs are the politics of starvation; they'd roll Christ Himself for a pound of salami. Polarization comes to West Sticksville. Watch out for these two contenders, though. They don't stay in the ring; they have a tendency to fight in the ten-dollar seats. Can we find a goat to hang up for both of them?

Slowly, rolling at thirty, Ben Richards passed between them.

... MINUS 038   and COUNTING ...

An hour passed. It was four o'clock. Shadows crawled across the road.

Richards, slumped down below eye level in his seat, floated in and out of consciousness effortlessly. He had clumsily pulled his shirt out of his pants to look at the new wound. The bullet had dug a deep and ugly canal in his side that had bled a great deal. The blood had clotted, but grudgingly. When he had to move quickly again, the wound would rip open and bleed a great deal more. Didn't matter. They were going to blow him up. In the face of this massive armory, his plan was a joke. He would go ahead with it, fill in the blanks until there was an 'accident' and the air car was blown into bent bolts and shards of metal ('. . . terrible accident . . . the trooper has been suspended pending a full investigation . . . regret the loss of innocent life . . .' – all this buried in the last newsie of the day, between the stock-market report and the Pope's latest pronouncement), but it was only reflex. He had become increasingly worried about Amelia Williams, whose big mistake had been picking Wednesday morning to do her marketing.

'There are tanks out there,' she said suddenly. Her voice was light, chatty, hysterical. 'Can you imagine it? Can you—' She began to cry.

Richards waited. Finally, he said: 'What town are we in?'

'W–W–Winterport, the sign s-said. Oh, I can't! I can't wait for them to do it! *I can't!*'

'Okay,' he said.

She blinked slowly, giving an infinitesimal shake of her head as if to clear it. 'What?'

'Stop. Get out.'

'But they'll kill y—'

'Yes. But there won't be any blood. You won't see any blood. They've got enough firepower out there to vaporize me and the car, too.'

'You're lying. You'll kill me.'

The gun had been dangling between his knees. He dropped it on the floor. It clunked harmlessly on the rubber floor-mat.

'I want some pot,' she said mindlessly. 'Oh God, I want to be high. Why didn't you wait for the next car? Jesus! Jesus!'

Richards began to laugh. He laughed in wheezy, shallow-chested heaves that still hurt his side. He closed his eyes and laughed until tears oozed out from under the lids.

'It's cold in here with that broken windshield,' she said irrelevantly. 'Turn on the heater.'

Her face was a pale blotch in the shadows of late afternoon.

... MINUS 037   and COUNTING ...

'We're in Derry,' she said.

The streets were black with people. They hung over roof ledges and sat on balconies and verandahs from which the summer furniture had been removed. They ate sandwiches and fried chicken from greasy buckets.

'Are there jetport signs?'

'Yes. I'm following them. They'll just close the gates.'

'I'll just threaten to kill you again if they do.'

'Are you going to skyjack a plane?'

'I'm going to try.'

'You can't.'

'I'm sure you're right.'

They made a right, then a left. Bullhorns exhorted the crowd monotonously to move back, to disperse.

'Is she really your wife? That woman in the pictures?'

'Yes. Her name is Sheila. Our baby, Cathy, is a year and a half old. She had the flu. Maybe she's better now. That's how I got into this.'

A helicopter buzzed them, leaving a huge arachnid shadow on the road ahead. A grossly amplified voice exhorted Richards to let the woman go. When it was gone and they could speak again, she said:

'Your wife looks like a little tramp. She could take better care of herself.'

'The picture was doctored,' Richards said tonelessly.

'They would do that?'

'They would do that.'

'The jetport. We're coming up to it.'

'Are the gates shut?'

'I can't see . . . wait . . . open but blocked. A tank. It's pointing its shooter at us.'

'Drive to within thirty feet of it and stop.'

The car crawled slowly down the four-lane access road between the parked police cars, between the ceaseless scream and babble of the crowd. A sign loomed over them: VOIGT AIRFIELD. The woman could see an electrified cyclone fence which crossed a marshy, worthless sort of field on both sides of the road. Straight ahead was a combination information booth and check-in point on a traffic island. Beyond that was the main gate, blocked by an A-62 tank capable of firing one-quarter-megaton shells from its cannon. Farther on, a confusion of roads and parking lots, all tending toward the complex jetline terminals that blocked the runways from view. A huge control tower bulked over everything like an H.G. Wells Martian, the westering sun glaring off its polarized bank of windows and turning them to fire. Employees and passengers alike had crowded down to the nearest parking lot where they were being held back by more police. There was a pulsing, heavy whine in their ears, and Amelia saw a steel-gray Lockheed/G-A Superbird rising into a flat, powerful climb from one of the runways behind the main buildings.

'RICHARDS!'

She jumped and looked at him, frightened. He waved his hand at her nonchalantly. It's all right, Ma. I'm only dying.

'YOU'RE NOT ALLOWED INSIDE,' the huge amplified voice admonished him. 'LET THE WOMAN GO. STEP OUT.'

'What now?' She asked. 'It's a stand-off. They'll just wait until—'

'Let's push them a little farther,' Richards said. 'They'll bluff along a little more. Lean out. Tell them I'm hurt and half-crazy. Tell them I want to give up to the Airline Police.'

'You want to do *what?*'

'The Airline Police are neither state enforcement nor federal. They've been international ever since the UN treaty of 1995. There used to be a story that if you gave up to them, you'd get amnesty. Sort of like landing on Free Parking in Monopoly. Full of shit, of course. They turn you over to the Hunters and the Hunters drag you out in back of the barn.'

She winced.

'But maybe they'll think I believe it. Or that I've fooled myself into believing it. Go ahead and tell them.'

She leaned out and Richards tensed. If there was going to be an 'unfortunate accident' which would remove Amelia from the picture, it would probably happen now. Her head and upper body were clearly and cleanly exposed to a thousand guns. One squeeze on one trigger and the entire farce would come to a quick end.

'Ben Richards wants to give up to the Airline Police!' She cried. 'He's shot in two places!' She threw a terrified glance over her shoulder and her voice broke, high and clear in the sudden silence the diminishing jet had left. 'He's been out of his mind half the time and God I'm so *frightened . . . please . . . please . . . PLEASE!*'

The cameras were recording it all, sending it on a live feed that would be broadcast all over North America and half the world in a matter of minutes. That was good. That was fine. Richards felt tension stiffen his limbs again and knew he was beginning to hope.

Silence for a moment; there was a conference going on behind the check-point booth.

'Very good,' Richards said softly.

She looked at him. 'Do you think it's hard to sound frightened? We're not in this together, whatever you think. I only want you to go away.'

Richards noticed for the first time how perfect her breasts were beneath the bloodstained black and green blouse. How perfect and how precious.

There was a sudden, grinding roar and she screamed aloud.

'It's the tank,' he said. 'It's okay. Just the tank.'

'It's moving,' she said. 'They're going to let us in.'

'RICHARDS! YOU WILL PROCEED TO LOT 16. AIRLINE POLICE WILL BE WAITING THERE TO TAKE YOU INTO CUSTODY!'

'All right,' he said thinly. 'Drive on. When you get a half a mile inside the gate, stop.'

'You're going to get me killed,' she said hopelessly. 'All I need to do is use the bathroom and you're going to get me killed.'

The air car lifted four inches and hummed smoothly forward. Richards crouched going through the gate, anticipating a possible ambush, but there was none. The smooth blacktop curved sedately toward the main buildings. A sign with a pointing arrow informed them that this was the way to Lots 16–20.

Here the police were standing and kneeling behind yellow barricades.

Richards knew that at the slightest suspicious move, they would tear the air car apart.

'Now stop,' he said, and she did.

The reaction was instantaneous. 'RICHARDS! MOVE IMMEDIATELY TO LOT 16!'

'Tell them that I want a bullhorn,' Richards said softly to her. 'They are to leave one in the road twenty yards up. I want to talk to them.'

She cried his message, and then they waited. A moment later, a man in a blue uniform trotted out into the road and laid an electric bullhorn down. He stood there for a moment, perhaps savoring the realization that he was being seen by five hundred million people, and then withdrew to barricaded anonymity again.

'Go ahead,' he told her.

They crept up to the bullhorn, and when the driver's side door was even with it, she opened the door and pulled it in. It was red and white. The letters G and A, embossed over a thunderbolt, were on the side.

'Okay,' he said. 'How far are we from the main building?'

She squinted. 'A quarter of a mile, I guess.'

'How far are we from Lot 16?'

'Half that.'

'Good. That's good. Yeah.' He realized he was compulsively biting his lips and tried to make himself stop. His head hurt; his entire body ached from adrenaline. 'Keep driving. Go up to the entrance of Lot 16 and then stop.'

'Then what?'

He smiled tightly and unhappily. 'That,' he said, 'is going to be the site of Richards's Last Stand.'

... MINUS 036   and COUNTING ...

When she stopped the car at the entrance of the parking lot, the reaction was quick and immediate. 'KEEP MOVING,' the bullhorn prodded. 'THE AIRPORT POLICE ARE INSIDE. AS SPECIFIED.'

Richards raised his own bullhorn for the first time. 'TEN MINUTES,' he said. 'I HAVE TO THINK.'

Silence again.

'Don't you realize you're pushing them to do it?' she asked him in a strange, controlled voice.

He uttered a weird, squeezed giggle that sounded like steam under high pressure escaping from a teapot. 'They know I'm getting set to screw them. They don't know how.'

'You can't,' she said. 'Don't you *see* that yet?'

'Maybe I can,' he said.

... MINUS 035   and COUNTING ...

'Listen:

'When the Games first started, people said they were

the world's greatest entertainment because there had never been anything like them. But nothing's that original. There were the gladiators in Rome who did the same thing. And there's another game, too. Poker. In poker the highest hand is a royal straight-flush in spades. And the toughest kind of poker is five-card stud. Four cards up on the table and one in the hole. For nickels and dimes anyone can stay in the game. It costs you maybe half a buck to see the other guy's hole card. But when you push the stakes up, the hole card starts to look bigger and bigger. After a dozen rounds of betting, with your life's savings and car and house on the line, that hole card stands taller than Mount Everest. *The Running Man* is like that. Only I'm not supposed to have any money to bet with. They've got the men, the firepower, and the time. We're playing with their cards and their chips in their casino. When I'm caught, I'm supposed to fold. But maybe I stacked the deck a bit. I called the newsie line in Rockland. The newsies, that's my ten of spades. They *had* to give me safe conduct, because everyone was watching. There were no more chances for neat disposal after that first roadblock. It's funny, too, because it's the Free-Vee that gives the Network the clout that it has. If you see it on the Free-Vee, it must be true. So if the whole country saw the police murder my hostage − a well-to-do, middle-class female hostage − they would have to believe it. They can't risk it; the system is laboring under too much suspension of belief now. Funny, huh? My people are here. There's been trouble on the road already. If the troopers and the Hunters turn all their guns on us, something nasty might happen. A man told me to stay near my own people. He was more right than he knew. One of the reasons they've been handling me with the kid gloves on is because my people are here.

'My people, they're the jack of spades.

'The queen, the lady in the affair, is you.

'I'm the king; the black man with the sword.

'These are my up cards. The media, the possibility of real trouble, you, me. Together they're nothing. A pair will take them. Without the ace of spades it's junk. With the ace, it's unbeatable.'

He suddenly picked up her handbag, an imitation alligator-skin clutch purse with a small silver chain. He stuffed it into his coat pocket where it bulged prominently.

'I haven't got the ace,' he said softly. 'With a little more forethought, I could have had it. But I *do* have a hole card – one they can't see. So I'm going to run a bluff.'

'You don't have a chance,' she said hollowly. 'What can you do with my bag? Shoot them with a lipstick?'

'I think that they've been playing a crooked game so long that they'll fold. I think they are yellow straight through from the back to belly.'

'RICHARDS! TEN MINUTES ARE UP!'

Richards put the bullhorn to his lips.

. . . MINUS 034   and COUNTING . . .

'LISTEN TO ME CAREFULLY!' His voice boomed and rolled across the flat jetport acres. Police waited tensely. The crowd shuffled. 'I AM CARRYING TWELVE POUNDS OF DYNACORE HI-IMPACT PLASTIC EXPLOSIVE IN MY COAT POCKET – THE VARIETY THEY CALL BLACK IRISH. TWELVE POUNDS IS ENOUGH TO TAKE OUT EVERYTHING AND EVERYONE WITHIN A THIRD OF A MILE AND PROBABLY ENOUGH TO EXPLODE THE JETPORT FUEL STORAGE TANKS. IF YOU DON'T FOLLOW

MY INSTRUCTIONS TO THE LETTER, I'LL BLOW YOU ALL TO HELL. A GENERAL ATOMICS IMPLODER RING IS SET INTO THE EXPLOSIVE. I HAVE IT PULLED OUT TO HALF-COCK. ONE JIGGLE AND YOU CAN ALL PUT YOUR HEADS BETWEEN YOUR LEGS AND KISS YOUR ASSES GOODBYE.'

There were screams from the crowd followed by sudden, tidelike movement. The police at the barricades suddenly found they had no one to hold back. Men and women were tearing across roads and fields, streaming out the gates and scaling the cyclone fence around the jetport. Their faces were blank and avid with panic.

The police shuffled uneasily. On no face did Amelia Williams see disbelief.

'RICHARDS?' The huge voice boomed. 'THAT'S A LIE. COME OUT.'

'I *AM* COMING OUT,' he boomed back. 'BUT BEFORE I DO, LET ME GIVE YOU YOUR MARCHING ORDERS. I WANT A JET FULLY FUELED AND READY TO FLY WITH A SKELETON CREW. THIS JET WILL BE A LOCKHEED/GA OR A DELTA SUPERSONIC. THE RANGE MUST BE AT LEAST TWO THOUSAND MILES. THIS WILL BE READY IN NINETY MINUTES.'

Cameras reeling and cranking away. Flashbulbs popping. The press looked uneasy too. But, of course, there was the psychic pressure of those five hundred million watchers to be considered. They were real. The job was real. And Richards's twelve pounds of Black Irish might be just a figment of his admirable criminal mentality.

'RICHARDS?' A man dressed only in dark slacks and a white shirt rolled up to the elbows in spite of the fall chill strolled out from behind a gaggle of unmarked cars fifty yards beyond Lot 16. He was carrying a bullhorn larger than Richards's. From this distance, Amelia could see only that he was wearing small spectacles; they flashed in the dying sunlight.

'I AM EVAN McCONE.'

He knew the name, of course. It was supposed to strike fear into his heart. He was not surprised to find that it *did* strike fear into his heart. Evan McCone was the Chief Hunter. A direct descendent of J. Edgar Hoover and Heinrich Himmler, he thought. The personification of the steel inside the Network's cathode glove. A boogeyman. A name to frighten bad children with. If you don't stop playing with matches, Johnny, I'll let Evan McCone out of your closet.

Fleetingly, in the eye of memory, he recalled a dream-voice. *Are you the man, little brother?*

'YOU'RE LYING, RICHARDS. WE KNOW IT. A MAN WITHOUT A G-A RATING HAS NO WAY OF GETTING DYNACORE. LET THE WOMAN GO AND COME OUT. WE DON'T WANT TO HAVE TO KILL HER, TOO.'

Amelia made a weak, wretched hissing noise.

Richards boomed: 'THAT MAY GO OVER IN SHAKER HEIGHTS, LITTLE MAN. IN THE STREETS YOU CAN BUY DYNACORE EVERY TWO BLOCKS IF YOU'VE GOT CASH ON THE LINE. AND I DID. GAMES FEDERATION MONEY. YOU HAVE EIGHTY-SIX MINUTES.'

'NO DEAL.'

'McCONE?'

'YES.'

'I'M SENDING THE WOMAN OUT NOW. SHE'S SEEN THE IRISH.' Amelia was looking at him with stunned horror. 'MEANWHILE, YOU BETTER GET IT IN GEAR. EIGHTY-FIVE MINUTES. I'M

NOT BLUFFING, ASSHOLE. ONE BULLET AND WE'RE ALL GOING TO THE MOON.'

'No,' she whispered. Her face was an unbelieving rictus. 'You can't believe I'm going to *lie* for you.'

'If you don't, I'm dead. I'm shot and broken and hardly conscious enough to know what I'm saying, but I know this is the best way, one way or the other. Now listen: Dynacore is white and solid, slightly greasy to the touch. It—'

'No, no! *No!*' She clapped her hands over her ears.

'It looks like a bar of Ivory soap. Very dense, though. Now I'm going to describe the imploder ring. It looks—'

She began to weep. 'I can't, don't you *know* that? I have my duty as a citizen. My conscience. I have my—'

'Yeah, and they might find out you lied,' he added dryly. 'Except they won't. Because if you back me, they'll cave in. I'll be off like a bigass bird.'

'*I can't!*'

'RICHARDS! SEND THE WOMAN OUT!'

'The imploder ring is gold,' he continued. 'About two inches in diameter. It looks like a keyring with no keys in it. Attached to it is a slim rod like a mechanical pencil with a G-A trigger device attached to it. The trigger device looks like the eraser on the pencil.'

She was rocking back and forth, moaning a little. She had a cheek in either hand and was twisting her flesh as if it were dough.

'I told them I had pulled out to half-cock. That means you would be able to see a single small notch just above the surface of the Irish. Got it?'

No answer; she wept and moaned and rocked.

'Sure you do,' he said softly. 'You're a bright girl, aren't you?'

'I'm not going to lie,' she said.

'If they ask you anything else, you don't know from

Rooty-Toot. You didn't see. You were too scared. Except for one thing: I've been holding the ring ever since that first roadblock. You didn't know what it was, but I had it in my hand.'

'Better kill me now.'

'Go on,' he said. 'Get out.'

She stared at him convulsively, her mouth working, her eyes dark holes. The pretty, self-assured woman with the wraparound shades was all gone. Richards wondered if that woman would ever reappear. He did not think so. Not wholly.

'Go,' he said. 'Go. Go.'

'I – I – *Ah, God*—'

She lunged against the door and half sprang, half fell out. She was on her feet instantly and running. Her hair streamed out behind her and she seemed very beautiful, almost goddesslike, and she ran into the lukewarm starburst of a million flashbulbs.

Carbines flashed up, ready, and were lowered as the crowd ate her. Richards risked cocking an eyebrow over the driver's side window but could see nothing.

He slouched back down, glanced at his watch, and waited for dissolution.

... MINUS 033   and COUNTING ...

The red second hand on his watch made two circles. Another two. Another two.

'RICHARDS!'

He raised the bullhorn to his lips. 'SEVENTY-NINE MINUTES, McCONE.'

Play it right up to the end. The *only* way to play it. Right up to the moment McCone gave the order to fire at will. It would be quick. And it didn't really seem to matter a whole hell of a lot.

After a long grudging, eternal pause: 'WE NEED MORE TIME. AT LEAST THREE HOURS. THERE ISN'T AN L/G-A OR A DELTA ON THIS FIELD. ONE WILL HAVE TO BE FLOWN IN.'

She had done it. O, amazing grace. The woman had looked into the abyss and then walked out across it. No net. No way back. Amazing.

Of course they didn't believe her. It was their business not to believe anyone about anything. Right now they would be hustling her to a private room in one of the terminals, half a dozen of McCone's picked interrogators waiting. And when they got her there, the litany would begin. *Of course you're upset, Mrs Williams, but just for the record ... would you mind going through this once more ... we're puzzled by one small thing here ... are you sure that wasn't the other way around ... how do you know ... why ... then what did he say ...*

So the correct move was to buy time. Fob Richards off with one excuse and then another. There's a fueling problem, we need more time. No crew is on the jetport grounds, we need more time. There's a flying saucer over Runway Zero-Seven, we need more time. And we haven't broken her yet. Haven't quite gotten her to admit that your high explosive consists of an alligator handbag stuffed with assorted Kleenex and change and cosmetics and credit cards. We need more time.

We can't take a chance on killing you yet. We need more time.

'RICHARDS?'

'LISTEN TO ME,' he megaphoned back. 'YOU HAVE SEVENTY-FIVE MINUTES. THEN IT ALL GOES UP.'

No reply.

Spectators had begun to creep back in spite of Armageddon's shadow. Their eyes were wide and wet and sexual. A number of portable spotlights had been requisitioned and focused on the little car, bathing it in a depthless glow and emphasizing the shattered windshield.

Richards tried to imagine the little room where they would be holding her, probing her for the truth, and could not. The press would be excluded, of course. McCone's men would be trying to scare the tits off her and undoubtedly would be succeeding. But how far would they dare go with a woman who did not belong to the ghetto society of the poor where people had no faces? Drugs. There were drugs, Richards knew, drugs that McCone could command immediately, drugs that could make a Yaqui Indian babble out his entire life story like a babe in arms. Drugs that would make a priest rattle off penitents' confessions like a stenographer's recording machine.

A little violence? The modified electric move-alongs that had worked so well in the Seattle riots of 2005? Or only the steady battering of their questions?

The thoughts served no purpose, but he could not shut them out or turn them off. Beyond the terminals there was the unmistakable whine of a Lockheed carrier being warmed up. His bird. The sound of it came in rising and falling cycles. When it cut off suddenly, he knew the fueling had begun. Twenty minutes if they were hurrying. Richards did not think they would be hurrying.

Well, well, well. Here we are. All the cards on the table but one.

McCone? McCone, are you peeking yet? Have you sliced into her mind yet?

Shadows lengthened across the field and everybody waited.

. . . MINUS 032 and COUNTING . . .

Richards discovered that the old cliché was a lie. Time did *not* stand still. In some ways it would have been better if it had. Then there at least would have been an end to hope.

Twice the amplified voice informed Richards that he was lying. He told them if it was so, they had better open up. Five minutes later a new amplified voice told him that the Lockheed's flaps were frozen and that fueling would have to begin with another plane. Richards told them that was fine. As long as the plane was ready to go by the original deadline.

The minutes crept by. Twenty-six left, twenty-five, twenty-two, twenty (*she hasn't broken yet, my God, maybe*—), eighteen, fifteen (the plane's engines again, rising to a strident howl as the ground crews went through fuel-system and pre-flight checks), ten minutes, then eight.

'RICHARDS?'

'HERE.'

'WE HAVE SIMPLY GOT TO HAVE MORE TIME. THE BIRD'S FLAPS ARE FROZEN SOLID. WE'RE GOING TO IRRIGATE THE VANES WITH LIQUID HYDROGEN BUT WE SIMPLY HAVE TO HAVE TIME.'

'YOU HAVE IT. SEVEN MINUTES. THEN I AM GOING TO PROCEED TO THE AIRFIELD USING THE SERVICE RAMP. I WILL BE DRIVING WITH ONE HAND ON THE WHEEL AND ONE HAND ON THE IMPLODER RING. ALL GATES WILL BE OPENED. AND REMEMBER

THAT I'LL BE GETTING CLOSER TO THOSE
FUEL TANKS ALL THE TIME.'

'YOU DON'T SEEM TO REALIZE THAT
WE—'

'I'M THROUGH TALKING, FELLOWS. SIX
MINUTES.'

The second hand made its orderly, regular turns. Three
minutes left, two, one. They would be going for broke
in the little room he could not imagine. He tried to call
Amelia's image up in his mind and failed. It was already
blurring into other faces. One composite face composed
of Stacey and Bradley and Elton and Virginia Parrakis and
the boy with the dog. All he could remember was that
she was soft and pretty in the uninspired way that so many
women can be thanks to Max Factor and Revlon and the
plastic surgeons who tuck and tie and smooth out and
unbend. Soft. Soft. But hard in some deep place. Where
did you go hard, WASP woman? Are you hard enough?
Or are you blowing the game right now?

He felt something warm running down his chin and
discovered he had bitten his lips through, not once but
several times.

He wiped his mouth absently, leaving a tear drop-
shaped smear of blood on his sleeve, and dropped the car
into gear. It rose obediently, lifters grumbling.

'RICHARDS! IF YOU MOVE THAT CAR,
WE'LL SHOOT! THE GIRL TALKED! WE
KNOW!'

No one fired a shot.

In a way, it was almost anticlimactic.

...MINUS 031 and COUNTING...

The service ramp described a rising arc around the glassine, futuristic Northern States Terminal. The way was lined with police holding everything from Mace-B and tear gas to heavy armor-piercing weaponry. Their faces were flat, dull, uniform. Richards drove slowly, sitting up straight now, and they looked at him with vacant, bovine awe. In much the same way, Richards thought, that cows must look at a farmer who had gone mad and lies kicking and sunfishing and screaming on the barn floor.

The gate to the service area (CAUTION – EMPLOYEES ONLY – NO SMOKING – UNAUTHORIZED PERSONS KEEP OUT) had been swung open, and Richards drove sedately through, passing ranks of high-octane tanker trucks and small private planes pulled up on their chocks. Beyond them was a taxiway, wide oil-blackened cement with expansion joints. Here his bird was waiting, a huge white jumbo jet with a dozen turbine engines softly grumbling. Beyond, runways stretched straight and clean into the gathering twilight, seeming to approach a meeting point on the horizon. The bird's roll-up stairway was just being put into place by four men wearing coveralls. To Richards, it looked like the stairs leading to a scaffold.

And, as if to complete the image, the executioner stepped neatly out of the shadows that the plane's huge belly threw. Evan McCone.

Richards looked at him with the curiosity of a man seeing a celebrity for the first time – no matter how many times you see his picture in the movie 3-D's you can't

188

believe his reality until he appears in the flesh – and then the reality takes on a curious tone of hallucination, as if entity had no right to exist separate from image.

He was a small man wearing rimless glasses, with a faint suggestion of a pot belly beneath his well-tailored suit. It was rumored that McCone wore elevator shoes, but if so, they were unobtrusive. There was a small silver flag-pin in his lapel. All in all, he did not look like a monster at all, the inheritor of such fearsome alphabet-soup bureaus as the FBI and the CIA. Not like a man who had mastered the technique of the black car in the night, the rubber club, the sly question about relatives back home. Not like a man who had mastered the entire spectrum of fear.

'Ben Richards?' He used no bullhorn, and without it his voice was soft and cultured without being effeminate in the slightest.

'Yes.'

'I have a sworn bill from the Games Federation, an accredited arm of the Network Communications Commission, for your apprehension and execution. Will you honor it?'

'Does a hen need a flag?'

'Ah.' McCone sounded pleased. 'The formalities are taken care of. I believe in formalities, don't you? No, of course you don't. You've been a very informal contestant. That's why you're still alive. Did you know you surpassed the standing *Running Man* record of eight days and five hours some two hours ago? Of course you don't. But you have. Yes. And your escape from the YMCA in Boston. Sterling. I understand the Nielsen rating on the program jumped twelve points.'

'Wonderful.'

'Of course, we almost had you during that Portland interlude. Bad luck. Parrakis swore with his dying breath that you had jumped ship in Auburn. We believed him; he was so obviously a frightened little man.'

'Obviously,' Richards echoed softly.

'But this last play has been simply brilliant. I salute you. In a way, I'm almost sorry the game has to end. I suspect I shall never run up against a more inventive opponent.'

'Too bad,' Richards said.

'It's over, you know,' McCone said. 'The woman broke. We used Sodium Pentothal on her. Old, but reliable.' He pulled a small automatic. 'Step out, Mr Richards. I will pay you the ultimate compliment. I'm going to do it right here, where no one can film it. Your death will be one of relative privacy.'

'Get ready, then,' Richards grinned.

He opened the door and stepped out. The two men faced each other across the blank service area cement.

. . . MINUS 030   and COUNTING . . .

It was McCone who broke the deadlock first. He threw back his head and laughed.

It was a very cultured laugh, soft and velvet. 'Oh, you are so good, Mr Richards. *Par excellence*. Raise, call, and raise again. I salute you with honesty: The woman has not broken. She maintains stubbornly that the bulge I see in your pocket there is Black Irish. We can't SAP her because it leaves a definable trace A single EEG on the woman and our secret would be out. We are in the process of lifting in three ampoules of Canogyn from New York. Leaves no trace. We expect it in forty minutes. Not in time to stop you, alas.

'She *is* lying. It's obvious. If you will pardon a touch of what your fellows like to call elitism, I will offer my observation that the middle class lies well only about sex. May I offer another observation? Of course I may. I am.' McCone smiled. 'I suspect it's her handbag. We noticed she had none, although she had been shopping. We're quite observant. What happened to her purse if it isn't in your pocket, Richards?'

He would not pick up the gambit. 'Shoot me if you're so sure.'

McCone spread his hands sorrowfully. 'How well I'd love to! But one does not take chances with human life, not even when the odds are fifty to one in your favor. Too much like Russian roulette. Human life has a certain *sacred* quality. The government – *our* government – realizes this. We are humane.'

'Yes, yes,' Richards said, and smiled ferally. McCone blinked.

'So you see—'

Richards started. The man was hypnotizing him. The minutes were flying, a helicopter was coming up from Boston loaded with three ampoules of jack-me-up-and-turn-me-over (and if McCone said forty minutes he meant twenty), and here he stood, listening to this man's tinkling little anthem. God, he *was* a monster.

'Listen to me,' Richards said harshly, interrupting. 'The speech is short, little man. When you inject her, she's going to sing the same tune. For the record, it's all here. Dig?'

He locked his gaze with McCone's and began to walk forward.

'I'll see you, shiteater.'

McCone stepped aside. Richards didn't even bother to look at him as he passed. Their coat sleeves brushed.

'For the record, I was told the pull on half-cock was about three pounds. I've got about two and a half on now. Give or take.'

He had the satisfaction of hearing the man's breath whistle a little faster.

'Richards?'

He looked back from the stairs and McCone was looking up at him, the gold edges of his glasses gleaming and flashing. 'When you get in the air, we're going to shoot you down with a ground-to-air missile. The story for the public will be that Richards got a little itchy on the trigger. RIP.'

'You won't, though.'

'No?'

Richards began to smile and gave half a reason. 'We're going to be very low and over heavily populated areas. Add twelve fuel pods to twelve pounds of Irish and you got a very big bang potential. Too big. You'd do it if you could get away with it, but you can't.' He paused. 'You're so bright. Did you anticipate me on the parachute?'

'Oh, yes,' McCone said calmly. 'It's in the forward passenger compartment. Such old hat, Mr Richards. Or do you have another trick in your bag?'

'You haven't been stupid enough to tamper with the chute, either, I'll bet.'

'Oh no. Too obvious. And you would pull that non-existent imploder ring just before you struck, I imagine. Quite an effective airburst.'

'Goodbye, little man.'

'Goodbye, Mr Richards. And *bon voyage*.' He chuckled. 'Yes, you do rate honesty. So I will show you one more card. Just one. We are going to wait for the Canogyn before taking action. You are absolutely right about the missile. For now, just a bluff. Call and raise again, eh? But I can afford to wait. You see, I am never wrong. Never. And I know you are bluffing. So we can afford to wait. But I'm keeping you. 'Voir, Mr Richards.' He waved.

'Soon,' Richards said, but not loud enough for McCone to hear. And he grinned.

... MINUS 029   and COUNTING ...

The first-class compartment was long and three aisles wide, paneled with real aged sequoia. A wine-colored rug which felt yards deep covered the floor. A 3-D movie screen was cranked up and out of the way on the far wall between the first class and the galley. In seat 100, the bulky parachute pack sat. Richards patted it briefly and went through the galley. Someone had even put coffee on.

He stepped through another door and stood in a short throat which led to the pilots' compartment. To the right the radio operator, a man of perhaps thirty with a care-lined face, looked at Richards bitterly and then back at his instruments. A few steps up and to the left, the navigator sat at his boards and grids and plastic-encased charts.

'The fellow who's going to get us all killed is coming up, fellas,' he said into his throat mike. He gazed coolly at Richards.

Richards said nothing. The man, after all, was almost certainly right. He limped into the nose of the plane.

The pilot was fifty or better, an old war-horse with the red nose of a steady drinker, and the clear, perceptive eyes of a man who was not even close to the alcoholic edge. His co-pilot was ten years younger, with a luxuriant growth of red hair spilling out from under his cap.

'Hello, Mr Richards,' the pilot said. He glanced at the bulge in Richards's pocket before he looked at his face. 'Pardon me if I don't shake hands. I'm Flight Captain Don Holloway. This is my co-pilot Wayne Duninger.'

'Under the circumstances, not very pleased to meet you,' Duninger said.

Richards's mouth quirked. 'In the same spirit, let me add that I'm sorry to be here. Captain Holloway, you're patched into communications with McCone, aren't you?'

'We sure are. Through Kippy Friedman, our communications man.'

'Give me something to talk into.'

Holloway handed him a microphone with infinite carefulness.

'Get going on your preflight,' Richards said. 'Five minutes.'

'Will you want the explosive bolts on the rear loading door armed?' Duninger said with great eagerness.

'Tend your knitting,' Richards said coldly. It was time to finish it off, make the final bet. His brain felt hot, overheated, on the verge of blowing a bearing. Call and raise, that was the game.

I'm going to sky's the limit right now, McCone.

'Mr Friedman?'

'Yes.'

'This is Richards. He wants to talk to McCone.'

Dead air for half a minute. Holloway and Duninger weren't watching him anymore; they were going through preflight, reading gauges and pressures, checking flaps, doors, switches. The rising and falling of the huge G-A turbines began again, but now much louder, strident. When McCone's voice finally came, it was small against the brute noise.

'McCone here.'

'Come on, maggot. You and the woman are going for a ride. Show up at the loading door in three minutes or I pull the ring.'

Duninger stiffened in his bucket seat as if he had been shot. When he went back to his numbers his voice was shaken and terrified.

If he's got guts, this is where he calls. Asking for the woman gives it away. If he's got guts.

Richards waited.

A clock was ticking in his head.

... MINUS 028   and COUNTING ...

When McCone's voice came, it contained a foreign, blustery note. Fear? Possibly. Richards's heart lurched in his chest. Maybe it was all going to fall together. Maybe.

'You're nuts, Richards. I'm not—'

'You *listen*,' Richards said, punching through McCone's voice. 'And while you are, remember that this conversation is being party-lined by every ham operator within sixty miles. The word is going to get around. You're not working in the dark, little man. You're right out on the big stage. You're coming because you're too chicken-shit to pull a double cross when you know it will get you dead. The woman's coming because I told her where I was going.'

Weak. Punch him harder. Don't let him think.

'Even if you should live when I pull the ring, you won't be able to get a job selling apples.' He was clutching the handbag in his pocket with frantic, maniacal tightness. 'So that's it. Three minutes. Signing off.'

'Richards, wait—'

He signed off, choking McCone's voice. He handed the mike back to Holloway, and Holloway took it with fingers that trembled only slightly.

'You've got guts,' Holloway said slowly. 'I'll say that. I don't think I ever saw so much guts.'

'There will be more guts than anyone ever saw if he pulls that ring,' Duninger said.

'Continue with your preflight, please,' Richards said. 'I am going back to welcome our guests. We go in five minutes.'

He went back and pushed the chute over to the window seat, then sat down watching the door between first class and second class. He would know very soon. He would know very soon.

His hand worked with steady, helpless restlessness on Amelia Williams's handbag.

Outside it was almost full dark.

... MINUS 027 and COUNTING ...

They came up the stairs with a full forty-five seconds to spare. Amelia was panting and frightened, her hair blown into a haphazard beehive by the steady wind that rolled this manmade flatland. McCone's appearance was outwardly unchanged; he remained neat and unaffected, unruffled you might say, but his eyes were dark with a hate that was nearly psychotic.

'You haven't won a thing, maggot,' he said quietly. 'We haven't even started to play our trump cards yet.'

'It's nice to see you again, Mrs Williams,' Richards said mildly.

As if he had given her a signal, pulled an invisible string, she began to weep. It was not a hysterical weeping; it was an entirely hopeless sound that came from her belly like hunks of slag. The force of it made her stagger, then crumple to the plush carpet of this plush first-class section with her face cupped in her hands, as if to hold it on. Richards's blood had dried to a tacky maroon smear on her blouse. Her full skirt, spread around her and hiding her legs, made her look like a wilted flower.

Richards felt sorry for her. It was a shallow emotion, feeling sorry, but the best he could manage.

'Mr Richards?' It was Holloway's voice over the cabin intercom.

'Yes.'

'Do we . . . are we green?'

'Yes.'

'Then I'm giving the service crew the order to remove the stairs and seal us up. Don't get nervous with that thing.'

'All right, Captain. Thank you.'

'You gave yourself away when you asked for the woman. You know that, don't you?' McCone seemed to be smiling and scowling at the same time; the overall effect was frighteningly paranoid. His hands were clenching and unclenching.

'Ah, so?' Richards said mildly. 'And since you're never wrong, you'll undoubtedly jump me before we take off. That way you'll be out of jeopardy and come up smelling like a rose, right?'

McCone's lips parted in a tiny snarl, and then pressed together until they went white. He made no move. The plane began to pick up a tiny vibration as the engines cycled higher and higher.

The noise was suddenly muted as the boarding door in second class was slammed shut. Leaning over slightly to peer out one of the circular windows on the port side, Richards could see the crew trundling away the stairs.

Now we're all on the scaffold, he thought.

. . . MINUS 026 and COUNTING . . .

The FASTEN SEAT BELTS/NO SMOKING sign to the right of the trundled-up movie screen flashed on.

The airplane began a slow, ponderous turn beneath them. Richards had gained all his knowledge of jets from the Free-Vee and from reading, much of it lurid adventure fiction, but this was only the second time he had ever been on one; and it made the shuttle from Harding to New York look like a bathtub toy. He found the huge motion beneath his feet disturbing.

'Amelia?'

She looked up slowly, her face ravaged and tear streaked. 'Uh?' Her voice was rusty, dazed, mucus clogged. As if she had forgotten where she was.

'Come forward. We're taking off.' He looked at McCone. 'You go wherever you please, little man. You have the run of the ship. Just don't bother the crew.'

McCone said nothing and sat down near the curtained divider between first and second class. Then, apparently thinking better of it, he pushed through into the next section and was gone.

Richards walked to the woman, using the high backs of the seats for support. 'I'd like the window seat,' he said. 'I've only flown once before.' He tried to smile but she only looked at him dumbly.

He slid in, and she sat next to him. She buckled his belt for him so his hand did not have to come out of his pocket.

'You're like a bad dream,' she said. 'One that never ends.'

'I'm sorry.'

'I didn't—' she began, and he clamped a hand over her mouth and shook his head. He mouthed the word *No*! at her eyes.

The plane swung around with slow, infinite care, turbines screaming, and began to trundle toward the runways like an ungainly duck about to enter the water. It was so big that Richards felt as if the plane were standing still and the earth itself was moving.

Maybe it's all illusion, he thought wildly. *Maybe they've rigged 3-D projectors outside all the windows and—*

He cut the thought off.

Now they had reached the end of the taxiway and the plane made a cumbersome right turn. They ran at right angles to the runways, passing Three and Two. At One they turned left and paused for a second.

Over the intercom Holloway said expressionlessly: 'Taking off, Mr Richards.'

The plane began to move slowly at first, at no more than air-car speed, and then there was a sudden terrifying burst of acceleration that made Richards want to scream aloud in terror.

He was driven back into the soft pile of his seat, and the landing lights outside suddenly began to leap by with dizzying speed. The scrub bushes and exhaust-stunted trees on the desolate, sunset-riven horizon roared toward them. The engines wound up and up and up. The floor began to vibrate again.

He suddenly realized that Amelia Williams was holding on to his shoulder with both hands, her face twisted into a miserable grimace of fear.

Dear God, she's never flown either!

'We're going,' he said. He found himself repeating it over and over and over, unable to stop. 'We're going. We're going.'

'Where?' She whispered.

He didn't answer. He was just beginning to know.

. . . MINUS 025   and COUNTING . . .

The two troopers on roadblock duty at the eastern entrance of the jetport watched the huge liner fling itself down the runway, gaining speed. Its lights blinked orange and green in the growing dark, and the howl of its engines buffeted their ears.

'He's going. Christ, he's going.'

'Where?' said the other.

They watched the dark shape as it separated from the ground. Its engines took on a curiously flat sound, like artillery practice on a cold morning. It rose at a steep angle, as real and as tangible and as prosaic as a cube of butter on a plate, yet improbable with flight.

'You think he's got it?'

'Hell, I don't know.'

The roar of the jet was now coming to them in falling cycles.

'I'll tell you one thing, though.' The first turned from the diminishing lights and turned up his collar. 'I'm glad he's got that bastard with him. That McCone.'

'Can I ask you a personal question?'

'As long as I don't have to answer it.'

'Would you like to see him pull it off?'

The trooper said nothing for a long time. The sound of the jet faded, faded, faded, until it disappeared into the underground hum of nerves at work.

'Yes.'

'Do you think he will?'

A crescent smile in the darkness. 'My friend, I think there's gonna be a big boom.'

. . . MINUS 024   and COUNTING . . .

The earth had dropped away below them.

Richards stared out wonderingly, unable to drink his fill; he had slept through the other flight as if in wait for this one. The sky had deepened to a shade that hung on the borderline between royal velvet and black. Stars poked through with hesitant brilliance. On the western horizon, the only remnant of the sun was a bitter orange line that illuminated the dark earth below not at all. There was a nestle of lights below he took to be Derry.

'Mr Richards?'

'Yes.' He jumped in his seat as if he had been poked.

'We are in a holding pattern right now. That means we are describing a large circle above the Voigt Jetport. Instructions?'

Richards thought carefully. It wouldn't do to give too much away.

'What's the absolute lowest you can fly this thing?'

There was a long pause for consultation. 'We could get away with two thousand feet,' Holloway said cautiously. 'It's against NSA regs, but—'

'Never mind that,' Richards said. 'I have to put myself in your hands to a certain extent, Mr Holloway. I know very little of flying and I'm sure you've been briefed on that. But please remember that the people who are full of bright ideas about how to bamboozle me are all on the ground and out of danger. If you lie to me about anything and I find out—'

'Nobody up here is going to do any lying,' Holloway said. 'We're only interested in getting this thing back down the way it went up.'

'Okay. Good.' He gave himself time to think. Amelia Williams sat rigidly beside him, her hands folded in her lap.

'Go due west,' he said abruptly. 'Two thousand feet. Point out the sights as we go along, please.'

'The sights?'

'What we're going over,' Richards said. 'I've only flown once before.'

'Oh.' Holloway sounded relieved.

The plane banked beneath their feet and the dark sunset line outside the window tilted on its ear. Richards watched, fascinated. Now it gleamed aslant the thick window, making odd, fugitive sungleams just beyond the glass. *We're chasing the sun,* he thought. *Isn't that amazing?*

It was thirty-five minutes after six.

... MINUS 023 and COUNTING ...

The back of the seat in front of Richards was a revelation in itself. There was a pocket with a safety handbook in it. In case of air turbulence, fasten your belt. If the cabin loses pressure, pull down the air mask directly over your head. In case of engine trouble, the stewardess will give you further instructions. In case of sudden explosive death, hope you have enough dental fillings to insure identification.

There was a small Free-Vee set into the seat panel at eye level. A metal card below it reminded the viewer that channels would come and go with a fair degree of speed. A touch-control channel selector was provided for the hungry viewer.

Below and to the right of the Free-Vee was a pad of airline stationery and a G-A stylus on a chain. Richards pulled out a sheet and wrote clumsily on his knee:

'Odds are 99 out of 100 that you're bugged, shoe mike or hair mike, maybe mesh transmitter on your sleeve. McCone listening and waiting for you to drop the other shoe, I bet. In a minute have a hysterical outburst and beg me not to pull the ring. It'll make our chances better. You game?'

She nodded and Richards hesitated, then wrote again:

'Why did you lie about it?'

She plucked the stylus out of his hand and held it over the paper on his knee for a moment and then wrote: 'Don't know. You made me feel like a murderer. Wife. And you seemed so' – the stylus paused, wavered and then scrawled – 'pitiful.'

Richards raised his eyebrows and grinned a little – it hurt. He offered her the stylus but she shook her head mutely. He wrote: 'Go into your act in about 5 minutes.'

She nodded and Richards crumpled the paper and stuffed it into the ashtray embedded in the armrest. He lit the paper. It puffed into flame and blazed brightly for a moment, kindling a tiny reflective glow in the window. Then it collapsed into ashes which Richards poked thoughtfully.

About five minutes later Amelia Williams began to moan. It sounded so real that for a moment Richards was startled. Then it flashed across his mind that it probably *was* real.

'Please don't,' she said. 'Please don't make that man . . . have to try you. I never did anything to you. I want to go home to my husband. We have a daughter, too. She's six. She'll wonder where her mommy is.'

Richards felt his eyebrow rise and fall twice in an involuntary tic. He didn't want her to be that good. Not *that* good.

'He's dumb,' he told her, trying not to speak for an unseen audience, 'but I don't think he's that dumb. It will be all right, Mrs Williams.'

'That's easy for you to say. You've got nothing to lose.'

He didn't answer her. She was so patently right. Nothing, anyway, that he hadn't lost already.

'Show it to him,' she pleaded. 'For God's sake, why don't you show it to him? Then he'd have to believe you

. . . call off the people on the ground. They're tracking us with missiles. I heard him say so.'

'I can't show him,' Richards said. 'To take it out of my pocket would mean putting the ring on safety or taking the full risk of blowing us up accidentally. Besides,' he added, injecting mockery into his voice, 'I don't think I'd show him if I could. He's the maggot with something to lose. Let him sweat it.'

'I don't think I can stand it,' she said dully. 'I almost think I'd rather joggle you and have it over. That's the way it's going to end anyway, isn't it?'

'You haven't—' he began, and then the door between first and second was snapped open and McCone half strode, half lunged through. His face was calm, but beneath the calm was an odd sheeny look which Richards recognized immediately. The sheen of fear, white and waxy and glowing.

'Mrs Williams,' he said briskly. 'Coffee, if you please. For seven. You'll have to play stewardess on this flight, I'm afraid.'

She got up without looking at either of them. 'Where?'

'Forward,' McCone said smoothly. 'Just follow your nose.' He was a mild, blinking sort of man – and ready to lunge at Amelia Williams the moment she showed a sign of going for Richards.

She made her way up the aisle without looking back.

McCone stared at Richards and said: 'Would you give this up if I could promise you amnesty, pal?'

'*Pal*. That word sounds really greasy in your mouth,' Richards marveled. He flexed his free hand, looked at it. The hand was caked with small runnels of dried blood, dotted with tiny scrapes and scratches from his broken-ankle hike through the southern Maine woods. 'Really greasy. You make it sound like two pounds of fatty hamburger cooking in the pan. The only kind you can get at the Welfare Stores in Co-Op City.' He looked at McCone's well-concealed pot. 'That, now. That looks more like a steak gut. Prime cut. No fat on prime cut except that crinkly little ring around the outside right?'

'Amnesty,' McCone repeated. 'How does that word sound?'

'Like a lie,' Richards said, smiling. 'Like a fat fucking lie. Don't you think I know you're nothing but the hired help?'

McCone flushed. It was not a soft flush at all; it was hard and red and bricklike. 'It's going to be good to have you on my home court,' he said. 'We've got hi-impact slugs that will make your head look like a pumpkin dropped on a sidewalk from the top floor of a skyscraper. Gas filled. They explode on contact. A gut shot, on the other hand—'

Richards screamed: *'Here it goes! I'm pulling the ring!'*

McCone screeched. He staggered back two steps, his rump hit the well-padded arm of seat number 95 across the way, he overbalanced and fell into it like a man into a sling, his arms flailing the air around his head in crazed warding-off gestures.

His hands froze about his head like petrified birds, splay fingered. His face stared through their grotesque frame like a plaster death-mask on which someone had hung a pair of gold-rimmed spectacles for a joke.

Richards began to laugh. The noise of it was cracked at first, hesitant, foreign to his own ears. How long had it been since he had had a real laugh, an honest one, the kind that comes freely and helplessly from the deepest root of the stomach? It seemed to him that he had never had one in his whole gray, struggling, earnest life. But he was having one now.

You bastard.

McCone's voice had failed him; he could only mouth

the words. His face was twisted and scrunched like the face of a badly used teddy bear.

Richards laughed. He held on to one arm of his seat with his free hand and just laughed and laughed and laughed.

...MINUS 022   and COUNTING...

When Holloway's voice informed Richards that the plane was crossing the border between Canada and the state of Vermont (Richards supposed he knew his business; he himself could see nothing but darkness below them, interrupted by occasional clusters of light), he set his coffee down carefully and said:

'Could you supply me with a map of North America, Captain Holloway?'

'Physical or political?' A new voice cut in. The navigator's, Richards supposed. Now he was supposed to play obligingly dumb and not know which map he wanted. Which he didn't.

'Both,' he said flatly.

'Are you going to send the woman up for them?'

'What's your name, pal?'

The hesitant pause of a man who realizes with sudden trepidation that he has been singled out. 'Donahue.'

'You've got legs, Donahue. Suppose you trot them back here yourself.'

Donahue trotted them back. He had long hair combed back greaser fashion and pants tailored tight enough to show what looked like a bag of golf balls at the crotch. The maps were encased in limp plastic. Richards didn't know what Donahue's balls were encased in.

'I didn't mean to mouth off,' he said unwillingly.

Richards thought he could peg him. Well-off young men with a lot of free time often spent much of it roaming the shabby pleasure areas of the big cities, roaming in well-heeled packs, sometimes on foot, more often on choppers. They were queer-stompers. Queers, of course, had to be eradicated. Save our bathrooms for democracy. They rarely ventured beyond the twilight pleasure areas into the full darkness of the ghettos. When they did, they got the shit kicked out of them.

Donahue shifted uneasily under Richards's long gaze. 'Anything else?'

'You a queer-stomper, pal?'

'*Huh?*'

'Never mind. Go on back. Help them fly the plane.'

Donahue went back at a fast shuffle.

Richards quickly discovered that the map with the towns and cities and roads was the political map. Pressing one finger down from Derry to the Canada-Vermont border in a western-reaching straightedge, he located their approximate position.

'Captain Holloway?'

'Yes.'

'Turn left.'

'Huh?' Holloway sounded frankly startled.

'South, I mean. Due south. And remember—'

'I'm remembering,' Holloway said. 'Don't worry.'

The plane banked. McCone sat hunched in the seat he had fallen into, staring at Richards with hungry, wanting eyes.

... MINUS 021 and COUNTING ...

Richards found himself drifting in and out of a daze, and it frightened him. The steady drone of the engines were insidious, hypnotic. McCone was aware of what was happening, and his leaning posture became more and more vulpine. Amelia was also aware. She cringed miserably in a forward seat near the galley, watching them both.

Richards drank two more cups of coffee. Not much help. It was becoming increasingly difficult to concentrate on the coordination of his map and Holloway's toneless commentary on their outlaw flight.

Finally he drove his fist into his side where the bullet had taken him. The pain was immediate and intense, like a dash of cold water in the face. A whistling half-whispered screech issued from either side of his clenched mouth, like stereo. Fresh blood wet his shirt and sieved through onto his hand.

Amelia moaned.

'We'll be passing over Albany in about six minutes,' Holloway said. 'If you look out, you'll see it coming up on your left.'

'Relax,' Richards said to no one, to himself. 'Relax. Just relax.'

God, will it be over soon? Yes. Quite soon.

It was quarter to eight.

... MINUS 020 and COUNTING ...

It could have been a bad dream, a nightmare that had crawled out of the dark and into the unhealthy limelight of his half-awake mind – more properly a vision or an hallucination. His brain was working and concentrating on one level, dealing with the problem of navigation and the constant danger of McCone. On another, something black was taking place. Things were moving in the dark.

Track on. Positive.

Huge, whining servomechanisms turning in the dark, in the night. Infrared eyes glowing in unknown spectrums. Pale green foxfire of dials and swinging radar scopes.

Lock. We have a lock.

Trucks rumbling along back-country roads, and on tri-angulated flatbeds two hundred miles apart, microwave dishes swing at the night sky. Endless streams of electrons fly out on invisible batwings. Bounce, echo. The strong blip and the fading afterimage lingering until the returning swing of light illuminates it in a slightly more southerly position.

Solid?

Yeah. Two hundred miles south of Newark. It could be Newark.

Newark's on Red, also southern New York.

Executive Hold still in effect?

That's right.

We had him dead-bang over Albany.

Be cool, pal.

Trucks thundering through closed towns where people look out of cardboard-patched windows with terrified, hating eyes. Roaring like prehistoric beasts in the night.

Open the holes.

Huge, grinding motors slide huge concrete duncecaps aside, shunting them down gleaming steel tracks. Circular silos like the entrances to the underworld of the Morlocks. Gasps of liquid hydrogen escaping into the air.

Tracking. We are tracking, Newark.

Roger, Springfield. Keep us in.

Drunks sleeping in alleys wake foggily to the thunder of the passing trucks and stare mutely at the slices of sky between close-leaning buildings. Their eyes are faded and yellow, their mouths are dripping lines. Hands pull with senile reflex for newsies to protect against the autumn cold, but the newsies are no longer there, the Free-Vee has killed the last of them. Free-Vee is king of the world. Hallelujah. Rich folks smoke Dokes. The yellow eyes catch an unknown glimpse of high, blinking lights in the sky. Flash, flash. Red and green, red and green. The thunder of the trucks has faded, ramming back and forth in the stone canyons like the fists of vandals. The drunks sleep again. Bitchin'.

We got him west of Springfield.

Go-no-go in five minutes.

From Harding?

Yes.

He's bracketed and braced.

All across the night the invisible batwings fly, drawing a glittering net across the northeast corner of America. Servos controlled by General Atomics computers function smoothly. The missiles turn and shift subtly in a thousand places to follow the blinking red and green lights that sketch the sky. They are like steel rattlesnakes filled with waiting venom.

Richards saw it all, and functioned even as he saw it.

The duality of his brain was oddly comforting, in a way. It induced a detachment that was much like insanity. His bloodcrusted finger followed their southward progress smoothly. Now south of Springfield, now west of Hartford, now—

Tracking.

. . . MINUS 019 and COUNTING . . .

'Mr Richards?'

'Yes.'

'We are over Newark, New Jersey.'

'Yes,' Richards said. 'I've been watching. Holloway?'

Holloway didn't reply, but Richards knew he was listening.

'They've got a bead drawn on us all the way, don't they?'

'Yes,' Holloway said.

Richards looked at McCone. 'I imagine they're trying to decide if they can afford to do away with their professional bloodhound here. Imagine they'll decide in the affirmative. After all, all they have to do is train a new one.'

McCone was snarling at him, but Richards thought it was a completely unconscious gesture, one that could probably be traced all the way to McCone's ancestors, the Neanderthals who had crept up behind their enemies with large rocks rather than battling to the death in the honorable but unintelligent manner.

'When do we get over open country again, Captain?'

'We won't. Not on a due south heading. We will strike open sea after we cross the offshore North Carolina drilling derricks, though.'

'Everything south of here is a suburb of New York City?'

'That's about the size of it,' Holloway said.

'Thank you.'

Newark was sprawled and groined below them like a handful of dirty jewelry thrown carelessly into some lady's black-velvet vanity box.

'Captain?'

Wearily: 'Yes.'

'You will now proceed due west.'

McCone jumped as if he had been goosed. Amelia made a surprised coughing noise in her throat.

'West?' Holloway asked. He sounded unhappy and frightened for the first time. 'You're asking for it, going that way. West takes us over pretty open county. Pennsylvania between Harrisburg and Pittsburgh is all farm country. There isn't another big city east of Cleveland.'

'Are you planning my strategy for me, Captain?'

'No, I—'

'Due west,' Richards repeated curtly.

Newark swung away beneath them.

'You're crazy,' McCone said. 'They'll blow us apart.'

'With you and five other innocent people on board? This honorable country?'

'It will be a mistake,' McCone said harshly. 'A mistake on purpose.'

'Don't you watch *The National Report?*' Richards asked, still smiling. 'We don't make mistakes. We haven't made a mistake since 1950.'

Newark was sliding away beneath the wing; darkness took its place.

'You're not laughing anymore,' Richards said.

... MINUS 018 and COUNTING ...

A half-hour later Holloway came on the voice-com again. He sounded excited.

'Richards, we've been informed by Harding Red that they want to beam a high-intensity broadcast at us. From Games Federation. I was told you would find it very much worth your while to turn on the Free-Vee.'

'Thank you.'

He regarded the blank Free-Vee screen and almost turned it on. He withdrew his hand as if the back of the next seat with its embedded screen was hot. A curious sense of dread and *déjà vu* filled him. It was too much like going back to the beginning, Sheila with her thin, worked face, the smell of Mrs Jenner's cabbage cooking down the hall. The blare of the games. *Treadmill to Bucks*. *Swim the Crocodiles*. Cathy's screams. There could never be another child, of course, not even if he could take all this back, withdraw it, and go back to the beginning. Even the one had been against fantastically high odds.

'Turn it on,' McCone said. 'Maybe they're going to offer us – you – a deal.'

'Shut up,' Richards said.

He waited, letting the dread fill him up like heavy water. The curious sense of presentiment. He hurt very badly. His wound was still bleeding, and his legs felt weak and far away. He didn't know if he could get up to finish this charade when the time came.

With a grunt, Richards leaned forward again and pushed the ON button. The Free-Vee sprang to incredibly clear, amplified-signal life. The face that filled the screen, patiently waiting, was very black and very familiar. Dan Killian. He was sitting at a kidney-shaped mahogany desk with the Games symbol on it.

'Hello there,' Richards said softly.

He could have fallen out of his seat when Killian straightened up, grinned, and said, 'Hello there yourself, Mr Richards.'

... MINUS 017   and COUNTING ...

'I can't see you,' Killian said, 'but I can hear you. The jet's voice-com is being relayed through the radio equipment in the cockpit. They tell me you're shot up.'

'It's not as bad as it looks,' Richards said. 'I got scratched up in the woods.'

'Oh yes,' Killian said. 'The famous Run Through the Woods. Bobby Thompson canonized it on the air just tonight – along with your current exploit, of course. Tomorrow those woods will be full of people looking for a scrap of your shirt, or maybe even a cartridge case.'

'That's too bad,' Richards said. 'I saw a rabbit.'

'You've been the greatest contestant we've ever had, Richards. Through a combination of luck and skill, you've been positively the greatest. Great enough for us to offer you a deal.'

'What deal? Nationally televised firing squad?'

'This plane hijack has been the most spectacular, but it's also been the dumbest. Do you know why? Because for the first time you're not near your own people. You left them behind when you left the ground. Even the woman that's protecting you. You may think she's yours. *She* may even think it. But she's not. There's no one up there but us, Richards. You're a dead duck. Finally.'

'People keep telling me that and I keep drawing breath.'

'You've been drawing breath for the last two hours strictly on Games Federation say-so. I did it. And I'm the one that finally shoved through the authorization for the deal I'm going to offer you. There was strong opposition from the old guard – this kind of thing has never been done – but I'm going through with it.

'You asked me who you could kill if you could go all the way to the top with a machine gun. One of them would have been me, Richards. Does that surprise you?'

'I suppose it does. I had you pegged for the house nigger.'

Killian threw back his head and laughed, but the laughter sounded forced – the laughter of a man playing for high stakes and laboring under a great tension.

'Here's the deal, Richards. Fly your plane to Harding. There will be a Games limo waiting at the airport. An execution will be performed – a fake. Then you join our team.'

There was a startled yelp of rage from McCone. 'You black bastard—'

Amelia Williams looked stunned.

'Very good,' Richards said. 'I knew you were good, but this is really great. What a fine used-car salesman you would have made, Killian.'

'Did McCone sound like I was lying?'

'McCone is a fine actor. He did a little song and dance at the airport that could have won an Academy Award.' Still, he was troubled. McCone's hustling away of Amelia for coffee when it appeared she might trip the Irish, McCone's steady, heavy antagonism – they didn't fit. Or did they? His mind began to pinwheel. 'Maybe you're springing this on him without his knowledge. Counting on his reaction to make it look even better.'

Killian said: 'You've done your song and dance with

the plastic explosive, Mr Richards. We know – *know* – that you are bluffing. But there is a button on this desk, a small red button, which is not a bluff. Twenty seconds after I push it, that place will be torn apart by surface-to-air Diamondback missiles carrying clean nuclear warheads.'

'The Irish isn't fake, either.' But there was a curdled taste in his mouth. The bluff was soured.

'Oh, it is. You couldn't get on a Lockheed G-A plane with a plastic explosive. Not without tripping the alarms. There are four separate detectors on the plane, installed to foil hijackers. A fifth was installed in the parachute you asked for. I can tell you that the alarm lights in the Voigt Field control tower were watched with great interest and trepidation when you got on. The consensus was that you probably had the Irish. You have proved so resourceful all the way up the line that it seemed like a fair assumption to make. There was more than a little relief when none of those lights went on. I assume you never had the opportunity to pick any up. Maybe you never thought of it until too late. Well, doesn't matter. It makes your position worse, but—'

McCone was suddenly standing beside Richards. 'Here it goes,' he said, grinning. 'Here is where I blow your fucking head off, donkey.' He pointed his gun at Richards's temple.

. . . MINUS 016   and COUNTING . . .

'You're dead if you do,' Killian said.

McCone hesitated, fell back a step, and stared at the Free-Vee unbelievingly. His face began to twist and crumple again. His lips writhed in a silent effort to gain speech. When it finally came, it was a whisper of thwarted rage.

'I can take him! Right now! Right here! We'll all be safe! We'll—'

Wearily, Killian said: 'You're safe now, you God damned fool. And Donahue could have taken him – if we wanted him taken.'

'This man is a criminal!' McCone's voice was rising. 'He's killed police officers! Commited acts of anarchy and air piracy! He's . . . he's publicly humiliated me and my department!'

'Sit down,' Killian said, and his voice was as cold as the deep space between planets. 'It's time you remembered who pays your salary, Mr Chief Hunter.'

'I'm going to the Council President with this!' McCone was raving now. Spittle flew from his lips. 'You're going to be chopping cotton when this is over, nig! You goddam worthless night-fighting sonofabitch—'

'Please throw your gun on the floor,' a new voice said. Richards looked around, startled. It was Donahue, the navigator, looking colder and deadlier than ever. His greased hair gleamed in the cabin's indirect lighting. He was holding a wire-stock Magnum/Springstun machine pistol, and it was trained on McCone. 'Robert S. Donahue, old-timer. Games Council Control. Throw it on the floor.'

. . . MINUS 015   and COUNTING . . .

McCone looked at him for a long second, and then the gun thumped on the heavy pile of the carpet. 'You—'

'I think we've heard all the rhetoric we need,' Donahue said. 'Go back into second class and sit down like a good boy.'

McCone backed up several paces, snarling futilely. He

217

looked to Richards like a vampire in an old horror movie that had been thwarted by a cross.

When he was gone, Donahue threw Richards a sardonic little salute with the barrel of his gun and smiled. 'He won't bother you again.'

'You still look like a queer-stomper,' Richards said evenly.

The small smile faded. Donahue stared at him with sudden, empty dislike for a moment, and then went forward again.

Richards turned back to the Free-Vee screen. He found that his pulse rate had remained perfectly steady. He had no shortness of breath, no rubber legs. Death had become a normality.

'Are you there, Mr Richards?' Killian asked.

'Yes I am.'

'The problem has been handled?'

'Yes.'

'Good. Let me get back to what I was saying.'

'Go ahead.'

Killian sighed at his tone. 'I was saying that our knowledge of your bluff makes your position worse, but makes our credibility better. Do you see why?'

'Yes,' Richards said detachedly. 'It means you could have blown this bird out of the sky anytime. Or you could have had Holloway set the plane down at will. McCone would have bumped me.'

'Exactly. Do you believe we know you are bluffing?'

'No. But you're better than McCone. Using your planted houseboy was a fine stroke.'

Killian laughed. 'Oh, Richards. You are such a peach. Such a rare, iridescent bird.' And yet again it sounded forced, tense, pressured. It came to Richards that Killian was holding information which he wanted badly not to tell.

'If you really had it, you would have pulled the string when McCone put the gun to your head. You knew he was going to kill you. Yet you sat there.'

Richards knew it was over, knew that they knew. A smile cracked his features. Killian would appreciate that. He was a man of a sharp and sardonic turn of mind. Make them pay to see the hole card, then.

'I'm not buying any of this. If you push me, everything goes bang.'

'And you wouldn't be the man you are if you didn't spin it out to the very end. Mr Donahue?'

'Yes, sir.' Donahue's cool, efficient, emotionless voice came over the voice-com and out of the Free-Vee almost simultaneously.

'Please go back and remove Mrs Williams's pocketbook from Mr Richards's pocket. You're not to harm him in any way.'

'Yes, sir.' Richards was eerily reminded of the plasti-punch that had stenciled his original ID card at Games headquarters. *Clitter-clitter-clitter.*

Donahue reappeared and walked toward Richards. His face was smooth and cold and empty. *Programmed.* The word leaped into Richards's mind.

'Stand right there, pretty boy,' Richards remarked, shifting the hand in his coat pocket slightly. 'The Man there is safe on the ground. You're the one that's going to the moon.'

He thought the steady stride might have faltered for just a second and the eyes seemed to have winced the tiniest uncertain bit, and then he came on again. He might have been promenading on the Côte d'Azur . . . or approaching a gibbering homosexual cowering at the end of a blind alley.

Briefly Richards considered grabbing the parachute and fleeing. Hopeless. Flee? Where? The men's bathroom at the far end of the third class was the end of the line.

'See you in hell,' he said softly, and made a pulling gesture in his pocket. This time the reaction was a little better. Not highly satisfactory, but better. Donahue made a grunting noise and threw his hands up to protect his face in an instinctive gesture as old as man himself. He lowered them, still in the land of the living, looking embarrassed and very angry.

Richards took Amelia Williams's pocketbook out of his muddy, torn coat pocket and threw it. It struck Donahue's chest and plopped at his feet like a dead bird. Richards's hand was slimed with sweat. Lying on his knee again, it looked strange and white and foreign. Donahue picked up the bag, looked in it perfunctorily, and handed it to Amelia. Richards felt a stupid sort of sadness at its passage. In a way, it was like losing an old friend.

'Boom,' he said softly.

. . . MINUS 014   and COUNTING . . .

'Your boy is very good,' Richards said tiredly, when Donahue had retreated again. 'I got him to flinch, but I was hoping he'd pee his pants.' He was beginning to notice an odd doubling of his vision. It came and went. He checked his side gingerly. It was clotting reluctantly for the second time. 'What now?' he asked. 'Do you set up cameras at the airport so everyone can watch the desperado get it?'

'Now the deal,' Killian said softly. His face was dark, unreadable. Whatever he had been holding back was now just below the surface. Richards knew it. And suddenly he was filled with dread again. He wanted to reach out and turn the Free-Vee off. Not hear it anymore. He felt his insides begin a slow and terrible quaking – an actual, literal quaking. But he could not turn it off. Of course not. It was, after all, Free.

'Get thee behind me, Satan,' he said thickly.

'What?' Killian looked startled.

'Nothing. Make your point.'

Killian did not speak. He looked down at his hands. He looked up again. Richards felt an unknown chamber of his mind groan with psychic presentiment. It seemed to him that the ghosts of the poor and the nameless, of the drunks sleeping in alleys, were calling his name.

'McCone is played out,' Killian said softly. 'You know it because you did it. Cracked him like a soft-shelled egg. We want you to take his place.'

Richards, who thought he had passed the point of all shock, found his mouth hanging open in utter, dazed incredulity. It was a lie. Had to be. Yet – Amelia had her purse back now. There was no reason for them to lie or offer false illusions. He was hurt and alone. Both McCone and Donahue were armed. One bullet administered just above the left ear would put a neat end to him with no fuss, no muss, or bother.

Conclusion: Killian was telling God's truth.

'You're nuts,' he muttered.

'No. You're the best runner we've ever had. And the best runner knows the best places to look. Open your eyes a little and you'll see that *The Running Man* is designed for something besides pleasuring the masses and getting rid of dangerous people. Richards, the Network is always in the market for fresh new talent. We have to be.'

Richards tried to speak, could say nothing. The dread was still in him, widening, heightening, thickening.

'There's never been a Chief Hunter with a family,' he finally said. 'You ought to know why. The possibilities for extortion—'

'Ben,' Killian said with infinite gentleness, 'your wife and daughter are dead. They've been dead for over ten days.'

. . . MINUS 013   and COUNTING . . .

Dan Killian was talking, had been perhaps for some time, but Richards heard him only distantly, distorted by an odd echo effect in his mind. It was like being trapped in a very deep well and hearing someone call down. His mind had gone midnight dark, and the darkness served as the background for a kind of scrapbook slide show. An old Kodak of Sheila wiggling in the halls of Trades High with a loose-leaf binder under her arm. Micro skirts had just come back into fashion then. A freeze-frame of the two of them sitting at the end of the Bay Pier (Admission: Free), backs to the camera, looking out at the water. Hands linked. Sepia-toned photo of a young man in an ill-fitting suit and a young woman in her mother's best dress – specially taken up – standing before a JP with a large wart on his nose. They had giggled at that wart on their wedding night. Stark black and white action photo of a sweating, bare-chested man wearing a lead apron and working heavy engine gear-levers in a huge, vaultlike underground chamber lit with arc lamps. Soft-toned color photo (soft to blur the stark, peeling surroundings) of a woman with a big belly standing at a window and looking out, ragged curtain held aside, watching for her man to come up the street. The light is a soft cat's paw on her cheek. Last picture: another old-timey Kodak of a thin fellow holding a tiny scrap of a baby high over his head in a curious mixture of triumph and love, his face split by a huge winning grin. The pictures began to flash by faster and faster, whirling, not bringing any sense of grief and love and loss, not yet, no, bringing only a cool Novocain numbness.

Killian assuring that the Network had nothing to do with their deaths, all a horrible accident. Richards supposed he believed him – not only because the story sounded too much like a lie not to be the truth, but because Killian knew that if Richards agreed to the job offer, his first stop would be Co-Op City, where a single hour on the streets would get him the straight of the matter.

Prowlers. Three of them. (Or tricks? Richards wondered, suddenly agonized. She had sounded slightly furtive on the telephone, as if holding something back—) They had been hopped up, probably. Perhaps they had made some threatening move toward Cathy and Sheila had tried to protect her daughter. They had both died of puncture wounds.

That had snapped him out of it. 'Don't feed me that shit!' He screamed suddenly. Amelia flinched backward and suddenly hid her face. 'What happened? Tell me what happened!'

'There's nothing more I can say. Your wife was stabbed over sixty times.'

'Cathy,' Richards said emptily, without thought, and Killian winced.

'Ben, would you like some time to think about all this?'

'Yes. Yes, I would.'

'I'm desperately, desperately sorry, pal. I swear on my mother that we had nothing to do with it. Our way would have been to set them up away from you, with visiting rights if you agreed. A man doesn't willingly work for the people who butchered his family. We know that.'

'I need time to think.'

'As Chief Hunter,' Killian said softly, 'you could get

those bastards and put them down a deep hole. And a lot of others just like them.'

'I want to think. Goodbye.'

'I—'

Richards reached out and thumbed the Free-Vee into blackness. He sat stonelike in his seat. His hands dangled loosely between his knees. The plane droned on into darkness.

So, he thought. It's all come unraveled. All of it.

. . . MINUS 012 and COUNTING . . .

An hour passed.

The time has come, the walrus said, to talk of many things . . . of sailing ships and sealing-wax, And whether pigs have wings.

Pictures flitted in and out of his mind. Stacey. Bradley. Elton Parrakis with his baby face. A nightmare of running. Lighting the newspapers in the basement of the YMCA with that last match. The gas-powered cars wheeling and screeching, the Sten gun spitting flame. Laughlin's sour voice. The pictures of those two kids, the junior Gestapo agents.

Well, why not?

No ties now, and certainly no morality. How could morality be an issue to a man cut loose and drifting? How wise Killian had been to see that, to show Richards with calm and gentle brutality just how alone he was. Bradley and his impassioned air-pollution pitch seemed distant, unreal, unimportant. Nose-filters. Yes. At one time the concept of nose-filters had seemed large, very important. Not so.

The poor you will have with you always.

True. Even Richards's loins had produced a specimen for the killing machine. Eventually the poor would adapt, mutate. Their lungs would produce their own filtration system in ten thousand years or in fifty thousand, and they would rise up, rip out the artificial filters and watch their owners flop and kick and drum their lives away, drowning in an atmosphere where oxygen played only a minor part, and what was futurity to Ben Richards? It was all only bitchin.

There would be a period of grief. They would expect that, provide for it. There would even be rages, moments of revolt. Abortive tries to make the knowledge of deliberate poison in the air public again? Maybe. They would take care of it. Take care of him – in anticipation of a time when he would take care of them. Instinctively he knew he could do it. He suspected he might even have a certain genius for the job. They would help him, heal him. Drugs and doctors. A change of mind.

Then, peace.

Contentiousness rooted out like bitterweed.

He regarded the peace longingly, the way a man in the desert regards water.

Amelia Williams cried steadily in her seat long after the time when all tears should have gone dry. He wondered indifferently what would become of her. She couldn't very well be returned to her husband and family in her present state; she simply was not the same lady who had pulled up to a routine stop sign with her mind all full of meals and meetings, clubs and cooking. She had Shown Red. He supposed there would be drugs and therapy, a patient showing off. The Place Where Two Roads Diverged, a pinpointing of the reason why the wrong path had been chosen. A carnival in dark mental browns.

He wanted suddenly to go to her, comfort her, tell her that she was not badly broken, that a single crisscrossing of psychic Band-Aids should fix her, make her even better than she had been before.

Sheila. Cathy.

Their names came and repeated, clanging in his mind like bells, like words repeated until they are reduced to nonsense. Say your name over two hundred times and discover you are no one. Grief was impossible; he could feel only a fuzzy sense of irritation and embarrassment: they had taken him, run him slack-lunged, and he had turned out to be nothing but a horse's ass after all. He remembered a boy from his grammar school days who had stood up to give the Pledge of Allegiance and his pants had fallen down.

The plane droned on and on. He sank into a three-quarter doze. Pictures came and went lazily, whole incidents were seen without any emotional color at all.

Then, a final scrapbook picture: a glossy eight-by-ten taken by a bored police photographer who had perhaps been chewing gum. Exhibit C, ladies and gentlemen of the jury. One ripped and sliced small body in a blood-drenched crib. Splatters and runnels on the cheap stucco walls and the broken Mother Goose mobile bought for a dime. A great sticky clot on the secondhand teddy bear with one eye.

He snapped awake, full awake and bolt upright, with his mouth propped wide in a blabbering scream. The force expelled from his lungs was great enough to make his tongue flap like a sail. Everything, everything in the first-class compartment was suddenly clear and plangently real, overpowering, awful. It had the grainy reality of a scare tabloid newsie clip. Laughlin being dragged out of that shed in Topeka, for instance. Everything, everything was very real and in Technicolor.

Amelia screamed affrightedly in unison, cringing back

in her seat with eyes as huge as cracked porcelain door-knobs, trying to cram a whole fist in her mouth.

Donahue came charging through the galley, his gun out. His eyes were small enthusiastic black beads. 'What is it? What's wrong? McCone?'

'No,' Richards said, feeling his heart slow just enough to keep his words from sounding squeezed and desperate. 'Bad dream. My little girl.'

'Oh.' Donahue's eyes softened in counterfeit sympathy. He didn't know how to do it very well. Perhaps he would be a goon all his life. Perhaps he would learn. He turned to go.

'Donahue?'

Donahue turned back warily.

'Had you pretty scared, didn't I?'

'No.' Donahue turned away on that short word. His neck was bunched. His buttocks in his tight blue uniform were as pretty as a girl's.

'I can scare you worse,' Richards remarked. 'I could threaten to take away your nose filter.'

Exeunt Donahue.

Richards closed his eyes tiredly. The glossy eight-by-ten came back. Opened them. Closed them. No glossy eight-by-ten. He waited, and when he was sure it was not going to come back (right away), he opened his eyes and thumbed on the Free-Vee.

It popped on and there was Killian.

. . . MINUS 011 and COUNTING . . .

'Richards.' Killian leaned forward, making no effort to conceal his tension.

'I've decided to accept,' Richards said.

Killian leaned back and nothing smiled but his eyes. 'I'm very glad,' he said.

. . . MINUS 010   and COUNTING . . .

'Jesus,' Richards said. He was standing in the doorway to the pilot's country.

Holloway turned around. 'Hi.' He had been speaking to something called Detroit VOR. Duninger was drinking coffee.

The twin control consoles were untended. Yet they swerved, tipped, and turned as if in response to ghost hands and feet. Dials swung. Lights flashed. There seemed to be a huge and constant input and output going on . . . to no one at all.

'Who's driving the bus?' Richards asked, fascinated.

'Otto,' Duninger said.

'Otto?'

'Otto the automatic pilot. Get it? Shitty pun.' Duninger suddenly smiled. 'Glad to have you on the team, fella. You may not believe this, but some of us guys were rooting for you pretty hard.'

Richards nodded noncommittally.

Holloway stepped into the slightly awkward breach by saying: 'Otto freaks me out, too. Even after twenty years of this. But he's dead safe. Sophisticated as hell. It would make one of the old ones look like . . . well, like an orange crate beside a Chippendale bureau.'

'Is that right?' Richards was staring out into the darkness.

'Yes. You lock on POD – point of destination – and Otto takes over, aided by Voice-Radar all the way. Makes the pilot pretty superfluous, except for takeoffs and landings. And in case of trouble.'

'Is there much you *can* do if there's trouble?' Richards asked.

'We can pray,' Holloway said. Perhaps it was meant to sound jocular, but it came out with a strange sincerity that hung in the cabin.

'Do those wheels actually steer the plane?' Richards asked.

'Only up and down,' Duninger said. 'The pedals control side-to-side motion.'

'Sounds like a kid's soapbox racer.'

'A little more complicated,' Holloway said. 'Let's just say there are a few more buttons to push.'

'What happens if Otto goes off his chump?'

'Never happens,' Duninger said with a grin. 'If it did, you'd just override him. But the computer is never wrong, pal.'

Richards wanted to leave, but the sight of the turning wheels, the minute, mindless adjustments of the pedals and switches, held him. Holloway and Duninger went back to their business – obscure numbers and communications filled with static.

Holloway looked back once, seemed surprised to see him still there. He grinned and pointed into the darkness. 'You'll see Harding coming up there soon.'

'How long?'

'You'll be able to see the horizon glow in five to six minutes.'

When Holloway turned around next, Richards was gone. He said to Duninger: 'I'll be glad when we set that guy down. He's a spook.'

Duninger looked down morosely, his face bathed in the green, luminescent glow of the controls. 'He didn't like Otto. You know that?'

'I know it,' Holloway said.

... MINUS 009 and COUNTING ...

Richards walked back down the narrow, hip-wide corridor. Friedman, the communications man, didn't look up. Neither did Donahue. Richards stepped through into the galley and then halted.

The smell of coffee was strong and good. He poured himself a cup, added some instant creamer, and sat down in one of the stewardess off-duty chairs. The Silex bubbled and steamed.

There was a complete stock of luxury frozen dinners in the see-through freezers. The liquor cabinet was fully stocked with midget airline bottles.

A man could have a good drunk, he thought.

He sipped his coffee. It was strong and fine. The Silex bubbled.

Here I am, he thought, and sipped. Yes, no question about it. Here he was, just sipping.

Pots and pans all neatly put away. The stainless steel sink gleaming like a chromium jewel in a Formica setting. And, of course, that Silex on the hotplate, bubbling and steaming. Sheila had always wanted a Silex. A Silex lasts, was her claim.

He was weeping.

There was a tiny toilet where only stewardess bottoms had squatted. The door was half ajar and he could see it, yes, even the blue, primly disinfected water in the bowl. Defecate in tasteful splendor at fifty thousand feet.

He drank his coffee and watched the Silex bubble and steam, and he wept. The weeping was very calm and completely silent. It and his cup of coffee ended at the same time.

He got up and put his cup in the stainless steel sink. He picked up the Silex, holding it by its brown plastic handle, and carefully dumped the coffee down the drain. Tiny beads of condensation clung to the thick glass.

He wiped his eyes with the sleeve of his jacket and went back into the narrow corridor. He stepped into Donahue's compartment, carrying the Silex in one hand.

'Want some coffee?' Richards asked.

'No,' Donahue said curtly, without looking up.

'Sure you do,' Richards said, and swung the heavy glass pot down on Donahue's bent head with all the force he could manage.

... MINUS 008 and COUNTING ...

The effort ripped open the wound in his side for the third time, but the pot didn't break. Richards wondered if it had been fortified with something (Vitamin B-12, perhaps?) to keep it from shattering in case of high-level turbulence. It did take a huge, amazing blot of Donahue's blood. He fell silently onto his map table. A runnel of blood ran across the plasticoating of the top one and began to drip.

'Roger five-by, C-one-niner-eight-four,' a radio voice said brightly.

Richards was still holding the Silex. It was matted with strands of Donahue's hair.

He dropped it, but there was no clunk. Carpeting even here. The glass bubble of the Silex rolled up at him, a winking, bloodshot eyeball. The glossy eight-by-ten of Cathy in her crib appeared unbidden and Richards shuddered.

He lifted Donahue's dead weight by the hair and rummaged inside his blue flight jacket. The gun was there. He was about to drop Donahue's head back to the map table, but paused, and yanked it up even further. Donahue's mouth hung unhinged, an idiot leer. Blood dripped into it.

Richards wiped blood from one nostril and stared in.

There it was – tiny, very tiny. A glitter of mesh.

'Acknowledge ETA, C-one-niner-eight-four,' the radio said.

'Hey, that's you!' Friedman called from across the hall. 'Donahue—'

Richards limped into the passage. He felt very weak. Friedman looked up. 'Will you tell Donahue to get off his butt and acknowledge—'

Richards shot him just above the upper lip. Teeth flew like a broken, savage necklace. Hair, blood, and brains splashed a Rorschach on the wall behind the chair, where a 3-D foldout girl was spreading eternal legs over a varnished mahogany bedpost.

There was a muffled exclamation from the pilot's compartment, and Holloway made a desperate, doomed lunge to shut the door. Richards noticed that he had a very small scar on his forehead, shaped like a question mark. It was the kind of scar a small, adventurous boy might get if he fell from a low branch while playing pilot.

He shot Holloway in the belly and Holloway made a great shocked noise: '*Whoooo-OOO!*' His feet flipped out from under him and he fell on his face.

Duninger was turned around in his chair, his face a slack moon. 'Don't shoot me, huh?' he said. There was not enough wind in him to make it a statement.

'Here,' Richards said kindly, and pulled the trigger. Something popped and flared with brief violence behind Duninger as he fell over.

Silence.

'Acknowledge ETA, C-one-niner-eight-four,' the radio said.

Richards suddenly whooped and threw up a great glut of coffee and bile. The muscular contraction ripped his wound open further, implanting a great, throbbing pain in his side.

He limped to the controls, still dipping and sliding in endless, complex tandem. So many dials and controls.

Wouldn't they have a communications link constantly open on such an important flight? Surely.

'Acknowledge,' Richards said conversationally.

'You got the Free-Vee on up there, C-one-niner-eight-four? We've been getting some garbled transmission. Everything okay?'

'Five-by,' Richards said.

'Tell Duninger he owes me a beer,' the voice said cryptically, and then there was only background static.

Otto was driving the bus.

Richards went back to finish his business.

... MINUS 007   and COUNTING ...

'Oh dear God,' Amelia Williams moaned.

Richards looked down at himself casually. His entire right side, from ribcage to calf, was a bright and sparkling red.

'Who would have thought the old man had so much blood in him?' Richards said.

McCone suddenly dashed through into first class. He took in Richards at a glance. McCone's gun was out. He and Richards fired at the same time.

McCone disappeared through the canvas between first

and second class. Richards sat down hard. He felt very tired. There was a large hole in his belly. He could see his intestines.

Amelia was screaming endlessly, her hands pulling her cheeks down into a plastic witch-face.

McCone came staggering back into first class. He was grinning. Half of his head appeared to be blown away, but he was grinning all the same.

He fired twice. The first bullet went over Richards's head. The second struck him just below the collar-bone.

Richards fired again. McCone staggered around twice in an aimless kind of dipsy-doodle. The gun fell from his fingers. McCone appeared to be observing the heavy white styrofoam ceiling of the first class compartment, perhaps comparing it to his own in second class. He fell over. The smell of burned powder and burned flesh was clear and crisp, as distinctive as apples in a cider press.

Amelia continued to scream. Richards thought how remarkably healthy she sounded.

... MINUS 006 and COUNTING ...

Richards got up very slowly, holding his intestines in. It felt as if someone was lighting matches in his stomach.

He went slowly up the aisle, bent over, one hand to his midriff, as if bowing. He picked up the parachute with one hand and dragged it behind him. A loop of gray sausage escaped his fingers and he pushed it back in. It hurt to push it in. It vaguely felt as if he might be shitting himself.

'Guh,' Amelia Williams was groaning. 'Guh-Guh-Guh-God. Oh God. Oh dear God.'

'Put this on,' Richards said.

She continued to rock and moan, not hearing him. He dropped the parachute and slapped her. He could get no force into it. He balled his fist and punched her. She shut up. Her eyes stared at him dazedly.

'Put this on,' he said again. 'Like a packsack. You see how?'

She nodded. 'I. Can't. Jump. Scared.'

'We're going down. You have to jump.'

'Can't.'

'All right. Shoot you then.'

She popped out of her seat, knocking him sideways, and began to pull the packsack on with wild, eye-rolling vigor. She backed away from him as she struggled with the straps.

'No. That one goes uh-under.'

She rearranged the strap with great speed, retreating toward McCone's body as Richards approached. Blood was dripping from his mouth.

'Now fasten the clip in the ringbolt. Around. Your buh-belly.'

She did it with trembling fingers, weeping when she missed the connection the first time. Her eyes stared madly into his face.

She skittered momentarily in McCone's blood and then stepped over him.

They backed through second class and into third class in the same way. Matches in his belly had been replaced by a steadily flaming lighter.

The emergency door was locked with explosive bolts and a pilot-controlled bar.

Richards handed her the gun. 'Shoot it. I . . . can't take the recoil.'

Closing her eyes and averting her face, she pulled the trigger of Donahue's gun twice. Then it was empty. The door stood closed, and Richards felt a faint, sick despair. Amelia Williams was holding the ripcord ring nervously, giving it tiny little twitches.

'Maybe—' she began, and the door suddenly blew away into the night, sucking her along with it.

. . . MINUS 005 and COUNTING . . .

Bent haglike, a man in a reverse hurricane, Richards made his way from the blown door, holding the backs of seats. If they had been flying higher, with a greater difference in air pressure, he would have been pulled out, too. As it was he was being badly buffeted, his poor old intestines accordioning out and trailing after him on the floor. The cool night air, thin and sharp at two thousand feet, was like a slap of cold water. The cigarette lighter had become a torch, and his insides were burning.

Through second class. Better. Suction not so great. Now over McCone's sprawled body (step *up*, please) and through first class. Blood ran loosely from his mouth.

He paused at the entrance to the galley and tried to gather up his intestines. He knew they didn't like it on the Outside. Not a bit. They were getting all dirty. He wanted to weep for his poor, fragile intestines, who had asked for none of this.

He couldn't pack them back inside. It was all wrong; they were all jumbled. Frightening images from high school biology books jetted past his eyes. He realized with dawning, stumbling truth, the fact of his own actual ending, and cried out miserably through a mouthful of blood.

There was no answer from the aircraft. Everyone was gone. Everyone but himself and Otto.

The world seemed to be draining of color as his body drained of its own bright fluid. Leaning crookedly against the galley entrance, like a drunk leaning against a lamppost, he saw the things around him go through a shifting, wraithlike grayout.

This is it. I'm going.

He screamed again, bringing the world back into excruciating focus. Not yet. Mustn't.

He lunged through the galley with his guts hanging in ropes around him. Amazing that there could be so much in there. So round, so firm, so fully packed.

He stepped on part of himself, and something inside *pulled*. The flare of pain was beyond belief, beyond the world, and he shrieked, splattering blood on the far wall. He lost his balance and would have fallen, had not the wall stopped him at sixty degrees.

Gutshot. I'm gutshot.

Insanely, his mind responded: *Clitter-clitter-clitter.*

One thing to do.

Gutshot was supposed to be one of the worst. They had had a discussion once about the worst ways to go on their midnight lunch break; that had been when he was a wiper. Hale and hearty and full of blood and piss and semen, all of them, gobbling sandwiches and comparing the relative merits of radiation poisoning, freezing, falling, bludgeoning, drowning. And someone had mentioned being gutshot. Harris, maybe. The fat one who drank illicit beer on the job.

It hurts in the belly, Harris had said. *It takes a long time.* And all of them nodding and agreeing solemnly, with no conception of Pain.

Richards lurched up the narrow corridor, holding both sides for support. Past Donahue. Past Friedman and his radical dental surgery. Numbness crawling up his arms, yet the pain in his belly (what *had* been his belly) growing worse. Still, even through all this he moved, and his ruptured body tried to carry out the commands of the insane Napoleon caged inside his skull.

My God, can this be the end of Rico?

He would not have believed he had so many death-bed clichés inside him. It seemed that his mind was turning inward, eating itself in its last fevered seconds.

One. More. Thing.

He fell over Holloway's sprawled body and lay there, suddenly sleepy. A nap. Yes. Just the ticket. Too hard to get up. Otto, humming. Singing the birthday boy to sleep. Shhh, shhh, shhh. The sheep's in the meadow, the cow's in the corn.

He lifted his head — tremendous effort, his head was steel, pig iron, lead — and stared at the twin controls going through their dance. Beyond him, in the plexiglass windows, Harding.

Too far.

He's under the haystack, fast asleep.

... MINUS 004 and COUNTING ...

The radio was squawking worriedly: 'Come in, C-one-niner-eight-four. You're too low. Acknowledge. Acknowledge. Shall we assume Guidance control? Acknowledge. Acknowledge. Ack—'

'Eat it,' Richards whispered.

He began to crawl toward the dipping, swaying controls. In and out went the pedals. Twitch-twitch went the wheels. He screamed as new agony flared. A loop of his intestines had caught under Holloway's chin. He crawled back. Freed them. Started to crawl again.

His arms went slack and for a moment he floated,

weightless, with his nose in the soft, deep-pile carpet. He pushed himself up and began to crawl again.

Getting up and into Holloway's seat was Everest.

... MINUS 003   and COUNTING ...

There it was. Huge, bulking square and tall into the night, silhouetted black above everything else. Moonlight had turned it alabaster.

He tweaked the wheel just a little. The floor fell away to the left. He lurched in Holloway's seat and almost fell out. He turned the wheel back, overcorrected again, and the floor fell away to the right. The horizon was tilting crazily.

Now the pedals. Yes. Better.

He pushed the wheel in gingerly. A dial in front of his eyes moved from 2000 to 1500 in the wink of an eye. He eased the wheel back. He had very little sight left. His right eye was almost completely gone. Strange that they should go one at a time.

He pushed the wheel in again. Now it seemed that the plane was floating, weightless. The dial slipped from 1500 to 1200 to 900. He pulled it back out.

'C-one-niner-eight-four.' The voice was very alarmed now. 'What's wrong? Acknowledge!'

'Speak, boy,' Richards croaked. 'Rowf! Rowf!'

. . . MINUS 002 and COUNTING . . .

The big plane cruised through the night like a sliver of ice and now Co-Op City was spread out below like a giant broken carton.

He was coming at it, coming at the Games Building.

. . . MINUS 001 and COUNTING . . .

Now the jet cruised across the canal, seemingly held up by the hand of God, giant, roaring. A Push freak in a doorway stared up and thought he was seeing a hallucination, the last dope dream, come to take him away, perhaps to General Atomics heaven where all the food was free and all the piles were clean breeders.

The sound of its engines drove people into doorways, their faces craning upwards like pale flames. Glass showwindows jingled and fell inward. Gutter litter was sucked down bowling-alley streets in dervishes. A cop dropped his move-along and wrapped his hands around his head and screamed and could not hear himself.

The plane was still dropping and now it moved over roof-tops like a cruising silver bat; the starboard wingtip missed the side of the Glamour Column Store by a bare twelve feet.

All over Harding, Free-Vees went white with interference and people stared at them with stupid, fearful incredulity.

The thunder filled the world.

Killian looked up from his desk and stared into the wall-to-wall window that formed one entire side of the room.

The twinkling vista of the city, from South City to Crescent, was gone. The entire window was filled with an oncoming Lockheed TriStar jet. Its running lights blinked on and off, and for just a moment, an insane moment of total surprise and horror and disbelief, he could see Richards staring out at him. His face smeared with blood, his black eyes burning like the eyes of a demon.

Richards was grinning.

And giving him the finger.

'—Jesus—' was all Killian had time to get out.

000

Heeling over slightly, the Lockheed struck the Games Building dead on, three quarters of the way up. Its tanks were still better than a quarter full. Its speed was slightly over five hundred miles an hour.

The explosion was tremendous, lighting up the night like the wrath of God, and it rained fire twenty blocks away.